IN THE WOLF'S MOUTH

IN THE
WOLF'S MOUTH

ADAM FOULDS

JONATHAN CAPE
LONDON

Published by Jonathan Cape 2014

2 4 6 8 10 9 7 5 3 1

First published in Great Britain in 2014 by
Jonathan Cape
Random House, 20 Vauxhall Bridge Road,
London SW1V 2SA

www.randomhouse.co.uk

Addresses for companies within The Random House Group Limited can be
found at: www.randomhouse.co.uk/offices.htm

The Random House Group Limited Reg. No. 954009

A CIP catalogue record for this book is available from the British Library

ISBN 9780224098281

The Random House Group Limited supports the Forest Stewardship
Council® (FSC®), the leading international forest-certification organisation.
Our books carrying the FSC label are printed on FSC®-certified paper.
FSC is the only forest-certification scheme supported by the leading
environmental organisations, including Greenpeace. Our paper procurement
policy can be found at www.randomhouse.co.uk/environment

Typeset in Bembo by Palimpsest Book Production Limited,
Falkirk, Stirlingshire

Printed and bound in Great Britain by
CPI Group (UK) Ltd, Croydon CR0 4YY

To Charla

There may be always a time of innocence.
There is never a place.

Wallace Stevens, *The Auroras of Autumn*

Prologue

The Shepherd

1926

He leaned forward, swung his shotgun carefully around from his back and raised it so that the stock rested firmly along his jawbone. His stubble rasped against the wood as he adjusted, setting the partridge floating on the two beads. Still there, panting in the heat. He fired. The bird was thrust sideways. It sat heavily, startled, like somebody suddenly shoved out of a chair. The blast rocked in echoes across the valley and knocked up into the air a crow that flew in wide evasive circles, crying out. Angilù thought of the other shepherds in the hills hearing the shot and wondering, frightened maybe. The partridge fluttered one wing as though thinking it might still fly away to safety, but while Angilù walked towards it the movement slowed to a feeble waving and by the time he reached it the bird was still, the clasp of its beak unfastened, its little black eye unblinking in the sun.

He picked up the bird and carried it back up to the ridge where the wind hit him then down the other side to his hut, his tethered mule, the sheep scuttling over stones looking for fresh growth. He sat in the shade of the opening and plucked the bird, the soft beautiful feathers blowing about his feet. When its pimpled flesh was as bare as a naked woman he took his knife and slit below the keel bone then pulled out the wet handful of innards. Ready to cook. Excellent. The partridge was good luck. Otherwise it would have been more salty cheese and hard bread or snails if he could be bothered to collect them. Or wild herbs. There was a place near here where they grew. He could see it in his mind: the clear light, the slender plants shaking in the wind.

He spatchcocked the bird, cracking open its small ribcage, and cooked it over a fire of quick-burning, sun-bleached stuff. He cut the meat and ate it from the side of his knife. He ate its delicate bones and sucked at the larger ones.

Winter had been a warm time back in the village, among people, with the cold silver rain darkening the earth, feeding it. But it was good to be alone again, up out of all the clamour of talk and obligation, families and rivalries and wrongs. The other shepherds missed home but he was young still and without a wife. There was loneliness, of course, and when he was a boy he'd hated it, feeling himself a prisoner in the hills, expelled from normal life, frightened of the bandits and the business he had to do. Back then he'd arranged stones on the ground near one of the huts to form faces and he'd talked to them, long conversations. He didn't do that any more but the place remained altered by it. There was a presence there, a charge in the air above the spot, a ghost of himself, perhaps.

As the sun set he watched the shadows pour down behind the hills, filling the valley. Then there were stars. His mule faded into the darkness, the pale sheep also. But the wind was always awake, vibrating over the hard ridges.

The following day, Gino drove his herd near enough in the east for Angilù to hear his singing rise up on the wind. Angilù put his hands to the side of his mouth and sang, 'Who's singing over there? Sounds like a sick dog.' There was a pause, then Gino's voice drifted back. 'Who's that singing up there? You sound like you've got toothache in every tooth.'

For a while they sang insults.

'You know nothing about singing. You'd better go and learn at school in Palermo.'

'You don't know how to sing. You need to go to school in Monreale.'

'When you were born behind a door I thought you were a stillborn dog.'

'When you were born in the middle of the street there was a terrible stink of shit.'

They sang for a while then Gino was gone.

The day after that at sunset Angilù saw his mule twitch its ears forwards and lift its head. He looked across the valley to see a man approaching on horse-back, the horse's big, jointed shadow moving over the stones in front of them as it snorted and laboured under a big man. One of the field guards. The Prince chose them for their size, in part, and how they would look in his livery. Angilù didn't have to look; he knew which one it would be before he arrived. He sat still and waited.

Finally, Angilù looked up at the huge silhouette of horse and man right in front of him, the sword hanging from the guard's hip, the feathers on his hat bending in the wind. The horse shifted sideways a little, finding sockets for its hooves in the ground.

'This evening,' the guard said, 'it would be better to let fate take its course.'

Angilù nodded. 'They're making it hard for themselves,' he said. 'There's no moon tonight.'

'Why should you worry?'

Angilù picked up a small pink pebble and rolled it in his palm. 'Are they bringing or taking?'

'Does it matter?'

Angilù didn't say anything.

The guard said. 'They're taking.'

'How many?'

'You've got a lot of questions.'

Angilù looked up at the horse's solid flank as it stepped back a pace. He could feel the guard staring down at the top of his head. The guard was smoking a cigarette now, an expensive one, sweet and fragrant.

'Let's say,' the guard said, 'that if it didn't happen the landlord wouldn't be happy.'

'I see,' Angilù said and let the pebble drop onto the ground. 'I see.'

The guard took off his hat and wiped the sweat from his hair with his forearm. 'You think too much up here. You worry. It's all arranged anyway. You'll be found in the morning.'

'Holy Mother.'

'It's best for your reputation if they tie you.'

'But why? They haven't done that before. Why do they need to do that? Jesus Christ.'

'What did I say about thinking? Maybe someone is worried that maybe somebody in the municipality is taking an interest. Things aren't like they were. It's best.'

'Best,' Angilù repeated.

'That's all,' the guard said. He flicked down the butt of his cigarette. It landed on the ground in front of Angilù as light and precise in its sudden stillness as a cricket. Angilù wondered if the guard was watching to see if he would reach across and pick it up.

The guard twisted his horse's reins and rode away down the hill, the horse resisting the gradient at first with stiff, straightened front legs. It took a long time for him to cross the valley, ride up the opposite slope and finally sink down behind it.

Darkness. The sky crowded on all sides with the countless bright stars of a moonless night. The wind sucked noisily at the fire. Angilù had nothing to do but wait.

When he finally heard them approaching he stood up to meet them. Different footsteps around him but he couldn't count how many of them there were. They spread out in different directions. Angilù saw in his mind spiders scattering from a lifted stone. They could see him perfectly clearly, as he intended, a man appearing in gusts of flame light as he stood by the fire. He wanted to show himself willing straightaway. The shape of one man approached directly and Angilù turned his back so as not to see the face, not to know. The man said nothing as he took hold of Angilù's wrists and started tying them. He had the sweet, acrid aroma of red wine on his breath. They would all have had a good meal in somebody's house in Sant'Attilio before travelling up. The man bent down to tie Angilù's ankles then thought better of it.

'Lie on your back and put your feet in the air.'

Angilù did as he was told. As the man spent a minute fastening the rope around his legs, Angilù felt a surprising pleasure at the intimacy of the contact with this stranger. He felt cared for. It was the same careful, practical touch his mother had when she cut his hair.

When he was tied the man turned and walked away.

'Hey!' Angilù shouted after him. 'Hey! Put me in the hut!' But the man didn't turn back and Angilù had to crawl like a caterpillar past the heat of the fire to get into the safe darkness of his shelter. Beyond its walls he could hear shouting, the snapping of whips, the bleating and scrambling of sheep driven away in the dark.

The men were busy for a while but eventually it was done and there was quiet, just the wind and the remaining sheep, spooked, rattling the stones. And suddenly his mule brayed into the emptiness, loud and angry. The dumb beast. He lay on his side so as not to lie on his hands and looked out at the diminishing flames and white ashes of the fire as they were torn away towards the stars. He relaxed slowly, slowly fell asleep past sudden painful jerks of his trussed legs.

He awoke before dawn and stretched the cramps out of his legs and arms then lay still and watched the cold red spill of light across the hills. As the sun climbed he smelled the dew on the ground as it burned away, the vegetation of his hut as it heated. He was thirsty but he couldn't think how to get the stopper from the skin of water without it emptying everywhere. Perhaps he could drink the whole thing.

Also he wanted to piss, but what could he do? He flipped himself over and squirmed and kicked towards the waterskin. Then he twisted upright so that it was behind him and within reach of his hands. His fingertips found the stopper, grasped it and pulled. He moved it by millimetres, with great concentration. When finally it suddenly came loose he had to spin around on the floor as quickly as he could, push his lips up against the weight of spilling water and fix his mouth over the hole. He lay there like a suckling infant, swallowing away as his stomach expanded with the cool darkness of the water. He detached himself, the water flowing over his face again, and crawled away. His hair was wet now, coarse and heavy with dust. He made his way over to the doorway and sat upright waiting to be discovered.

Angilù squinted out over the hills. No one. Nothing. He stared into the blue and pink distances and looked for figures. Nothing. The world was only just creeping awake. His mule quivered its flanks to shake off the first flies. Angilù really needed to pee now and there was no way to get his hands round to the front of his body. He could try lying back with his knife under him but surely someone would come soon. He kicked himself back into the shade of his hut, found a dry area the spilled water hadn't soaked and lay still.

He woke up with one image roaring in his mind – a stream exploding over a rock. There was no choice now. He wrestled his knife out of his belt, gripped it with the blade upright against the rope and lay back over it. He rocked from side to side, crushing his fingers, feeling the blade bite into the rope, its tip sting against his back. He pushed with his heels so all his weight came down on it, and when it was almost through he rolled onto his face and pulled his arms apart as hard as he could. After three exertions his arms flew apart and he used them to drag himself out of the hut. He fell on his side, pulled open his trousers and let himself go in a long, loud stream that rolled over the ground as thick as a sheet of glass.

The sun was well past its highest point. They had forgotten him. Angilù shouted as loudly as he could, separating each syllable, 'Motherfuckers!'

He crawled back inside his wet, disordered hut and took the knife to cut the rope at his ankles. His arms were weak. His fingers trembled inaccurately. He saw that the dirt floor was churned, marked with the tracks of his struggle. He pushed the stopper back into the flaccid skin and picked it up. He collected his gun and left to ride his sombre, patient mule back to the estate to report the stolen sheep to the man who had ordered the theft.

Climbing onto his mule, he felt a hot fluttering pain in the small of his back. He checked with his fingertips: fine wet lines where his knife had cut him. He kicked the beast forwards, patting its strong neck as it collected itself under his weight and lunged.

Sant'Attilio appeared by stages, sliding behind slopes, emerging at other angles. From one ridge, Angilù saw the landlord's separate house, close to the palace, its outer walls and olive trees. From another, the whole of Sant'Attilio was disclosed – cubes of flaking yellow and grey, red roofs, the white church tower, the empty stripe of the roadway, the palace large on its outskirts.

Everything he knew was down there, every name, every person, every secret.

He rode straight to the landlord's house to do it quickly and get it over with. He got down from his mule at the gate and led it by the bridle between the hissing silver leaves of his beloved olive trees. He walked up to the front door and pulled the bell. He heard the sound of shaken brass pass through the house and frightened himself by imagining the landlord's presence moving in response through the interior darkness and no way of knowing how close he was, shifting closer and closer. The door opened. The landlord, smoking, looked down at him from the step then out over the top of his head. A clean white shirt and braces. Angilù thought of the dust in his hair, the dirt on his clothes, his shirt plastered to the small of his back with stiff dried blood. *Best for your reputation.*

Angilù began, 'Sir, last night . . .'

Cirò Albanese seemed bored. He raised a languid upturned palm and curled his fingers to summon the story he already knew out of Angilù.

'Last night,' Angilù began again. 'Bandits. The sheep. They took most of my sheep.'

'How many?'

'I don't . . .' Angilù didn't know what to say. He couldn't say, *I didn't count them because I thought they'd tell you.* He said, 'I didn't count.'

'You didn't count.'

'No.'

'Mother of God. All right. You go straight back up. Don't talk to anyone in the village. You understand me? I'll let the Prince know next time I see him.' The landlord leaned backwards and closed the door.

Angilù wanted to go and see his mother, to wash, to eat, to be comforted, to get a new saint for the string around his neck because he was worried that the one he had on was losing power. But he'd been told. He climbed back onto his mule and kicked its belly with his heels, kicked again and again until it bounced up into a trot and carried him up and away, the heavy pull of his unvisited home dragging at his back. It carried him up to many days of heat and silence, the noon sun pressing the colours flat to the ground, nights of stars and the sharp points of the returning moon. He drove the remaining sheep on with a whirling whip and they stumbled before him, nervous, thick-skulled, reeking. When he paused they stopped where they were, haggard, and stared down at their own shadows as if wanting to crawl into them. Angilù drove them on past his place of faces in the ground. He looked across and felt a surge of communication from them. He couldn't say what it was they were telling him. The impulse was dark, opaque, but it was commanding. It felt as though they recognised him and what it was had something to do with his shame, trussed up and helpless, forgotten by the world. He should . . . what? He touched the weakening saint on his collarbone and said a prayer.

Finally they reached a hollow full of prickly pears and the sheep hurried towards them, their tatty rumps swaying as they ran. This was now the far west of the estate, the dangerous edge. Bandits here were not the friends of friends. They would be stealing to sell or even eat. He would have to sleep lightly in the day and try to keep watch at night, his gun close at hand.

He was up there for days before anything happened, more days than it would take for him to be seen and word to spread so he was past his fear when they came, having assumed that no one cared. He'd even started sleeping at night for hours at a time, a decision he made collecting snails one day. He detached their light bodies from a rock, dropped them into his bag, then lay down in the shade and drifted into sleep. When he awoke he found his little prisoners crawling out again in laborious escape. Their long grey feet fully extended, their tiny eyes circling on their stalks, they strived forwards as quickly as they could. He laughed as he picked them up again, unsuckering them from the stones, and kept on laughing, finding it hilarious, and that laughter rinsed right through him, made him careless and light-hearted. He laughed at the thought of himself up in the hills, picturing the top of his head from above as God might see it and whatever, fuck it, whatever would happen would happen. He wiped tears from his cheeks.

They came early so he'd only just fallen asleep. He saw their grey shapes moving in the moonlight. He shouted, 'I have only thirteen sheep! The others were stolen! They're not worth taking.' There was a yellow flash, a jump in the dirt near his feet and he fell away onto his face, his hands over the back of his head. 'Don't shoot! I won't do anything! Don't shoot!' They fired again. He could still see the ghost of the muzzle flash smeared across the darkness when he heard his mule growl and stagger and fall hard onto its knees. To the rhythm of its heart, blood was pumping out of the poor beast, masses of blood, a sound like a fountain or like a basin emptied over and over onto the ground. The mule wheezed, snarling and snoring, and struggled to stay upright. Angilù saw its head flail down onto one side as the blood continued to gush. 'Why did you?' he shouted and reached for his gun. Another shot thumped into the ground right by him. Angilù aimed at one of the hurrying grey shapes and fired. A twisting fall. He'd hit him. There were curses, two more shots from different places, running feet. Angilù fired again. He saw the men, heads low, arms half raised, racing down into the darkness and disappearing.

Then Angilù was alone with the man he'd shot and had to listen to him dying. Angilù was cursed, forgotten, all his luck gone. His saint was painted tin. In the moonlight he could see the man lying on the ground by a dark irregular shape of blood, his loose legs and outflung arms like a dropped puppet's. The man chattered to himself and cried. Angilù didn't know what to do. He sang to drown out the sound. He thought of the man lying there, was suddenly himself inside the dark cave of his dying mind, hearing the man who'd killed him singing. It was terrible. But what else could he do? After a while he sensed silence beyond the sound of his voice and stopped. Stillness. The bandits gone. The shape of the mountains and the moon. His dead mule. A dead man.

Everything had ended. It was all over. And there was nothing Angilù could do, no way to alter one thing. All the time there had been death, he'd heard gunshots and stories, but he'd always been apart, hidden in the hills, in his gleaming good fortune. Now he was himself forced to eat death. Now he was taking part. His life was over. He felt tiny sitting there in the dark, his head hanging forwards, the round bones of his neck exposed to the wind. The world had its huge thumb on the back of his neck. It pressed down. It would never release him.

In the faint, frayed light of dawn, Angilù went over to look at the body to see if he recognised the man. He didn't. The shape of the man's skull was distinctive, tall and narrow and accented along the jaw with tufts of beard. His eyes had already sunk under the ridge of bone. His mouth was open showing yellow teeth, surprisingly long, like a sheep's. Angilù crossed himself. The son of some mother, some woman who would beat her head with open hands when she knew, who would clasp her rosary and howl, held up by her daughters. Probably word had already reached her.

Angilù had to go and tell someone. He had, at the very least, to be away from there so that the bandit's people could climb up and collect the body. He picked up his gun and bag and whip and scared the sheep into a huddle and drove them past the fallen body of the mule towards the village. Leaving now, not stopping, they could be back by nightfall.

After the thick, surging colours of sunrise, two little birds joined them, wagtails, hunting the insects that whirred up where the sheep trod. They twitched their yellow tails and emitted their one bright, repetitive note. They kept flying a foot or two in the air and landing again, maintaining a precise distance from

15

Angilù and the animals. Where they landed was the exact midpoint between their hunger and their fear.

Cirò Albanese rode to a nearby town to talk to somebody, a large stationary man who sat with a boulder of stomach resting on his thighs. This man, Alvaro Zuffo, modestly dressed and inconspicuous as he was, made a centre wherever he sat. Any chair enthroned him. Cirò found him in the clean-cut rectangle of shade cast by the awning of a particular bar on the square. This man had a surprisingly delicate way of smoking. He puffed, the cigarette held low in an open hand of evenly spread fingers. The man talked elliptically but to the point. Birds. Barking dogs. Stones. Fishermen. He spoke in proverbs. Only when Cirò mentioned the posters around the town did he speak directly, with rage. His anger was so large and powerful it seemed to tire him like an illness. He half closed his eyes. That mule-jawed, cuckolded son of a whore had appointed a Fascist governor to Sicily, as Cirò knew, and now disappearances, torture, order destroyed. So the decision Cirò was making was very wise. Cirò didn't know he had made a decision. He thought, rather, that he had come for advice. The man told Cirò where to go. There was a coffin maker down in the harbour who arranged things. Cirò shouldn't say one word to anyone, not even his wife, just slip away there and go.

Angilù pulled hard at the bell of the landlord's house. The jangling faded. He rang again. Silence solidified on the other side of the door. He was relieved, for the moment. He was alone. Nothing was happening. He walked back through the olive trees to the pillared gate. Beyond it he saw a motor car, dark green, its gleaming polish filmed with road dust. Beside it there was a tall man in a brown suit wearing bright shoes of two different colours of leather.

The tall man saw him. Their eyes met. Angilù wished that hadn't happened. He should have just hidden. He had no wish to meet any unknown friends of the landlord. He hung his head down between his shoulders, an insignificant peasant, and pushed through the gate.

The tall man said, in good Italian, 'He isn't here?'

Angilù answered, as he had to, in Sicilian. 'No one answered.' He tried to walk away.

'What business do you have with him?' The tall man bent down towards Angilù. His face was composed of neat triangles, a clipped beard and moustache, a sharp nose and arched eyebrows. He put his hands in the soft checkered fabric of his pockets, leaning forwards.

'I . . . I have to talk to him, to tell him, about my flock.'

'But as he's not here, why don't you tell me?'

'I should go now, sir, and . . .'

'He's not here. Tell me instead.'

'I'm sorry, sir.' Angilù scratched his head. 'I need to speak . . .'

'What do you do?' The man kept his eyes on Angilù's face, stepping with him as he tried to shift away, preventing him.

'I'm a shepherd, here on the estate.'

17

'I see.' The man smiled. 'And do you know who I am?'

'No, sir. I can't say I do.'

'That's my fault,' the man said, producing a gold pocket watch as smooth as a river pebble from his waistcoat pocket. He checked it and flipped shut its thin gold door. 'But that will change. I'm your Prince, you see. You work for me.'

'I'm sorry, sir. I didn't . . . I saw you once as a child, at harvest . . .'

'My fault, as I say. Spending all my time away in Palermo like every other fool. What was it you had to tell Albanese?'

'I was in the hills last night with the sheep. West part of the hills, your hills, and bandits came to steal them and shot my mule and tried to shoot me and I defended myself, as I had to, Lord Jesus Christ forgive me, and I fired in the darkness and shot one who lies dead there now. The others ran away. I've penned the sheep above the village.'

'You shot one?'

'God forgive me, I did. He's up there. He's dead.' The long teeth in the half-light. The shadowed eyes. Flies up there now. The mother.

'I see. It's what you should have done. You've been brave. How old are you? Still a boy, really.' He put a clean hand on Angilù's shoulder. 'Why don't you come with me? I'd like to talk to you some more.'

'Come with you? In that?' Angilù nodded towards the motor car.

'Yes, yes. In this. Albanese's not here. Probably a good thing. Come on, then. Let's go.'

Prince Adriano held open the door for him and

Angilù sat down on the chair inside, awkwardly gathering his gun and bag between his knees. The Prince shut the door, walked briskly round the front of the car and fired its motor with a violent twist of a metal handle. Angilù was surprised to see a prince bend down and use inelegant physical force. The Prince then got in and sat in the driving position beside him. He moved some levers and then, without any effort of man or animal, not even the visible pistoning of the train, they moved along the road, bouncing over its rough surface on soft leather chairs, all the way to the Prince's palace.

The palace was the largest building Angilù had been inside, larger even than any church. He'd seen it countless times, of course, from nearby or up above. He knew the shape of the plain, extensive roofs edged with gutters, the two sides that thrust forwards like a crab's claws, the patterned garden at the back with statues in it, but he'd never properly considered that its outward size must be matched by a vastness inside. As the Prince led him through, ceilings flew high overhead, some with paintings on them, false skies and angels, and he saw rooms on either side big enough for whole families.

A dog loped out to meet them, huge and rough-coated. Petted by the Prince, it trotted ahead on high, narrow legs. It turned, mouth open, to check that they were following. The beast was at home here. It lived in this place.

The Prince showed Angilù into a room, indicated a chair for him to sit on, and stood himself in front of a mirror the size of a dining table so that Angilù could see the back of his cleanly groomed head also. The mirror was surrounded by a thick, ornate golden frame at the corners of which fat little angels were stuck like flies in honey. The dog settled itself on a rug, looped around nose to tail and seemed, by the twitching of its eyebrows, to be listening to its master. Angilù's seat felt treacherously soft beneath him, as though there were nothing there. He had the strange feeling that some of his sensations were disappearing. The heat and wind in which he always lived were gone, shut outside this airy, airtight place. He looked around him at the polished furniture and patterns and realised that the Prince had been talking for some time. It turned out that the tall man's elegant beard was wagging to a great hymn of praise to Angilù himself and not only to Angilù: all shepherds were great, the true and ancient Sicily, classical Sicily. Someone had described Sicilian shepherds in a poem a long time ago. Angilù had shown great courage defending his flock against the bandits and it was the Prince's turn to do the same, to return from Palermo to protect his flock. Now that the Fascists were in power things would be different. There would be no room for people like Albanese who came between the Prince and his people, exploiting them both. The Prince gave Angilù a cigarette of soft French tobacco. Another vanishing sensation: the smoke passed down Angilù's throat in such a light, cool, unabrasive stream that he hardly felt he was smoking at all.

'Here,' the Prince said. 'I'm going to give you a gift, a pledge if you like. Wait a moment.'

He left the room. Angilù and the dog were alone,

silent together. The dog lay on the rug, wet-eyed, its long muzzle resting along its forepaws. Angilù wondered what the dog could smell on him. Sheep, snails, gunpowder, blood, the mule, herbs, sweat.

Quick stuttering footsteps. The dog raised its head. Angilù looked round. A small child stood in the doorway, a girl with big dark eyes set in skin that was pale and yellow. A child who was kept out of the sun, who was never hungry. She wore a dress that stuck out around her legs in stiff rustling layers and pleats. She held the door frame and opened her mouth slowly with a slight popping sound as though to say something, staring with frank curiosity at the stranger. A servant rushed up behind to collect her, a woman with a watch on a short chain that hung on the breast of her dark dress. Everyone here knew the exact time. She caught sight of Angilù and nodded in acknowledgement, a quick tuck of her chin that was more to conceal her flinching in shock than to greet the dirty stranger in the Prince's drawing room. She took hold of the child's hand and led her away.

The Prince returned holding something small high up in front of him like a lantern. 'Here,' he said. 'Open your hand.'

Angilù did as he was told. The Prince dropped onto Angilù's palm a heavy gold ring, a small thing but as heavy as a pigeon. The gold looked soft, buttery, as though Angilù would be able to cut through it with his knife.

'It's Roman, less ancient than your craft but there you are. I had it just the other day from a dealer from Smyrna.'

'I don't know . . .'

'You can show it to other people in the village, tell them that it's a gift from me, that I've returned. There'll be no more landlords coming between me and them, no more leases bought in crooked auctions with violence and intimidation and the profits from the land going to the landlord and his friends.'

Angilù nodded, knowing that he would never show the ring to anyone ever. It would have to be hidden. One day, when he knew how, he could sell it.

'And you and I will meet now and again,' the Prince said. 'And you can help me get to know the land. You see, I'd like to know what you know.'

Cirò Albanese walked through his house with one hand outstretched, his fingertips touching the wall, feeling the silky whitewash as he moved. Three generations to get into this house. He knew its forms, its sounds, where it was cool, where the warmth collected in winter. His children should grow up here. He should have had them already, a check to his brother's sons. He was heading for a little storeroom in which he picked up a bottle of his olive oil. He looked at it, holding it towards the window to see its colour. He opened it and swigged. A flash of green-gold light above his eyes. The smoothness as he swallowed, the peppery flavour in the after-gasp. He licked his slippery lips, savoured the hours that had gone into its making, sunlight and labour, the possession of the trees.

In his bedroom he went to a particular drawer and collected money which he put in two different pockets and more still in the lining of his jacket. He folded a handkerchief and fixed its neat peak in his breast pocket. He looked at himself in the smoky reflection of the old dressing-table mirror and smoothed his hair back at the sides, straightened his lapels, plucked his cuffs.

Take nothing. Say nothing to anyone. Go.

People were disappearing. This was true enough. Life was becoming impossible. People knew his name. That's why he had to go this way. And better to do it, better to act for yourself, be the captain of your own fate. This was about staying alive.

He found his wife busy at the kitchen table, her hair pinned up out of the way, an ordinary day six months into their marriage. Teresa was small and voluptuous, as though she had been assembled quickly and greedily. This on top of that on top of that. Breasts, belly and behind. He took her waist in his hands and laid his face against the warm skin of her bare neck.

'Baby, I can't really . . .' She raised floured hands, adjusted her fringe with her wrists as she turned inside his grip. 'You're dressed up.' He kissed her hard on the mouth. She squeaked complaint then acquiesced, softening under the force of him. He pushed his tongue into her mouth, pressed it up against her front teeth so that they raked the surface as he withdrew.

'I've got business,' he said. 'I'll see you later. What are we having?' he asked, peering over her shoulder.

'You'll find out,' she said.

Hours later Cirò had found the coffin maker's down in the city harbour. He stopped outside to smoke a cigarette and think for a moment and look at the water. This wasn't nothing he was doing. He was even afraid. Big boats standing there. Big white seabirds flying athletically overhead. The stevedores' voices bounced with a prompt, echoless lightness over the surface of the water. Cirò was an inland Sicilian. For him the sea was strange, dangerous, dazzling and beyond his calculations. It meant travel to invisible places. It meant the edge of his world, the end of it.

He threw down his cigarette then knocked on the door. He gave the name of the mutual friend who had sent him. They nodded. A boy made him coffee while they waited for a weeping widow to finish her order and leave. She pressed the tears from her cheeks with a black-bordered handkerchief and argued them down to a good price in dignified whispers. Cirò smiled at her sharpness. When she was gone they locked the door and showed Cirò his coffin and how it worked, the latches and hinges inside, the sliding panels to open the vents. They made out documents with the name and address of a family. He would be their uncle. They told him to urinate and then climb in. Standing over the drain at the back he found he couldn't pee. He came back and stepped up on a chair then into the coffin. It was a little tight at the shoulders of his strong, short-levered body but otherwise fine. He lay there and looked up at the wooden planks of the ceiling and their faces bending over him. 'Don't open the latch,' they said, 'until five hours after you feel the motion of the sea. Then you just climb out and mingle in the crowd. You're just another passenger.'

They put on the lid with its false screw heads. He latched it inside and opened the vents. It worked: he could breathe. After a minute or two he felt himself lifted up and processing out on a trolley. He began to feel very calm in an enclosing darkness that was safe and simple. He felt more protected than he had for many years. After days of much agitation arranging everything for this moment, hiding things, instructing people, he relaxed. The motion lulled him. Cirò Albanese was almost asleep when they loaded him onto a ship bound for America.

Part One

North Africa

1942

1

And here was a world intact, like a dream of his childhood. After years of war, not a sign except the intriguing sight from the train of numerous unfamiliar young women in the fields, land girls brought in presumably from Birmingham and Coventry, too distant to be seen properly, labouring silently. In London there were shelters, sandbags, militarised parks, blacked-out windows and gun emplacements. Here, nothing, trees washed through with sunshine and bird-song, the smell of the ground breathing upwards through the thick moist heat. As Will started out, his feet remembered the exact rise and fall of the walk home from the station. How perfectly his senses interlocked with the place. He knew that when he rounded this corner, yes, here it was, the peppery smell of the river before he could see it. He could picture the dim bed of round stones, the swaying weeds, its surface braided with currents. *A full-fed river.* Behind his left shoulder, away up for a couple of miles, was the rippled shape of an Iron Age hill fort where he'd played as a child, battling his brother down from the top. Everything here was still clean and fresh and in place, the countryside sincere and vigorous. It was as though he were walking through the first chapter of a future biography, with his kitbag on his shoulder.

Will decided to avoid the village and headed down through the wood. According to his father this was a recent planting, maybe only a hundred years old. It was still coppiced in this section, which had a peculiar regularity. The evenly spaced, slender trees always made him think of stage scenery. When the wind died the coppice had an indoor quiet, the quiet of an empty room.

'And where do you think you're going?'

Startled, Will turned to see his younger brother, Ed, wearing his hunting waistcoat, his open shotgun hooked over his shoulder. 'For God's sake, Ed.'

Ed smiled. They shook hands.

'You didn't hear me, did you?'

'Can't say I did.'

'Makes a fellow wonder who's been in training and who hasn't.'

Ed was much given to stealth. He loved hunting and had a straightforward aptitude for it that Will sometimes envied, often mocked. Ed would appear suddenly in a room, quiet in his body, his senses splayed around him, then smile and go out again without saying anything. Father had been in a way similar, although sharply clever, a quiet grammarian indoors but a sportsman outside, hard-riding, red-faced, breathing great volumes of air, his hair sweated to his head. A mere schoolmaster, he'd been invited to join the hunt after the last war when he'd returned with a medal, with *the* medal. It was outdoors that Will was allowed glimpses of what he took to be his father's mysterious heroism, that undiscussable subject. There was a kind of calculated rampaging, his movements very hard and linear. Ed had a different quality. He was less reflective, less troubled by thought, simply a live moving part of the world of trees and creatures and water. Will wasn't sure how he himself would be described. He wasn't a natural sportsman although he was efficient and strong enough. He always noticed the moment of commitment, the threshold he had to cross between thought and action, his mind instigating his body. He didn't think he should notice; it made him feel slightly fraudulent. His movements were effective but too invented. He was playing a part.

'Why aren't you fishing?' Will asked. 'I can't imagine there's anything left to shoot. I thought the woods would be stripped bare with rationing having everyone setting snares and popping their shotguns.'

'Ah, but for them wot knows the old woods like I does.' He opened his waistcoat to show hanging inside its left panel a rabbit, teeth bared and eyes half closed. 'And,' he said, reaching into his front pocket and carefully lifting out a bird, '. . . there's this.'

'You little tinker. A woodcock. When everyone else is working on the nth permutation of bully beef.'

Will took the bird from him. Its head, weighted by its long bill, hung over Will's fingers on the loose cord of its neck. The small body was still warm, the plumage shining with the airy burnish of a living bird. Will's senses were lighting up, home again after weeks of training grounds, weapons drills, diagrams, distempered huts and dismal food. 'That's a very kind homecoming gift,' Will said.

'It isn't any such thing,' Ed said and took the bird back, refolding its wings to fit into his pocket.

'All for you. You going to sell it on the black market?'

'No.' Ed was impatient. 'I'll give it to Mother. You'll probably eat it tonight in a pie.'

'Did she send you out to meet me?'

'Er, no. How could she if we didn't know you were coming?'

They walked out of the wood, the shadowy trees gently breaking apart to reveal the river, there with the sun on its back, the fields glowing beyond.

Will narrowed his eyes at the view.

'Ah, yes.'

'Pleased to be home?'

'I won't be back for long.'

They turned away from the riverside and up a rise to come out into the lane. Either side of them as they walked back to the house the hedgerows were lively with small birds, the verges starred with the blues and purples of wild flowers.

As they entered the front garden, Will called out, 'Ma! Mother!' They rounded the side of the house and entered through the back door. Immediately he was inside, dropping his kitbag down beside the boots and walking sticks and umbrellas, Will felt himself claimed by the familiar aroma of the place. It was a combination of many things – carpets, dogs, wood, the garden, the damp in the cellar – too subtle to be separated. It was more a mood, a life. It contained his school holidays, his father's presence, his father's death. A world intact.

'Oh, Mother! Where art thou?'

He found her in the kitchen, leaning over the table with palms pressed flat either side of the newspaper.

'Surprise.'

'Oh, crikey, yes. It's this one. Here he is. William of Arabia,' she said, lifting her spectacles and fixing them on top of her head before reaching her arms towards him, and waiting. That annoyed him, the quick flash accusation of emulation. As though T. E. Lawrence were the only man in the world to learn Arabic, to be a soldier. He walked towards her and she took hold of his shoulders with hands that were scalded red. She must have just been busy in the sink. He looked into that emotional round face, her eyes moist and diffuse with poor sight, her heavy cheeks hanging. She pulled him forwards over the long incline of her bosom and kissed him vividly on the temple.

'So you've survived training?'

'Outwardly I seem fine, don't I?'

'Near enough.'

'Some chaps broke significant limbs with the motor-cycle training.'

'Motorcycles?'

Hearing the voices or scenting him, perhaps, the dogs came shambling in. Will bent to Rex first. The King Charles spaniel squirmed down onto its haunches and whisked its feathery tail. He rubbed the soft upholstery of its ears. Will had a voice he used for the dogs, clear, enthusiastic and mocking. 'Look at you. Look at you. Yes, indeed.' Teddy, the black Labrador, his large mouth loosely open, panted and bumped against Will's legs, trying to insinuate his sleek head under Will's hands. 'Oh, and you. Yes, boy. Yes, Teddy. Oh, I've missed you too. Yes, I have. I have.'

Squatting down now, Will combed his fingers through the rich, oily fur at Teddy's nape. He felt the upswept rough warm wetness of Teddy's tongue against his chin.

'Don't overexcite them, darling.'

'They're dogs, Mother. They overexcite themselves. You do. Yes, you do. Pea-brained beasts. They're just pleased to see me again.'

'Broken limbs on motorcycles, you said.'

'Off motorcycles. Up a hill as fast as you can, whizz round then down again likewise. They disconnected the brakes to make it more difficult. There were chaps strewn all over. And they call it "Intelligence".'

'Do they? Ah, would you look at that.'

Will glanced up to see Ed laying his kills on the table, the woodcock's wings dropping open, the rabbit stiff and grimacing, the fur on one side blasted.

'Number two son brings great treasure.'

The predicted pie appeared for supper, the fine dark meat of the woodcock, with its flavours of dusk and decaying leaves, and the clean tang of the rabbit were both impaired by a horrible margarine pastry. They ate economically without candles or lights. Through the windows floated a soft lilac light. It hung in the room, almost as heavy as mist, and made the striped wallpaper glow with dreamy colour. Will realised how tired he was at the end of his training, at the end of a lot of things, and posted now, although Mother was yet to ask, off to the war finally. His mother spoke as though overhearing his thoughts.

'You know I had hoped the war would have finished before you got dragged into it.'

Will sat up. He was horrified. 'But you wouldn't want me to miss my chance.'

'I think I could cope.'

Ed said solemnly, 'A man wants to fight', and Will laughed.

'And how would you know?'

'Boys.'

'Look, it's my duty, isn't it? It needs to be done. It's what Father would have wanted.'

'I'm not so sure you know that about him,' Will's mother said quietly.

'Why wouldn't he?'

'You're his son.'

'I know that. All somewhat academic, anyway. I've been posted.'

His mother looked up at him, her dim eyes watery, a rose flush blotching her neck. 'Have you?'

'Yes.'

'And?'

It wasn't what he'd wanted. It was not what he deserved, with his Arabic and ambition. He had been warned by one NCO during training, a sly and adroit Cockney who seemed to be having the war he wanted, who had friends in the kitchens and spat at the end of definitive statements. 'You need blue eyes,' he'd said, smoking a conical hand-rolled cigarette, 'to get a commission. Take my word for it. You'll end up in the dustbin with the rest of them.' There was a look for the officer class and Will didn't have it. Five feet nine inches tall, he had dark hair and dark eyes, a handsomely groomed round head and a low centre of gravity. This was unfair. In his soul he was tall, a traveller, a keen, wind-honed figure.

35

The man who sat at the last in a sequence of desks Will had visited, the man who decided Will's future, considered the paperwork through small spectacles and made quiet grunting noises like a rootling pig. Finally he looked up. 'All very commendable. Languages. I'm putting you in for the Field Security Services.' The dustbin.

Will pinched the bridge of his nose. 'If I may, sir, I was hoping for the Special Operations Executive, you see, I . . .'

'The duty to which we are assigned,' the man interrupted, as though finishing Will's sentence, 'is where we must do our duty.'

And so Will had humiliated himself precisely in the way he'd told himself he never would.

'Sir?'

'What?'

'Sir, I'm not sure I should mention this but my father, you see, in the last war . . .'

'Yes?'

'Distinguished himself. He was awarded the VC. I . . .'

'Oh, excellent. Jolly good. You should try to be like him.'

The personnel of the unit to which Will was assigned was like a saloon bar joke. *An Englishman, a Welshman and a Jew . . .* And lo and behold his commanding officer was tall, blue-eyed, a wistful blond, younger than Will by a couple of years, an Oxford rower, perfectly friendly, unobjectionable and unprepared. To Will he said, 'And suddenly we're all soldiers. All a bit unreal, isn't it?' But they weren't soldiers. Not really.

The only danger Will could perceive with the FSS was spending the remainder of the war guarding an English airbase doing nothing at all.

Will considered how much of this to tell his mother as she asked again, 'And?'

'You needn't look so worried. I'm not going far just yet. Port protection sort of thing. Security.'

'Isn't that police work?'

Ed, leaning low over his plate, looked across to see Will's reaction.

Will felt an urge to throw his drink in his mother's face. He pictured vividly the water lashing out from his cup and striking. It was a thought he had now and then, in different company, just picking up his cup and hurling its contents into the face of whoever it was who had provoked him. He wouldn't ever do it but in those moments the vision of it was so clear and fulfilling that he had to resist. 'It is what I have been assigned to do until I am posted abroad.'

After supper they listened to the wireless, angling their heads just a little towards its glow and chiselled voices, their eyes vaguely involved in the carpet or what their hands were doing, his mother sewing, the needle rising and sinking, thread pulled tight with little tugs. The dogs slouched around the room, lay down and got up again. Will called Teddy to him and patted his smooth, hard head. The wireless made Will crave action and involvement with a physical feeling akin to hunger, an emptiness and readiness in his tightened nerves. He was very alert. He'd had years of this now: battle reports, a burning, piecemeal geography of the war, and war leaders and chaos, victories and defeats. And propaganda, of course. You couldn't really know what was going on, but Will with his intelligence, deep reading and cynicism made shrewd guesses. The reports on the wireless were so charged with possibility and vibrant with what was never said or admitted about the battles, the terror and exaltation. The mere cheering of victories didn't come close to what Will supposed the reality must be. The war was large and endlessly turbulent. There was room in it for someone like Will, for his kind of independent mastery. He could make elegant and decisive shapes out of the shapelessness. He wanted in. *By it and with it and on it and in it.*

When the news reports gave way to dance band music, Will got up to go into his father's study.

The room had its own stillness. The book spines. The vertical pleats of the heavy blue curtains. The solidity of the desk with its paperweight, mother-of-pearl-handled paper knife, the blotter and wooden trays. Behind Will, the sofa on which his father had died.

Somewhere in a drawer in this room was the medal his father never took out. The room's composed silence was like Will's father. He had always raised a hand halfway to his mouth and coughed quietly before he spoke, preparing himself to do so. Sometimes Will felt as though the empty study might do the same, clear its throat delicately and say something neat and short, something devastating. A terrifying rupture of his reserve had presaged Will's father's death. He'd come back from the hunt after being unhorsed. He'd landed badly, apparently, and sat down to dinner looking pale with a deep red scratch trenching his cheek just beside his nose. There was a small notch taken out of his forehead also. Ed asked what had happened.

'What do you bloody well think happened?'

'Darling . . .'

'What are you leaping into the breach for? Damnfool question. And I have a pounding headache. Christ.'

He leaned over and vomited onto the carpet right there at his feet. They all sat there waiting through the noise, the wrenching up out of his body. Teddy ambled over afterwards and sniffed at it.

Father sat up straight and gulped water. 'Don't all gawk at me like that. I'm obviously ill. I'm going to lie down.'

He stood up, swayed, and stalked out to his study. Half an hour later, Will's mother found him dead on the study sofa. Dead and gone having hardly ever said anything at all to his sons. There was much to cherish, of course, in Will's memories but he was gone, a man who had always known more than he said.

Will read along a shelf. Something fine and sharply enhancing of his intellect. Lucretius on the nature of the universe? Why not? It had that fine brilliance and fearlessness as a description of the world, bright bodies in space. Distinctive also. Let the other fellows always be quoting Cicero and Virgil. And reading Latin would keep his mind active. Will would have this and his Arabic poetry. The Lucretius was a squarish, green-covered volume. Inside he saw his father's pasted *ex libris*, signed with his fastidious, vertical pen strokes. *Henry Walker, 1921.*

He began reading it that night under the low, sloping

ceiling of his boyhood bedroom, intending to remember and look up the words he didn't know.

In the morning he drew the curtains. A neutral day, the light white and even. There was none of the gorgeous lustre of the previous day and this was almost a relief. The world was a realer place, more practical. Then he noticed in the glass of one pane of the window the twist of bubbles. He'd forgotten about them, or felt as though he had, but if asked at any time he could have sketched their exact distribution, rising through the clearness. They had been a small magic of his childhood, catching the light differently, sparkling a little. And they were part of his room, his world. As a child he'd almost felt them inside himself, a sensation of excitement spiralling up in his breast. And they connected his room to the river, as though his windows were formed from panels of the river's surface. That river there, brown and steady, rather work-manlike today. The bubbles in the window filled him, even before he'd gone, with a large nostalgia for this house and the landscape and his childhood. It was poetical at first but gradually he became aware of a dark outline around that feeling, a constriction, and realised that it was fear. His life, unexciting as it may have been so far, was still a detailed, complicated thing. In its own way, for him, it was precious. It would be a lot to lose.

He turned away and examined the small bookshelf in this room painted with creamy white paint that showed the tracks of the brush. How to. Boys' adventures. *Alice. The Wind in the Willows.* Ah, yes. He realised that it had been in his mind since his return. *A full-fed*

river. By it and with it and on it and in it. He'd loved
that book as a boy with its small engrossing illustra-
tions, darkly cross-hatched and tangled like nests
holding the forms of the characters. Sentimental, of
course, but he decided to take it too.

At breakfast Will told his mother that he was off
that day to his posting and she fell silent. They chewed
through their rough and watery meal of national loaf
and powdered eggs – here, in the countryside, they
were eating powdered eggs – and after that she disappeared. Will was used to interpreting her silences,
particularly those of the stricken widow period, and
he knew what she was saying. A stiff, stoical farewell
was all that was required but instead she would force
him to think of her, helpless and alone in this pristine
place in the middle of England that the dark, droning
bombers had swept over on their way to flatten
Coventry. She would be here all the while imagining
him blown to bits. This thought demanded that he
imagine his own death also and that was deeply point-
less and unhelpful. Typical: her determination never
to make a scene often resulted in strange, cramped,
unresolved scenes like this. Useless woman. A boy
going away to war without a goodbye from his mother.

Ed walked with Will towards the station, putting
on a flat cap when light rain began to fall from the
low unbroken clouds. The dismal, factual light looked
to Will like something issued by the War Office. They
walked together through the quiet coppice with the
dogs snuffling at the ground and there they parted
with a firm handshake. Will thought that Ed may have
held onto his hand a fraction longer than necessary

and said, 'Let's not be silly about this. I'll probably be back before you know it. There'll probably be some administrative delays. There generally are.'

Ed put his hands in his pockets and called the dogs. 'It's all delays for me.'

Will smiled. 'Nice for Mother, though.'

Ed hitched an eyebrow, saying nothing, then called the dogs again. They gathered, breathing, at his feet. Will petted them a final time and Ed turned to go, the dogs following after in a wide swirling train. Will watched his brother vanishing and appearing through the trees, slightly hunched, the rain pattering on his cap. Ed was heading home, sinking back into his place. Then Will turned himself and headed towards the station, out into the world and the war, and he was glad to be going.

2

On deck, out of sight, Ray had his notebook open and was trying to concentrate, to collect. It was difficult. The ship's engines were loud and the wind thumped off the Atlantic making the corners of the pages buzz and blur. Ray became engrossed in that sight. When he was beat, which in the army was most of the time, he found these small impressions dilating in his mind and filling his attention. Often they brought with them forgotten things of his childhood. Back in training, at night, his body tired and tight, twitching into sleep, the blanket he lay under brought back exactly one he'd seen in a cowboy picture when he was small. In the scene, a cowboy placed the blanket over a sleeping boy, a small courageous boy who had followed him out on a journey and now lay in front of a fire. Ray had in his mind the exact weight of the blanket, the rounded, smooth solidity where it was folded over at the top and rested on the boy's shoulder. Those few seconds of that movie had obviously gone deeply into him. He remembered how he'd imagined himself as that boy after he'd seen it – achieving that perfection of sleep, eyelids perfectly still, the blanket heavy and calm, the fire's busy, watchful light in all that dark space. Sometimes waking in the Quonset hut he found himself lost in a still earlier time. He expected to see in front of him his brother's face puffed out with sleep or the hollow in the back of his neck, his sharp shoulder blades, before he woke up and got mean. Ray remembered waking in a new day and lying there in the peace before his brother was up, hearing his father pissing in the bathroom before leaving for the leather workshop, the husky sound of his sister Monica brushing her hair in the hallway, shouts and early traffic outside, pigeons grumbling on the window ledge, their shadows shifting.

In Ray's notebook were written his ideas for movies, sometimes whole stories, sometimes single scenes or images, things he'd put in if he were making a movie. On some pages were drawings of exactly what he wanted to see on the screen, profiles of faces against backgrounds, landscapes, men walking between streetcars, between skyscrapers. He didn't expect he ever could or would be but he loved inventing, was susceptible to deep reveries in which things occurred with the glossy smoothness and sureness of movies. He kept having these ideas, ideas he'd wanted to hang on to. Sometimes he wrote down actors' names, people with the right mood in their faces for the characters. A while ago he'd bought this particular small notebook with a blue and white hardboard cover and he'd brought it with him to war where he expected many ideas to come to him. He held it open at a blank page beneath the left side of which he could see the ink of his last jottings. There was a complete scenario that he was pleased with, an idea for a picture about a boxer, a scrappy kid from the neighbourhood, maybe one of the tough kids his brother hung around with on the corners getting into trouble until one day he wandered into a gym and found discipline, focus, ambition. Of course the boxer couldn't separate himself entirely from his old ways and friends. In the lead-up to the big fight he gets caught up in a robbery and his trainer, an old guy, a real father figure, gives up on him and quits. The boxer almost gives up on himself also and has a wild night on the booze before pulling himself together, going it alone with guts and determination, and winning. Ray hadn't yet decided if that was it or maybe even better would be that the old trainer is there at the fight, appearing in his corner after a brutal round, and tells him that he hadn't given up on him but had said so to shake the kid into showing his real spirit and decency.

Ray liked that story because it was so complete, a very satisfying tale of a bad kid turning out to be good and kind. Every scene fell into place as soon as he started thinking about it. He had the entire picture in his head and could run it any time. That was the only place it would ever be. He had no idea how a picture got made and certainly didn't think that someone like him would get to make one. He just loved the movies. Lots of people did, for sure, but not like him. Ray didn't think they really got them in the same way. He'd sneak in through a fire escape and sit with his whole soul wide open in the darkness and filling with the characters, the silver and black, the music, the streets, interiors and landscapes, the camera winding its way through the world, seeing things. Other people there, eating and fooling around and puffing the projector beam full with curling smoke, didn't seem to get it. They were moved all right and they laughed but the scale of the magic, its possibilities, they didn't think about that.

The other idea he'd had in his mind recently was a love story but for this he only had a scene, a beginning. He wanted to work out where it would go. All he had was this guy, a Fifth Avenue office type, small-time and hard-working. Every day he eats his lunch in the same city park, on the same bench. This young secretary appears each day at the next bench, takes her sandwich out of a paper bag and eats it. They start greeting each other, little nods. They sit separately and take quick furtive glances. And one day they say hello and another day the young man plucks up courage and sits on her bench and they talk. Ray could see the girl, her face in the soft light of a close-up: chalk-white skin, sculpted hair, large intimate hopeful shining eyes. The man is handsome but not too handsome, ordinary really. They sit together and sparrows peck around their feet and old ladies with little dogs walk by. All the possibilities of the future surround them, leaning in close. It's in the way they're photographed, a hazy brightness, summer light hitting off them. She smiles and turns her head a half-inch and it means the whole world.

That was all he had.

Ray inhaled sharply. The cold ocean air shocked him awake. Now he was in the army, there was a moment of panic when he caught himself sinking into his imagination. He came to and was in actual fact on a warship heading for battle. True and unbelievable.

He'd opened his notebook because he thought he might use it like a journal, to record historic things and make observations about the characters he was meeting. There were plenty that fascinated him. The army had taken him from the cramped, complicated, disorderly world of his Italian neighbourhood and introduced him to the rest of America, to people like George.

Usually Ray kept himself to himself, hiding in the dark, preferring invisibility. He liked to be quiet and think. The army, then, was not a natural place for him. He could be seen all the time. Powerful, watching people shouted at him, making him run and crawl and stand thrusting himself upwards at attention and repeat things after them. Just shouting, 'Yes, sir!' was difficult for Ray. Flinging his voice out loud and clear made his heart race. Every day in the army there were terrors to confront. At night he fell fast asleep.

Back home, Ray's brother was unpredictable and not a pleasant person and much more at home in the neighbourhood than Ray was. He had tough and aimless friends whose attention you did not want to attract. They knew precise ways to twist your skin and take your money from you. They would encircle you and dare you to do something. 'Dare' was not the right word – you had to do it or suffer some penalty. They enjoyed themselves. They were street life and that meant they were out there, in places you needed to be. Walking past, Ray could get from his own brother a cold, empty stare, sometimes a kind of malevolent indifference that was the best of it, other times an annihilation, a threat that made him sick to his stomach. Ray hid from his brother and his friends, in different places and inside himself. Until the draft came and he was taken out of that place and put into one so raw and unfamiliar he started to miss home.

From his assumed position of invisibility, Ray looked out at the other men and found them fascinating. They came from all over, from worlds Ray had never seen. Some of them talked with him and Ray replied as best as he could. But there was something different about George. When George noticed him and spoke to him, Ray didn't feel frightened. He was the opposite of his brother, the opposite of a bully. George was tall, mellow, a decent Midwesterner, the kind of American they put in propaganda films. He had a round-cheeked face, eyelids that hung at a slight diagonal down to the outer edges of his eyes and a small mouth. His neat ears, exposed by his crew-cut, were sometimes comical, sometimes sad. Gentle and unassuming, his easy way with friendly gestures had a powerful effect on Ray. The first time Ray really noticed this was at the end of an assault course. He crossed the line nauseous with effort. His lungs were a tight burning thickness that he couldn't get air into. He bent double and drooled onto the ground. When he straightened up again, George winked at him. 'Nice day for a stroll.' Nothing clever or out of the ordinary. Just a little humour.

When they played cards together, the slow courtesy of George's manners made Ray think of the real America that he came from, evenings spent talking softly and watching the sun set from rural porches. It was nice to get a feel of that. Ray thought that if you

48

put George in a cowboy picture, he would be the store owner who becomes the sheriff when the sheriff is shot, a man who just knows what is right and sticks to that.

In westerns Ray liked the huge skies. His own had been crowded by buildings, ranks of windows and zigzagging fire escapes, pigeons, laundry, faces. In the cowboy pictures the skies were barred with streaks of cloud or brilliantly hot and empty with hungry vultures spiralling through space. Under those skies the strong, simple stories, men moving with their animals.

Closing his buzzing notebook, hushing the pages together and fitting it back into his pocket, Ray squinted up at the sky. Being on a ship in the middle of the Atlantic, no larger sky was possible. A dome, it dropped round to horizon on all sides. Clouds made its colours similar to that of the troopship's paintwork, sober greys and blues. The ocean churned beneath him. It was easy to think about eternity here, big things of life and death, in this fateful vastness, or if not to think about them at least to say their names. Time. Fate. Courage. Journey.

Ray returned to the noise and smells below decks. Most had stopped vomiting now but odours lingered in pockets, acrid with a tang of burned iron and bleach. When Ray first entered the ship it had reminded him of going down into the subway, that same flickering roar and riveted, heavy, hard-working metal. Ray walked past card games and letter writing, push-ups and smoking and comic book reading to find the boys of his squad. He found half of them together.

A conversation about women. Their shapes, their smells, sweetness and deceit, the variations across nationalities, whores, wives, girls. Women were so exhaustively discussed that Ray felt them almost materialising, wished into existence. Randall was on the subject of freckles, apropos of a girl he knew back home, and what amount of freckles was the right amount. This girl had the perfect number.

Floyd, squatting on his heels, said, 'Sounds like everybody'd be wanting to fuck her. How many guys are hanging around her now, you reckon? Right now? I bet right now this kid ain't even vertical.'

Randall leaned back and punched his shoulder.

'What's her address?' Floyd went on. 'Texas, by the beef cow by the cactus. That it? Maybe if I get a light injury I'll go pay her a visit.'

Randall put his hand to the side of Floyd's head and shoved. 'You've got bad morals, boy. No wonder no woman ever touched you.'

Randall was a disappointing Texan. Ray had always imagined them as tall and square, squinting, sun-weathered. Randall had the look of poverty, grey and small. His body was tightly knit, with jerking reflexes. In his bleak wrists and the clever joints of his fingers, Ray saw Randall's grip on things. Firing at the range, Randall produced the quick rhythmical *chuck-chuck* sound of a well-handled weapon. There were odd nicks like blows of a chisel in Randall's scalp where the hair didn't grow. Ray couldn't remember what it was Randall did back home, probably because he was cagey about it. Most likely he was living on welfare. What he'd tell you was how great a pitcher he was, how women shed their clothes for him or were devoted sweethearts. That was the army for you. Everyone was at it, being new men, lying freely, old selves left behind with their soft civilian clothes. Not George, though. He was honest, a Christian man who crossed his hands in front of his chest, bowed his head and concentrated when the padre said prayers.

'You're making that stuff up. You've seen that girl with, like, her boyfriend or something,' Ray said. George smiled.

'What are you talking about? Ignorant. Don't know anything.'

'So what's her name?'

'Daisy.'

'Daisy?' Ray laughed, emboldened by the flow of conversation. 'I knew you was making it up. Daisy is, like, a cow you had or something. Why didn't you even say something we could believe, Mary–Ellen or Elizabeth–May or something? Daisy.'

'Listen. Fuck. Goddamn it, listen. You're a little wop virgin, Marfione.'

'That's Italian virgin to you,' Ray said.

'That's nice,' George said. 'Like a Leonardo da Vinci.'

Floyd held a cigarette in his left hand. With his right he lit a match against his teeth, poking it far back into his mouth and dragging it along the underside of his molars. A tussle of brightness inside his mouth then he held up a match in full flame. Nonchalantly, he lit his cigarette. That was Floyd announcing he was bored with Daisy. 'Out of our hands anyway,' he said. 'The war will decide if we get to see any of these people again.'

'Don't talk that way.'

'Where are we even going? Nobody knows. Officers don't tell us.'

'We're going to fight, to land. We know that.'

'Too busy eating that gourmet shit upstairs.'

'Fuckin' right.'

'I've got to say I'm looking forward to some fighting. Get some fresh air at least.'

Fear thickened in the ship over the coming days. You could feel it. The men got angry, exercising furiously or stalled, torpid, their faces seizing up. After they were briefed about the operation they had at least a target to think about, an object in mind, procedures. But still in his dreams Ray flailed forwards on the training ground, sweat stinging his eyes and loosening his grip on his rifle. Impotent with his bayonet, he was unable to drive it into the dummy or scream his battle cry. Other indistinct men ran past him into the danger he wasn't ready to meet.

Bad weather took hold of the ship two days before the landings. The men hung on as the dark interior sank suddenly sideways, rose, slid across, plunged. There were rumours of torpedoes but none came. Vomit rolled across the floors. There was a kind of mad festivity about it as they puked and shouted, kicked about inside a turbulence equal to their dread. Rain clattered onto the metal hull and decks. The engines churned. Men vocalised as they retched, barking, moaning, almost singing. George held onto his bunk. For comfort, Ray watched him. George's eyes were closed. He seemed to be speaking a prayer. Dunphy, the big machine-gunner in Ray's squad, fell badly and sat and cursed, holding his wrist. A few of the men had started cheering as the ship reached the summit of its tilt and fell down, like it was all a ride at Coney Island.

When the storm let go of them there was cleaning up to be done, heads to be cleared, as after a wild, violent party.

In the final hours before landing on the North African coast, the boys listened to their instructions again and again, readied their weapons and kit. They were consumed with practical thoughts, or at least attempted to be, thinking things through with a determined sanity: materialist, mechanical, rational, so clear and potent it was as dizzying as moonshine. Army sanity. This was how you did it. This was how you got through. Drills and procedures. There was an opportunity to automate yourself and just fit in. This was what Ray's urge to hide counselled him – the hope that he could disappear into the military machine and present no individual target. Religion was there to cover the part of them that remained exposed. The padre said prayers. Ray looked at George, standing there, praying along. His ears looked small and serious. There was a Catholic priest as well for the boys who wanted him. Ray was not really a church guy. The priests back home were too friendly with the tough guys, both types parading around the neighbourhood in their fancy outfits, accepting the tributes of the people. But he went for a blessing anyway. His mother would want him to.

3

The waiting to land, like all the interminable waiting, felt like it would never end and then suddenly did. Ray found himself on deck loaded with his equipment waiting to climb down into a landing craft. In a grid all around him in the darkness the others were waiting to do the same. So many of them, Ray felt for the first time the pent-up strength of the force. They couldn't lose. Men went over the side and everyone stepped forward. Then Ray went over the side, clambering down from square to warping square of netting. Beside him, a soldier Ray didn't know mistimed the jump and fell between the troopship and the landing craft. His helmet struck the hull with a ringing sound and before he had time to cry out he was gone, disappeared into the black water, and didn't resurface. A quiet, rapid, weird death – the first Ray witnessed – that no one had time to remark on. It made Ray pant with terror for a minute. This was it. This was battle. This was where men died.

Ray dropped into the craft as it was rising on a wave so that it caught the bottom of his feet and almost threw him. He stepped forward, gripped the handle where he stood. Beside him, Floyd whispered, 'Let's hope the Frenchies are sleeping.'

'They'll wake up.'

'Look up at those.'

'What?' Ray glanced up: the huge side of the ship, the night sky. 'What?'

'Those stars. If I knew astrology then what could I know about what's coming.'

'We are.'

'Maybe it's all up there already.'

'Shut the fuck up, you two.' Another voice, tight with fear.

'I agree with that guy,' Ray said.

'Okay, men.' That was Sergeant Carlson, standing right behind Ray. 'Settle down. God bless us and our victory.'

The craft surged forward. For the long ride of five miles to the port that was their target, Ray stood and thought and tried not to think. He noticed how strange it was that this was the same world, the same wind blowing against them, the same sea they were moving over, but now everything was different. All the rules were different. And that falling man – had that happened? Maybe he dreamed it. No dreaming. Look. Think forwards. Think weapons. This was a night-time attack, an attack on sleep. Only the sentries would be standing upright with their eyes open. Enemies. He had a picture in his head suddenly of his older brother with his friends from the corner, different when he was with his friends, hostile. At night Ray and Tony's breath mingled in the small bed. During the day they separated. The look in his eye, hard and distant, when his kid brother walked by. That was the space you had to shoot across, corner to corner. Ray's mind was too busy. He had his rifle in his hands. He gripped it, feeling the solidity, wood and metal, remembering the parts, the action. That was all he needed to know. Until they reached the target he should be empty like a movie camera pushing forwards into the world, seeing things. *I'm in a war!* he thought to himself. *I'm in a movie!*

Now out. Okay. Just the tiniest moment between knowing he had to get out and his muscles responding, a refusal he overcame. Ray was in the cold sea, taking long slow strides to get out of it, holding his rifle over his head. Then he was on the beach, lying down on the smooth sand. The fort was where it should be, up on the right, smaller than he had pictured it. The sentries weren't firing. Ray wasn't firing. Other soldiers started firing and the sentries responded, a *put-put-put* sound that didn't seem to be hurting anyone. Soldiers were running up the steps, waving others after them. One of the sentries fell. Then the other stopped firing. Ray was running up the stone steps with the others into the fort where people were already corralled outside with their hands up. Flashlights showed their faces soft with sleep. Hearing American voices ahead, one soldier arrived up the steps shouting 'Geronimo!' There was laughter. Cigarettes were lit. Everyone was panting, airy with relief. Randall punched Ray on the arm.

'I think I shot one of those guys.'

'Well, it wasn't me. How do you know, though? Lots of shots, Randall.'

'Yeah, but the timing. When he fell. Think I got him right in the heart.'

'I'm shaking. Are you shaking?'

'Why the fuck would I be shaking?'

'It's the sea.' George appeared. 'We're not on a boat any more. Feel how solid the ground is. It's weird.'

'That's it,' Ray said. 'That must be why. I feel like I'm on waves.'

Sergeant Carlson collected his men together. His squad was one of three ordered to patrol the town and respond to any signs of resistance. A French soldier was issued to him to translate if necessary, a man now already civilian in his indifferent slouch and muttered opinions. Carlson, a head taller with white-gold hair that sparkled in the darkness, patted him on the shoulder with heavy, meaningful friendliness.

'Tell him, if he tries anything . . .' Floyd said.

'He knows,' Carlson said. 'And don't be talking about anything.'

They walked through old stone streets, alert for some danger from doorways or alleys but none came. Ray looked up at the ancient buildings of pitted stone. They walked across a deserted square, the sound of their boots echoing back from store fronts, the high façade of a great basilica.

Ray wanted to see it all but by the time the sun was up and the town was alive – Ray imagined shy, fascinated children, dark women – he and the others were in pup tents on the outskirts of the town waiting for tanks and vehicles to be landed before the army headed east. Ray stared across low, faded, biblical-looking hills and turned slowly round to the north, watching the town come into view and rocks, sea, sky. He wasn't the first to hear the planes but as soon as someone did the reaction was general, people either staring or running. Up in the heights Ray saw glinting fuselages. A formation of small planes around a couple of bombers. As they approached, the Stukas – that was what they were – went into their dive like something sliding off a table, falling then powering down towards the town. They roared overhead. Their bay doors opened and elegant, pointed bombs dropped silently out, turning end over end. Ray fell onto his face in time to feel the first explosion buck through the ground. Then again and again, a fit, an attack. Any one of them could be the end of him, any second. He listened to the detonations and in the gaps between them felt a strange swimming uplift, himself exposed, expanding, until the next one fell. The earth beneath him was blackness, oblivion. He lay on the thin, bouncing surface waiting to die. A frantic, dry popping sound was small arms fire discharged at the sky. He should be doing that, he should be up on his feet. He pushed himself up onto his knees and went to the tent for his rifle, keeping low, running round-shouldered, shrinking from the sky. There was smoke rising from the town as German aircraft made snarling, curving runs and flew away. He wrestled his gun up to his shoulder, chose one plane and shot pointlessly at it. An artillery weapon, possibly in the fort, was being fired with effect: a fighter plane cartwheeled chaotically into the sea. A bomb landed close, less than a hundred yards away, a dark speeding freefalling object that vanished inside a blast that Ray felt against his face and hands. The power was tremendous. It could kill him so easily. Bullying, shaking, the biggest thing he'd ever felt and it was personal, it meant him, it wanted to kill him.

That was the last explosion. Aircraft engines droned into the distance. Gunfire thinned. Soldiers shouted at each other and vehicles raced. No one among the tents had been killed but in the town things were different. Someone said 'bodies'. The word 'bodies' was repeated. Ray heard it. Bodies on the beach, apparently, and in the water. Smoke rose from one place in the town, thick and black, not like woodsmoke or cigarette smoke or anything but dense, full of matter, poisonous, chugging upwards.

Sergeant Carlson was right there, forming his men together. Floyd, Randall, George, Sorenson, Coyne, Dunphy, Wosniak, they were all there. Orders were to get the tents down and be ready to move out. Those not needed in town would be clearing the area. Either way, clear the camp. Carlson walked away to get further orders himself from higher up the chain.

Randall said, 'Now I got good reason to kill some of them sons of bitches.'

'Ready and willing,' Floyd said. He spat hard, checked the backs of his hands a couple of times. 'I wanna keep on invading. I wanna invade the hell out of those motherfuckers.'

George said, 'Well, we have come all this way.'

Sorenson said, 'Would you faggots actually shift and get this shit cleared up.'

'Invasion time,' Ray said, wanting to join in and convince himself. 'You better believe it.' And he did feel it inside, the havoc he wanted to wreak, maybe it was the fear thrashing away but it wanted out, it wanted action, even though the raid had left something in his mind he knew he wouldn't get rid of. A small hard certainty was lodged in his brain that he'd just have to ignore. Ray knew that he wouldn't live long. There was no way. Not against all that.

On the road into the desert, Ray knew his death had come. Planes tore down low over them and the whole column of men fell onto their faces, crawled under vehicles. Strafing fire chattered down, kicking up stones, whining off armour. Ray felt his back blown open in a ragged circle of heat. The planes angled up, turned, overflew again, firing, and flew away as guns chased them from the ground. Crying quietly, Ray felt for the wound. His fingers touched hot metal but it was loose. It was nothing, an empty shell case. He stood up, alive. Some other men weren't. There was blood, stillness, twitching, moaning, running men. Wosniak was one of them, a red foam of blood around his mouth, eyes open and blank. *Just let's do it again. Another chance. Just go back a minute.*

Artillery, guns bucking, jumping back, men feeding them, cringing away from the blast with hands to their ears, reloading, firing, volley after volley. The smell of it drifting back, the blasts felt in the soles of the men's feet, the spasming light in darkness. And then, into the incoming fire, the tanks rolled forward with a high-pitched continuous mechanical noise. It was like the surface of another planet and a war between machines, like something from the alien adventure comics some of the boys had with them, death rays and strange technologies. Ray felt small, and human. A shell landed near, thumping some men to pieces,

60

and his bowels opened warmly into his pants as the infantry squads jogged forward behind the tanks. Their task was to mop up, to catch any enemy fleeing their burning tanks or whatnot, when eventually they crossed their line. The squad jogged over the soft ground together, only eight of them now with no replacement yet for Wosniak. Sergeant Carlson set the pace. Dunphy bounced up and down with the big Browning at his hip. The tanks, whining, ground forwards, firing shells. It was like herding, Randall had said, pretending to be a cowboy. It was like. It was like. It was like nothing on earth.

One grey exhausted evening, George said to Ray, 'You know what this is like?'

'No.'

'You ever look after a baby? Ever been out on the street with a stroller with a baby in it?'

'I didn't know you got kids.'

'I don't. My sister has a baby. You're out there and this tiny thing is right there and you're totally focused on it, totally preoccupied.'

'I wanna eat something.'

'So the whole world is a danger around you. Everything.'

'I understand.'

'Yeah, but it's bigger than that, the feeling. I don't know. The whole world and the little baby, little fingers, little eyes, you know?'

'I think so, George. We should . . . I think we should find out if we can sleep.'

'It's everything. That's what I'm saying.'

Mostly the infantry couldn't do much, running

among the machines. It kept them warm was one good thing. At night, cold space pressed down on them in the desert. The air was full of freezing stars. Heat came from the machines, from the fires, from their bodies. Ray ran past a burning tank once that pushed a furnace heat against him. It was hotter than a stove, so hot that red rivets were weeping out of the metal and sparks fizzed above the turret. Ray pictured white bones inside, luminescent, soldiers heated until they became ghosts. A good way to go, maybe. At least there'd be nothing left. They had passed tanks in the daytime that were loud with flies. They had passed bodies and parts of bodies. The artillery hacked into the distance. Tanks whirred forwards. They jogged after, looking for people loose on the other side. The landscape changed around them. Once they trotted through masses of paper that fluttered and blew around them, a silent storm. Some of the pages were scorched and black. They raced in spirals on the wind. They were letters. An enemy vehicle full of mail, presumably thinking the front line further forward, had been hit. It was a smoking hulk with exploded tyres, flapping shreds of canvas. The driver was still at the wheel, a harrowed figure of red and black. The way his teeth were exposed in his burned face made him look like a rat trying to gnaw at something. The squad was making good progress, covering ground. Ray was getting closer to his death.

4

Battle forms had broken up now. It was pure chasing
at all hours. Through glassy morning air Ray and the
boys set off in their quiet hunting party. Their uniforms
were stiff with sweat and excrement but they'd been
promised they were almost out of the desert and
anyway they loosened as they moved. Ray felt thin
and sinewy, light-headed, lucid, dumb. They were on
some sort of rock shelf, the ground beneath them
hard, rippled, glittering with tiny crystals. It lasted for
hours. Ahead of them they could see mountains now,
a greener world rearing up, toppling and fracturing in
hard peaks and facets. Ray was looking up at them,
dreaming them, when they were suddenly fired on
from the right and all dived down. Dunphy let go
with a wide swinging arc of automatic fire. Ray,
ignoring the pain in his arms from throwing himself
onto the rock, squirmed around to see what was what.
Floyd was to his right and he was lying there moaning,
in trouble, his legs obviously too relaxed like he
couldn't move them. Randall was crawling forwards
as shots came chipping across. He pulled a grenade
from his belt and threw it. Ray heard it skittering
across the rock before it exploded.

'Got 'em,' Randall shouted. 'They're down in a hole.'

'Floyd's bad,' George shouted.

Sergeant Carlson ordered them forwards. Ray had to get past Floyd who looked across at him with wild eyes. His head was jerking. 'Please,' he said.

Ray shot into the oncoming fire. Another grenade was thrown which disappeared down into the enemy hole and sent up handfuls of rock and gravel and maybe some human stuff. Afterwards, a strange sight – hands rising up out of the ground. Small and simple human hands wavered at the tops of arms, empty.

'They're surrendering,' Ray said it to himself then shouted, his voice hoarse and cracking. 'They're surrendering!'

Sergeant Carlson shouted, 'Stay careful! We don't know. I'm . . . Randall!'

Randall was up on his feet walking towards the hands that were persisting in the air. He walked until he was standing over them. 'They are!' he shouted back. 'Fuckers are just giving up.'

The others, all but Floyd, ran forward to see. There were four Germans standing in a cleft in the rock with three dead bodies at their feet. There must have been more of them to start with but in a part of the trench hit by a grenade it was hard to work out from the remains.

'What do we do, sarge?'

Ray stared down at the shaven head of one of them, at the fingerprint pattern of growth visible in the little sparks of hair. The German looked back up at Ray. The whites of his eyes were red. There was a gum of white spit in the corners of his mouth that jerked as he babbled in German. Ray's bayonet was swinging in front of them. One little stab.

A shot. Then another. Randall was shooting them, point-blank shots bursting down into them. He shot the one at Ray's feet then Carlson grabbed Randall round the arms and fell with him to the ground. 'For God's sake, Randall.'

The last living German was shaking, dancing on the spot, his hands at either side of his head, fingers paralysed into claws. He was trying to lift his feet out of the wetness around him.

'Ray, watch Randall,' Carlson said. 'No fucking choice now.'

Sergeant Carlson stepped forward and shot the last one.

From behind them George called out, 'Floyd's dead.'

5

What was he remembering? He had the picture in his mind but couldn't locate it – paint running in a gutter, white paint very clean against the pasted greys of the street. Ray could only have been four or five. It was Mitchell's. That was it. The storefront was being painted. Men were washing out the cans and emptying them into the drains. A smooth clean chemical smell. Looking up, a man in overalls smiling. Ray's brain relaxed with pleasure as the memory came back whole. They were running past a burned-out fighter plane that had crashed onto its face, its tail in the air. Wosniak had been replaced now by a boy they called Red. Floyd had been replaced also: a boy called Alex who insisted on his own name. They called him Alice instead.

Almost there, almost into the colourful upheaval of the mountains. This might be it, the last day. They kept moving under Carlson's command, his hair now white from the sun. Aircraft, their aircraft, growled overhead on raids. They saw men, prisoners, sitting on the ground with their hands in the air, weaponless, unburdened and exempt. Bodies they kept running past. Some were blackened and swollen, bursting their skin, others neat on a dry stain of red blood. Sometimes their clothes had been blown off and they were randomly naked from the waist down or across the back. Ray was still alive which didn't make sense. Several times Stukas had spilled down towards them and let out their bombs and the earth had jumped, towering upward for a second, roaring. Men died all around him and he was fine. Once he felt himself inflating, growing larger and larger, filling the deadly space around him and still nothing, no bullet or bomb or shrapnel pierced him.

Such were his thoughts now, big and weird. His mind no longer raced as it had at first. Instead single images, memories, kept catching as in a malfunctioning projector, the actors slowing down nonsensically and stopping, the images blistering and burning through as his mind gave way to exhaustion.

And it was over. The tanks were leaguered. All the surviving soldiers were together. They dropped down to sleep on the ground without pitching tents. They woke up to find themselves in an actual place with facilities being built and a town nearby. Here they'd be rested, refreshed, let loose for a night before the next push.

6

After a shave, Ray's cheeks felt numb and glassy under his fingertips. After a shower, blasted clean, he felt very small and bare. He looked down at his unhurt body, his white stomach shrunken hard around cubes of muscle, his meekly hanging genitals, his long thighs and bony feet. The only signs of war on him were a few notches in the skin of his hands and arms and the fact that he was slimmer, more sinewy, healthier. He dried himself fiercely, scrubbing at his surface with the thin army towel and dressed for town.

Soldiers in clean uniforms were everywhere. The streets thronged with them, their voices caught and echoing between stone walls. There were so many of them, all loudly alive. Ray looked around at them and saw repetition, like a natural phenomenon with lots of the same thing coming at once, like birds or rain. Around him George, Coyne and Randall were wearing the same uniforms, were talking in the same way, smiling and gesturing. It was a good thing to get lost in. It was safe. A prod in his back startled him. Beside him a small boy stood with cupped palms saying, 'Joe, Joe, you have cigarette for me?'

'Sure. Why not?' Ray tapped one out of his pack and handed it over.

The boy took the gift without thanks and pocketed

it, absorbing it quickly into his possession the way the ground absorbs water. 'Joe, you want fuck?'

'Not now, kid. Scram.'

'Hey, you made a friend,' George said.

'Not really, I haven't.'

'Hey, mister, you want fuck?'

'Now, son . . .' George began and Randall interrupted.

'Tell him we'll see his sister later. Right now we want drink.'

The boy circled around them as they walked until Coyne shoved him with his boot. After that he moved on to another group ahead of them, catching the hand of a Negro soldier and examining it.

It seemed there was a bar ahead but already it was too full with a great still crowd formed around it. They couldn't get close so turned to try another direction. On the top of a wall, looking down at him, Ray noticed a cat. Its large eyes catching the sun were lit a startling green. Its striped velvet face, with wide whiskers and pink fastidious nose, rested just above its forepaws. It shifted as they strode past, holding Ray's gaze, its shoulder blades undulating under its loose skin. Just a cat living its cat's life in silence, half out of sight, doing its thing. Ray felt his throat tighten against the threat of tears.

'Here's a place,' Coyne announced.

Excepting one occasion as a child when he and his brother had got sick on their father's grappa, Ray had never really drunk. A little red wine at weddings and that was that. But tonight he would drink as a man and as a soldier, battle-hardened and deserving.

With the first glass they toasted victory, then Wosniak and Floyd, and after that to dispel the quickly enclosing gloom George offered 'Wild nights!' The wine was cool with a pleasant innocuous fruit flavour. Ray knocked it back as he would any other drink to quench the thirst he now noticed he had. As the wine washed through him, he felt a fibrous stiffness in his face and scalp start to loosen. The tension in his body drifted outside of him as he drank, surrounding him, buzzing pleasantly. Later glasses of wine tasted less and less wholesome, growing acrid with the residue each one left in his throat and the many cigarettes Ray smoked.

With a soft steady fire the sun set along the narrow street, enriching the texture of the bricks, lighting the men, their blue smoke, the red wine, glasses sparkling, everything haloed. Ray was on a chair now, leaning back on its rear legs with his head resting on the rough wall.

'Would you look at that,' he said.

George answered. 'At what?'

'Just look at it all. At the look of it.'

'Oh, indeed.' From his nostrils, George exhaled smoke down around his collar.

'Man, if I had a camera, a movie camera . . .'

'Or you could draw a picture.'

'You know how sometimes in a movie you can really see what the air's like, like it's soft or how much breeze there is? Right now would be perfect for that.'

'You wanna get into the movie business?'

'Sure.' Ray swigged from his glass. 'But whoever heard of a person . . .'

'Seems all I ever hear about is people. People in Hollywood gotta come from someplace. I can see it now.' George shaped a banner across the air in front of him. 'Decorated military hero and movie director . . .'

'Hey, what the fuck. Why's Randall always gotta be making trouble? Christ.'

Coming towards them held under the arm of another man, Randall's head was a strangled bloody red with thick veins in his brow and temples. Rocking and heaving, reaching up, Randall was trying to throw him.

'Gentlemen, gentlemen.' George stood with his hands a loud hailer at the sides of his mouth. 'Save it for Fritz and the Eyeties.'

In the darkness Ray said, 'Sun's down.'

'Planet's turned,' George said.

'Big light gone,' Coyne said. 'Big light in hole.'

They were very much drunk now, all four of them. Coyne had in his hand a bottle of wine he'd swiped from a table. He blew across the top of it. 'Listen up, men,' he said. 'And listen good. Good men.' He swayed. 'That's what you are.' He jerked to his full height, wine sloshing in the bottle. 'To fallen fucking heroes!'

'To fallen heroes!'

The bottle was passed around. It kept arriving in Ray's hand after new toasts were made, grand, senti-mental, patriotic toasts. A part of Ray cringed from them and didn't want to have to say them with the others. He couldn't have said what but there was something in them defiling of his feelings. At the same time, he couldn't stop; another part of Ray did want to roar them out with the others and he did so, although each time he registered inside a small violation of his soul.

Randall was spanking his own forehead incredibly hard. 'Dang,' he said. 'Dang.' He stopped hitting himself. 'Y'all know what? Battle, fellers, you know. True as Christ Jesus, I used to be dirty, all dirty and torn up. Clean now. Clean ole motherfucker. Fire. Fire coming at you, all around.' He laughed. 'It's a job is what it is. I needed a job and I sure as shit got one now. It's a thing you gotta do. I'm doing it.'

'That's nice,' Coyne said. 'I like listening to your pretty talk but really I'd like to fuck a lady.'

Randall reared up, eyes wide. 'That's a good idea. We should get one of them kids running around selling the whores. Gotta take your chances when fortune presents itself.'

'What do you say, George?' Coyne asked. Ray looked up, waiting for George's answer.

'I think it's what you fellows need.'

'Why not?' Ray said. 'Why not? Could be dying tomorrow.'

A boy was easy to find. Puffing on a cigarette Randall gave him, the kid led them through alleyways on a winding journey that filled Ray with dread. A virgin, Ray had once been permitted to squeeze the breast of a cousin called Rosa, under the blouse but on top of a stout brassiere. That was about the extent of his experience with women. What he knew of the rest was hard to fit together. There was the dirty, mechanical, implausible and disgusting talk of his brother and friends, and in movies the disembodying swerve of a camera away from a kissing couple up into the sky or to a scene of playing fountains. Well, he would know soon enough. They were through a door, handing over money, walking upstairs as other soldiers walked down.

While Coyne and Randall chattered, George was quiet. Ray wondered if he was disgusted and wouldn't take part but that didn't turn out to be the case. Frowning, as if at a bad headache, George entered the whore's room before Ray and the others, even despite Randall's obscene objections. He emerged ten minutes later drying his forehead with his handkerchief, making Ray wonder what on earth went on in there. 'She's a good girl,' George said, taking out and lighting a cigarette. 'Don't you all be scared now. And act like the gentlemen you aren't.'

Ray was scared. The fear had drained the swagger and abandon out of him and left him with an unwieldy, unwanted drunkenness that he felt trapped inside. Too soon it was his turn inside the room. He entered, struggled to fix his eyes on the girl and to take in the dim surroundings. The girl was small, plump, tired, with loose black hair, lipstick, tin rings on her short fingers. She wore two large pieces of black underwear that she must have replaced between each visitor. There was a basin where she rinsed herself. A large crack forked across the wall over the plain crumpled bed where she had laid some sort of towel or protective cloth to keep the sheets clean. On the wall above the bedstead, Ray saw that she had tacked a picture postcard of some mountains with snow on them.

She looked at Ray standing there. She nodded at him, her mouth hanging open, and reached behind her back to unfasten her brassiere. 'Yes, Joe,' she said. 'Happy time now.' The garment loosened and slid from her shoulders, revealing two large, soft, unevenly sized breasts that ended with startling nipples of dark brown. Their haloes were textured with little bumps. The bits that stuck out were dented in the middle. Ray stared at them, grimacing. Significant, female nipples. So many facts in the world, so much he didn't know. Briefly, he thought of the Germans in the trench wilting down into their own blood, the people emptying out of the bodies. The prostitute came forward, seeing him stuck there, and kept coming until the weight of her was pressed against him, her breasts shaping like dough against his chest, her smell floating up and enclosing him. She reached down and undid his belt, opened him up and put her bare hand directly on the nerves of his penis. Ray shivered. He took hold of one of her breasts and tried to kiss her on the side of her forehead as she pulled at him, pulling him out from his centre, unravelling him. Then abruptly she stopped, walked over to the bed, pulled down her drawers and lay down. Ray looked at her, at the breasts spilling off her chest, then he glanced down between her parted legs but was frightened by the dark, split, complicated shape inside a messy tuft of black hair – it had an awful kind of leer to it – and he jerked his gaze away. He decided to close his eyes, to go by sensations. Carefully, he climbed on top of her with his pants round his knees and she touched him again, arranging him in position to push which he did and found he could push still further and then his penis was inside her body, was covered with her, gripped all around. He pushed again, testing. It was fine. She didn't seem to mind. This was it. This was doing it. He kept pushing and looked down at her face, staring at her dark eyes until he noticed that she was looking back at him. He saw her looking out from inside herself. For a moment they saw each other then Ray hid his face in the damp hair around her neck. He decided not to be ashamed and to try and screw her like a man, to go at it with vigour, but almost as soon as he started he was helpless and it was over. He lay on top of her twitching. She patted his back like he was a little boy. 'Good Joe,' she said. 'Good soldier.' She squirmed and he slid out and got to his feet, buckling his pants. As he collected himself, wiping the sweat from his face, and walked to the door, he could hear her splashing water up inside herself to wash him out. He glanced back to see her at it, her jaw set, concentrating, a woman at a task. It might've been laundry or scrubbing a stove.

After that, what was there to do but drink more? The boys found more wine and then a bottle of some kind of spirit. Ray drank and shouted until he was sick, leaning his forearms against a wall as he retched again and again, exhausting heaves that lifted one foot off the ground, a burning rope slowly hauled out of his guts and leaving him clean and empty, his face wet with saliva and tears.

7

Ray sat staring at the table top, sipping coffee with sugar, remembering snatches of the ghost train ride of the night before. He didn't know what to make of it all. It was just more, more stuff, more of all of this. He'd fucked a girl; that was a fact. That had happened. Now he knew that at least he wouldn't die a virgin.

Mail arrived. For Ray there was the moral prod of a parcel from home. Inside was a letter, a bit of an envelope with a Cuban stamp on it and a movie fan magazine called *Screenland*. The letter was really a short note written by his father entirely in capital letters. It didn't have much to say. YOUR MA SHE'S WORRIED SICK AND MISERABLE EVERY NIGHT I TELL HER HER SONS A HERO SHE SHOULD BE PROUD. There was news about a dying uncle Luigi (still alive) and he explained about getting the stamp from a neighbour with a cousin in Cuba. Ray's father was under the impression that Ray collected stamps. This wasn't true. He had collected them, half-heartedly, for about six months when it seemed that everybody was. Ray's father must have noticed at the time and this was now a thing he remembered about his son who was away fighting in the war. Ray looked closely at the stamp, its image formed from delicate lines of

76

ink finer than hairs. It showed a woman in flowing clothes holding a baby aloft in front of a double cross. 'Republica de Cuba' was printed across the bottom. Beneath the stamp was the carefully torn square of envelope. His father's fingers had done that. The stamp had travelled the unimaginable distance from home. Ray felt the reality of that suddenly. Somehow, it was like the moment of seeing the prostitute inside her eyes looking out at him. He blushed, heat curdling in his face, and picked up the magazine.

Keep 'Em Smiling! Bob Hope Tells How. Coyne read it aloud over his shoulder and commented, 'Looks like Claire Trevor's got some better ideas.' The actress was pictured on the cover with her neat small breasts snugly defined by a winter jersey. Standing by a white fence with blue sky behind her, she smiled encouragingly at the reader. 'And would you look at that,' Coyne went on. 'Gene Tierney's Honeymoon Home! Scoop photos! Ain't that a thrill. I didn't know you were into these sissy mags, Marfione.'

'I don't read 'em.'

'Evidence is stacking up the other way.'

'I don't. My folks know I like movies is all.'

'Movies and sweet, sweet American titties.'

Later, George saw Ray with the magazine and said, 'Planning your future.'

'What?'

'The movies. Last night we were talking and you were talking about movies. You had a whole theory going about how movies should look more like photos in newspapers. And that thing about the air. Remember?'

'Drunk is what I was.'

'Made sense to me. What else are you gonna do when you get back?'

'Come on.'

'I'm serious.'

Ray didn't know what to say. Those words and ideas coming out of another person, coming out of George, made them seem real, seem possible. Ray's scenarios, the boxer and the lovers unfolded afresh in his imagination, full of light and life.

8

Ray looked out through the back of the truck at the cold white rain, the road shining into mud and the snarling face of the truck behind. They were in foothills on an uncomfortable twisting drive. Either side there was forest, dark and inward, loud under the rain. Actually, through the gasoline and wet uniforms the world smelled good. The main thing was not to jump out of the truck, not to try and escape into the woods. Ray concentrated on not moving and allowing himself to be safely carried to his death. Thoughts kept coming to him, convulsions of his mind that showed bodies, explosions, Wosniak and Floyd ripped and dead, their eyes empty.

They shouldn't have had that time off. It made it so much harder to go back to running and killing, to a world of possible annihilation from three hundred and sixty degrees at any split second in time. Strangely, one of the hardest things was pulling the trigger, to open fire. Ray had only ever had to do it at a distance, his bullets flicking forwards into so much empty space it seemed they could only land harmlessly. Not like Randall and Carlson who had fired point blank through hair, skin, bone and blood, men swaying and falling, no longer men. 'Point Blank Range' was maybe a good name for a movie. Ray would hesitate at such a moment and maybe that is what would kill him, soon, up there in the mountains. He smiled to himself. Going up into the mountains to die.

That night, before the dawn attack, under a tarp drumming with the rain, George spoke seriously to Ray. They were standing together. Ray could tell from the way they were breathing and not saying anything that they were both thinking about the fighting to come and how things had been in the desert. He could tell because there wasn't much else they could be thinking about. When he said slowly to himself, 'Yep, yep,' George answered, 'Oh, yes, indeed.'

Ray went on. 'Hell of a . . .'

'Sure was.'

'I'm pleased that part's over.'

'Oh, it's over. Came and went.'

'Came and fucking went. Boom.'

'I've been thinking, though.'

'Not sure you ought to be doing that,' Ray said.

'Things got awful clear for a while out there. Couldn't help it, I suppose. I'm going to tell you, Ray.'

'What?'

George pressed his palm against his forehead then looked at it. 'It's about the fighting.'

'Yes?'

'I'm thinking if it's a straight out question of you against another man.'

'Yes?'

'Then you shouldn't do it. You should let yourself be killed. I mean me. I don't want to kill the other guy.'

'Holy crap, George. Don't fucking say that. In a fucking war?'

'You can shoot, I'm not saying that, only above them or to the side. Take them prisoner. But I don't want to shoot the man. It's not right. Like I said, it came clear.'

'George, you son of a bitch, don't say this. What do you think that does to your chances?'

'Really? Ray, statistically what do you think it does to your chances, killing or not killing? Do you think it makes a blind bit of difference? And anyway, chances, fuck 'em. You can't steer by chances.'

'George, come on,' Ray pleaded. 'I think you should change your mind. We'll be out there in a couple hours.'

'Change it. Just throw a switch and change it. I can't.'

'Goddammit George, I don't want you . . .'

'I know, I know. But what are we gonna do?'

9

The gull lifted its wings, leaned into the wind and floated up from the harbour wall.

Will watched it adjust its angles and move, sliding away, rising up and backwards on a gust. With its pale, shallow eyes, its long yellow bill switching from side to side, it scanned the scene. Its breast feathers flickered as it hung there, thinking, then it planed down, raced low over the water, circled around and settled back on the wall, folding its grey wings away. It tilted its head back and called at nothing.

For Will it was painful to find himself so engrossed, registering this bird's flight as an event in his day. Boredom this profound was painful. Standing there on guard for long hours of empty daylight made his chest tight, his hands feel weak.

The sea shifted quietly inside the square arms of the harbour wall, restless colour inside a shape. Changing clouds and birds.

The perimeters had to be secure. When cargo came in, as it did every so often, Will or one of the other Field Security men would give it the once over and then try to prevent any of it from being stolen. It was with this task that Will was coming to understand something of the large, rambling incompetence of the war effort. Frequently it was misdirected cargo that arrived. He had checked in a shipload of desert fighting equipment that had arrived from a port in North Africa, sent away for no apparent reason from precisely the place where it would have been of use. Theft was impossible to stop. Moving equipment and supplies was evidently like carrying water in your cupped palms. Several times in one of the town's dismal pubs, Will had been offered tinned foods that he had checked off earlier that day and which were addressed to foreign theatres of operation.

A kind of low comedy seemed to have taken hold of the town. Petty crime, overworked prostitutes, talkative invalids, suspect fishermen, vain girls. Some Americans were stationed there and the local women had been surfeited with attention. As far as Will could see it had made them all prone to overestimate their own charms, vulgarly capricious and avid for gifts. The girl who enlivened Will's imagination was not to be found among them. She was dark, different, intelligent, aloof. Will pictured a sharp refinement to her beauty: aquiline, subtly expressive, almost like speech; it spoke to him. She would have little time for the common run of people but she would notice him, she would recognise him, his complexity and command. She would be passionate. Perhaps she was the daughter of a vicar or a medical man. She read into the night and walked along the coastline. She was nothing like the laughing dollies of the pubs, smelling of face powder and cigarettes and beer.

Sergeant Major Henderson wasn't interested in these women either. He was a practical man and preferred the prostitutes. The other night he had received the men in his room, stripped from the waist down, sitting open-legged in front of the fire, a razor rasping through his pubic hair as he shaved it off. 'For the avoidance of crabs,' he informed them. 'I suggest you strip your area as well. Don't give 'em anything to hold onto.' His legs were large and white as wax. Between his feet dropped dry curls of coppery hair. He had similarly forthright advice about dealing with civilians and fellow soldiers. 'You'll want to get off on a good footing. I find it helps give the idea if you refer to them as "You fuckers".'

Will nodded. That was what a sergeant major was for: to inculcate the coarseness and expeditious brutality of military manners. Not that Sergeant Major Henderson would have thought in those terms. He simply was brutal and coarse. His shaving left him with scalded pink genitals, nude and obscene. He tried to look away while Henderson stood up swinging to pull on his underpants. At this point Captain Draycott entered and froze, blinking, trying to work out what he had walked into. Henderson calmly buckled his trousers. 'Lessons in hygiene, sir,' he said.

Captain Draycott was a very different man, a DPhil in Icelandic Literature from a military family but a man who wouldn't have entered the army if it hadn't been for the war. He was gifted with a natural physical prowess that was apparently accidental. He rowed and played handball. With his eyes of clear, rinsed blue, he was obvious leadership material. His eyes weren't piercing, however, but sensitive, vulnerable. Confronted with the gross, obtuse, often perverse demands of the army, he would halt, blink, and look around as though to catch the attention of someone reasonable who could never be found. Will would certainly have made a better captain than Draycott. Perhaps one day, war being what it is, he would get his chance.

The wind had strengthened, cuffing the water into little waves that raced endlessly into the harbour wall. The gull had been joined by two others. They circled in the air and settled, bowing and calling.

'Afternoon, squire.' Travis, come to relieve him. 'Anything of note? U-boats among the mackerel fleet?'

'No activity of any kind. Shit all, as Henderson would say.'

'Smoke?'

'Abso-bloody-lutely.'

Travis tapped a couple of cigarettes from his pack and flipped open his lighter. Will lit his from the ragged, blustery flame. Travis snapped the lighter shut. He smiled, tilting upwards the cigarette between his lips.

'Least we're not in any bother,' he said.

'True enough. I detect no immediate peril.'

'That's right. And you get to keep all your limbs that way. No sliding about outside Woolworth's on a wooden tray begging with a tin cup.'

'Can't argue with that. You can just stand here and enjoy the view.'

'Exactly.'

'And we'll all die as old men in our beds with nothing on our minds.'

'Sounds ideal.'

Back in the hut, Will found Samuels reading a magazine, head bent, a cigarette held at his temple, exhaling smoke onto the opened pages. 'Afternoon,' he said without looking up. 'Enjoy the ozone?'

'Bored. Bored. Bored. Bored. Bored. Couldn't find a book to read?'

'My apologies, professor.' Samuels imitated Travis's voice: 'But we're all safe and sound, ain't we?'

'I know. Awfully cheering, isn't it.'

Samuels turned a page cleanly, slowly, with his skilled fingers. A Jew, Samuels' father was the proprietor of a wireless shop in London and the young Raphael – who liked to be called 'Rafe' in the English manner; Will called him Samuels – had grown up fiddling with valves and wires. He loved the machines and the broadcasts and could be quite poetic on the subject, talking of the invisible radio waves that surrounded them all, beamed through the air and separated into electrical impulses by these beautiful machines. Will suspected that all Samuels knew, admittedly quite a lot, he had gleaned from his listening rather than reading or a real education. An automatic, fastidious recoil from Samuels sometimes occurred in Will. He wanted to distinguish between them. They were not the same thing, not to be confused, even if they shared a stature, an eye colour and a rank in this unsatisfactory unit.

Will sat down and looked at the bustling clouds. The bright window pane shook.

'I want to do something,' he said.

'I know you do. But this won't last for ever,' Samuels said. 'It can't, can it? Nothing does.'

Will lit one of his own cigarettes, dragging the match aflame with a slow, vindictive scrape. The hut hummed in the wind.

For the next three days nothing happened except the theft from a vessel of a couple of crates of prosthetic limbs. There were jokes about that – checking the town for men with three legs, and so on – but Will didn't find them amusing. Standing in the hold inspecting an open crate full of arms had given Will a very unpleasant feeling. It was one sudden thought, that those unnatural smooth forms, parodies of human flesh, actually embodied real pain in real men, men with their limbs blown off, or – even more powerful to realise – men whose limbs hadn't yet been blown off but would be, any moment, possibly that very moment. It was the way the boat rocked as he stood in it. It was all mixed up with Lucretius and the swerving atoms that make up the world and its events and it all came home to him. He was enclosed in the thought as in a dream. The war was very large and complicated and, in some important ways, wrong. The scale of it was disclosed by this one tiny detail, this one negligible fragment of the chaos. The prosthetic limbs lay in the open crate in front of him like bits of outsized dolls, marionettes, things for the theatre. Thoughts thronged in his mind with such force they almost unbalanced him. He said nothing. He told the man he could close the case again. Outside, in the sea air, he breathed and felt better.

That night Captain Draycott gave them the news. They were off. Finally, a proper posting – to liberated North Africa.

10

Two nauseous weeks on board ship, more digression and delay. But beneath the leaden hours, Will could feel, flashing, impatient, the bright incipience of adventure, of the action he was sailing towards.

The first view of the town showed a delicate white human construction set above the sea, very intricate and appealing after the monotonous, elemental voyage. The soldiers disembarked, were processed and billeted and walked through a pretty Islamic place of domes and minarets and blue shadows across whitewashed walls. There were shell holes and craters, pockmarks of bullets in plaster. A late-flowering plant grew everywhere, in gardens and high places, hung with spidery red blossoms. Frenchmen in white suits and straw hats observed the troops with an effortful nonchalance. Will smiled at one, was scowled at. They seemed without gratitude or energy. A strange atmosphere. Lassitude and recent death. The Arab children were more alive, smiling, running up, running away. Will tried an Arabic phrase on one little girl. She caught her sudden laugh in a cupped hand, stopped still and stared as he walked on with the others.

The Field Security unit were given a fine seaside mansion to inhabit. They weren't told who had been there before. It was simply now theirs, capacious and comfortable with a steep stony garden, grand vistas of the sea and an ideal policeman's view of the town below to the right. The first sensation was of trespass. The tiled floors gave a clipped response, the high ceilings seemed to know something. It took the men's loud appropriation, curses, thrown kitbags and slammed doors, to take possession of the place. They discovered a dining room with a long walnut table and mirrors, several bathrooms with baths on clawed feet, canopied beds and simple servants' beds.

Will and a few others were sent back to the waterfront to collect motorbikes. They returned roaring up the coast after a couple of hours to learn that Draycott had found them a cook. That evening they sat around the long table and ate a meal that would have seemed a hallucination back home: fresh meat, wine from small tulip-shaped glasses, fruits – nectarines and peaches – and soft cheese. The fruit was so colourful, like a platter of tiny Chinese lanterns glowing golden and rose, and so full of juice and flavour. They sucked and gasped.

'We're being seduced,' Will said. 'They're trying to soften us up.'

'That comes later,' Travis said. 'With the dusky maidens.'

'Not tonight it doesn't, I'm afraid, chaps,' Draycott said. 'Meeting in the town hall. Everyone's got to be there. Laying down the law sort of affair. Apparently I've got to make a speech.'

The town hall was filled with voices and different uniforms. With sidelong glances the defeated French assessed the free French, the town's police, the military police, the Senegalese soldiers, the Arabs, the stiff Englishmen, New Zealanders and Indians. It soon settled into a dullness, however, as speech after tedious speech was made. Captain Draycott had the pleasure of informing the assembly that Field Security now represented the highest civil authority in the city. Whether this was understood was hard to determine although it seemed unlikely. To overcome the language barrier, Captain Draycott had decided to address the audience in carefully correct schoolboy Latin. Will looked around at the various bored, attentive or murmuring faces. He thought that they weren't really there to find out how the town would be run. They were there to show themselves, to see the others and draw their own conclusions. Later, outside, they would find out the rest.

11

Despite Draycott's Latin, enough of what he'd said had been understood for the Field Security office to be immediately busy with visitors. The first to arrive was a small man with short, dense, dark hair, as smooth as velvet, rippling twice over rolls of flesh at the top of his nape. He held a leather portfolio with both hands and spoke rapid French from a puckering mouth. With none of the French speakers in the office, it fell to Will to try to determine the reason for his presence. Possibly Will would have understood the man if he'd been able to slow the tempo of his speech but each time Will tried to staunch the flow of words with outspread hands the man fell silent, watched, and then started again with the same incomprehensible gabble. He ended by pointing at himself with his thumb and nodding with great sincerity, drawing up his shoulders, the pantomime of a dignified man denying some affront.

'I didn't understand a word of that,' Will said loudly. 'You'll have to wait.'

The man raised questioning eyebrows.

'Sit,' Will said and pointed to a chair. The man understood. He sat down, arranging his portfolio square across his lap.

Will returned to unloading into cabinets the prefabricated filing system.

The next visitor was a Monsieur Girardot, tall, with a kindly, vicarish stoop to his shoulders and fingers dappled yellow with nicotine stains. He spoke excellent English and explained that he was a landowner in a small way.

'I hope that what I say to you now,' he went on, 'will be treated as a matter of confidence.'

'Indeed.'

'Because you see, I want to tell you what it is here. There are not many people for you to trust in this town. The truth is that everybody, ev-er-y-bo-dy, in this town is pro-Vichy. Of course they don't say this to you now because you are here and you have the guns. Fine. So, I can give you details of the people to watch, for reasons of security. I can give you evidence of every person of substance, including, I am ashamed to say, my own brother Guillaume Girardot, being in league with the enemy.'

'Can you?'

'I am afraid so.'

'I think perhaps I ought to introduce you to my superior, Captain Draycott. I'm sure he'd be very interested in what you have to say. Follow me.'

Will led M. Girardot – who was expressing his pleasure at the moral superiority of the English – down the corridor to Draycott's room. He knocked, heard 'come', and entered.

'Captain, this is M. Girardot. He is sympathetic to our cause and has some very interesting information about the local inhabitants.'

An hour later, Will heard Draycott ushering Girardot out of the building. Will went out to see Draycott, his face hanging heavily with relief, returning up the stairs. He caught sight of Will and tutted. 'Why on earth did you send that awful man in to see me? He sat down without asking and betrayed pretty much everyone he knew, immediately, incontinently, including close family.'

I'm sorry, sir. I thought he might have some useful information. Sir, I've just had a thought. Will you excuse me a moment? He can be of use.' Will dashed out past Draycott and called out after M. Girardot, still just within sight, about to turn a corner between crumbling white buildings. Will beckoned him back.

'Thank you. I wonder, could you possibly translate for us what this chap's trying to say.'

'Of course I will help you.'

Shown the small man with the portfolio, M. Girardot said, 'But I know him.' The two men chatted in French for a moment. Girardot turned and said, 'This is Monsieur Dusapin. He has been trying to explain to you that he is an executioner. He built his own guillotine so it is his property. He can work for you, it's not a problem. He has photographs with him of his work he can show to you.'

'He has photographs?'

'Yes, he has.'

Hearing the word 'photographs', M. Dusapin began fiddling at the strings of his portfolio. 'Tell him to stop,' Will said. 'Tell him I don't want to see his disgusting photographs. Tell him we won't be needing his services. There are thousands of our soldiers in the vicinity. A firing squad won't be hard to find. There's no need for us to recreate the terror of the French Revolution.'

Girardot, with a pained expression, translated. Dusapin began objecting. Head tilted to one side, looking at Will, Girardot listened and conveyed the executioner's meaning to Will.

Will stopped him. 'I've said we don't want him. It's time for him to leave.'

When they'd gone, Will plucked at his uniform, pulling it straight. Nausea surged with the anger that rose in him. Obscene, that executioner – soft, ingratiating, ambitious, argumentative, delicate. The rich hair on his head was somehow particularly sickening. Deeply, sinisterly French. He was precisely why the French should not have an empire. They weren't clean and decent. Their order was that of a petty, sordid regime.

Will's opinion of the French was reinforced rather than challenged by each of the colonials he encountered in the town. With little to occupy them, they drank too much, fornicated in shuttered rooms and paid frequent visits to the office to denounce each other as traitors. They drank so much that occasionally one of them would fall from a bar stool and die on the floor. Draycott mentioned a couple of distressing recent incidences of this happening in a morning meeting and Samuels raised his hand to say, 'It's the anisette, sir. It's not safe.'

Will and Samuels had gone to a bar together one evening. Will requested beers. While they were served, Samuels watched the preparation of a drink for their neighbour at the bar. A glass of clear spirit was handed to a customer who added a dash of water, turning the whole concoction cloudy white. The man noticed

Samuels looking at him and said, 'Anisette. You like to try? Very strong. Is good.' He took the cigarette holder from between his teeth and knocked back the drink, closing his eyes, leaning forwards, tucking in his chin and shuddering. He reopened watery eyes and laughed. 'Yes, yes, two for you, for victory heroes.'

'That's kind,' Samuels replied. 'I'm not sure . . .'

'But why not?' Will said, always alert to detect any hint of unmanliness in Samuels, with the urge to punish any that appeared. Will said to the Frenchman, 'That's good of you. For victory heroes.' To Samuels he went on, 'What are you scared of?'

'Nothing. I . . .'

'Might as well try it. New experiences and all that. See the world. Worried it'll be too strong for your delicate constitution?'

'No. It's not that. I . . .'

'So there we are, then.'

The Frenchman was already conferring with the barman. It seemed that some discussion was necessary, some persuasion. Finally, the barman shrugged his shoulders and reached for an unmarked bottle.

'He is not certain for you,' the Frenchman laughed. 'In Vichy time, it was not legal. Now it comes back to legal. But only the pharmacist makes it. Very very strong alcohol.'

Two small glasses were set before Will and Samuels. They added water and observed the colour change like schoolboys in a chemistry lesson.

'Right,' Will said. 'On one.'

'It smells like pure ethanol with a dash of aniseed twists.'

'On one. One.'

The drink fell in clouds of flame into Will's chest. 'Haaa.'

'There goes my tongue,' Samuels croaked.

'That's awful.'

'The second one is always better,' the Frenchman said, laughing. 'You will see.' He ordered two more.

Later, the Frenchman was telling something deeply secret into Will's ear, his breath hot, his lips wet and explosive. It was something about a particular woman's vagina, someone's wife. Will couldn't really follow. Something to do with the vagina and a kind of fruit. Outside the bar, the Frenchman called over an Arab boy and reached into a pocket musical with loose change. 'Look at this,' he said to Will. When the boy was close, the man jerked up one leg and stamped as hard as he could onto the boy's bare toes. The boy squeaked and fell over holding his foot.

'Did you see what that fucker did?' Samuels spiralled into Will's vision. 'I'm going to stamp on his fucking toes.' Samuels staggered towards the man and tried to do the same but missed, banging his own foot on the pavement. 'I missed.'

'Why?' the Frenchman protested, looking hurt. 'It is normal. It is good for them.'

'Try again,' Will instructed. Samuels did but the man backed away as he approached and then turned and kept walking.

Will remembered hurtling home on his motorbike after that, zooming up the slope to the villa and arriving suddenly stock still beside the machine with the engine running. He made himself vomit into the elegant floral lavatory of the villa and went to bed.

The following morning, when called into Draycott's office, Will's head felt both hollow and filled with pain. Light drilled into him. He squinted as he saluted and sat carefully on the chair Draycott indicated. Draycott had good news. As an Arabic speaker, Will's new job was to compile a report on local attitudes to the Allies. Get out of town on a motorcycle and see what he could find out. Talk to the tribal bigwigs. Will watched with increasing interest as Draycott's fingers swirled over a very sizeable area of the map.

'All of that?'

'Yes.'

'How long?'

'However long it takes, I suppose. Not too long. If we need you for anything we'll let you know.'

'Thank you, sir.' Will stood up and saluted again, suddenly cleared of pain by a rush of real happiness.

12

Frightened by the noise of Will's motorcycle, a deer flew up the mountainside. He watched it go, the pulsing of its strong body, its delicate legs flung out, gathered under. Will shut off the engine and stood on the balls of his feet, the bike balanced beneath him. The winter's day was as clear as spring water. In the forests of cork oak on either side, every tree was distinct, clarified. He could see the texture of the bark, the shivering leaves, insects twirling in shafts of sunlight. Above, a raptor glided along the valley's channel of sky. Will tipped his head back and breathed in through his nostrils. Fresh cold air, wood-scented, tainted with the faint reek of petrol and hot metal. He was further inland than any of the Allies had yet reached, out on his own, the first. As he drove between fields, startled women had turned their backs on him, hiding their unveiled faces. The stillness in the forest was wonderful. It reminded him of being home in the wood by the river. Peace settled gently over his shoulders like a shawl. He allowed himself a moment more then kicked the motorcycle alive. There was somewhere he had to get to. The bike rattled and shook, firing up. The Norton was not a powerful machine but it was dogged up the inclines, chugging away. Will was getting to like its dumb, stubborn character as he would a horse.

Standing in the sleepy Esso station, petrol splashing into the hot empty tank of the Norton, it occurred to Will that the open lorry he'd just seen driving away with barrels roped to its back was probably delivering stolen fuel. Petrol was going missing in large quantities from the Allied shipments, soaking quickly out of sight. Of course that was what he'd just seen happen but he hadn't realised it at the time because he lacked the nasty immediate suspiciousness of a policeman. He hadn't thought of it until it was too late. He wouldn't go after the truck now. He didn't have time and, anyway, if it was delivering there'd be no evidence. He had better things to do, an appointment to keep.

In the next valley, Will terrified a man walking with a few goats by riding at him, even as he tried to get out of the way, stopping and shouting the tribal leader's name into his face. Eventually the man understood. He took his stick from across his shoulder blades and pointed with it, adding words Will couldn't understand. Will nodded and gave him a cigarette then drove off, his motorcycle sliding under him as it struggled for purchase in the dust.

Will found a huddle of tents surrounded by animals and children who ran up to him to examine the motorcycle and take hold of his hands and laugh and try to grab the pistol in his belt. Will repeated the elder's name at them. A man approached, very stately in a long swathe of cloth, and bowed with his right palm over his heart. He beckoned Will to come in, delaying him at the low entrance to remove his boots. Inside, Will felt underfoot the luxury of thick carpets. Seated on cushions were several men smoking and drinking tea. Will assumed the eldest of them to be the man he had come to see and he bowed deeply, his hand over his heart. The man smiled and gestured for him to sit. Will lowered himself into a cross-legged position on a cushion and looked around, carefully smiling at everyone in turn. The soft, rich carpets, the luminous low walls of the tent, the scent of tea and smoke, made a cosiness as piquant, Will thought, as that of an English cottage with a lively fire and rain beating on small panes of leaded glass. In his classical Arabic, he said that he thanked Allah for bringing him to this place and for the honour of being their guest. Some tension seemed to be induced by this greeting. Polite smiles stiffened and betrayed incomprehension. Of course, Will's accent might not be too accurate. He was a reader of Arabic first and a speaker second. The faces arranged around him in the tent were similar enough for Will to think he saw signs of interbreeding. Recurring round the circle were the same sharp, deeply cleft chins and large watery green eyes. A young lad offered fresh glasses of tea on a brass plate. Will took one and held it by the burning rim. The head man immediately sucked at his glass and growled quietly. Behind him, in Will's line of sight, an open panel in the tent showed the world outside with browsing goats shaking off flies, low sunlight clinging to the stones and plants and goat fur, and blue smoke rolling across from a fire out of sight.

The old man said something to Will. Will listened but could not understand. The man repeated himself. This time Will managed to hear the breaks between the words and understood that what he'd been asked, a little surprisingly, was whether he was a German.

'No. I'm British. The Germans are our enemy.'

'Ah.' The man reached into his glass with long fingers and pulled out a sprig of mint, chewed it. 'Tell me, my brother, who will Allah give victory to in this war?'

'To us.'

'Ah. Are there many of you?'

'Yes. Very many. Many thousands. We have many cannons, aeroplanes, bombs and ships. The enemy, the Germans, cannot resist.'

'Ah. This is what I thought.' The old man turned to his fellows. He said, 'They will win.'

Through the bright gap in the tent wall, Will saw a goat suddenly start to piss, a thick jet of liquid, while it lifted its tail and a few turds extruded and dropped softly in a pile. Will had the urge to comment, to make a little joke perhaps, in the English way, but stopped himself. He felt the flat heat of embarrassment pressing under his skin at the thought of the misstep he might have just made. It would have been gauche and he arraigned himself for his superficial civilisation, degenerate, that was scandalised by natural processes. These tribal men in their tent, mixing regal postures, ceremony and unaffected natural squalor, were truly aristocratic, like figures from epic or Arabic hunting poetry. But he hadn't said anything. All was well. The moment passed. He sipped his tea and imagined in his own eyes, narrowed at the steam, the same far-seeing, blue-green clarity of the eyes around him. 'Yes,' he said slowly. 'We will win.'

A thoughtful silence. Outside the tent, the dry ripping sounds of a wood fire, the voices of those tending to it.

'I can offer you,' the old man said, slapping his palm on the carpet beside him, 'one hundred horsemen to help you win the war.'

'Thank you. I will tell the general of your offer. He will be very pleased and honoured.' Will had no idea whether the man could raise a hundred horsemen. It sounded suspiciously like a symbolic figure but it hardly mattered. Even if they existed, there was no need for them. No, what this exchange meant was that Will had created an alliance, a pact between warriors.

'Good. Then that is settled. Come outside now.'

The men all stood up and Will followed them in his socks out into the light and air. He thought for a moment of retrieving his shoes but decided he couldn't double back. He absorbed, with slight tremors, the discomfort of the ground beneath him. Several men lit new cigarettes and Will did also, offering his around. A couple of the men already smoking took one of Will's for later. That smell: across the fire lay the scorched carcase of a goat, blackened, cracking, its posture rigid as though still resisting giving up its life. Evidently Will was being treated to full tribal hospitality.

More tea was brought by a woman whose similar eyes looked out, downcast, from the gap in her veil. One of the men patted Will on the shoulder and led him over to squat down by the fire and start picking shreds of meat to eat. The other men joined them, sinking onto their heels and laughing. A hawk called overhead, keen, austere, poignant. Evening moisture had started giving body to the air. After this successful mission, Will would get back on his motorcycle and ride down from the mountains to the coast. At the villa, he would lie on his bed and read more classical philosophy. Here he was sitting among newly made allies, tribesmen. At home in Warwickshire was a famous river by which he'd grown up. He was the son of a war hero. Overhead an eagle (probably) was flying. He was eating roasted goat. He was where he'd always wanted to be, in the middle of his life's adventure and standing at its prow, pushing forwards.

Before he left, they told Will that they wanted to present him with a gift. Two men left and Will filled the silence with expressions of his gratitude and how unnecessary a gift was for him, it was he who should have brought them a gift and so on. They returned accompanied by a young girl and Will, smiling, looked at them each in turn and waited for them to present the gift. 'Please,' one of the men said and gestured at the girl. 'No,' Will said. 'No, you can't mean . . .' She was about fourteen years old, short with strong bare feet and thin gold rings in her ears. The expressions of the men seemed to confirm that they were serious, that she was a gift. Will didn't know what to say. The living presence of the girl, staring down, waiting, her toes contracting to grip the carpet, disabled thought. Will didn't want to offend the men and forfeit his achievement with them. Still not knowing what he would do, he thanked them with his right hand over his heart. He took the girl to his motorbike, followed by the tribesmen, thanked them again and sat down, arranging her behind him with her arms around his waist. He had to pull her arms around him; they were knotted with fear or shame or some terrible emotion. He waved and they drove off down the valley, Will's heart pounding, the girl's breath on the back of his neck.

When they were out of sight, he slowed to a halt to consider the situation. Again he had to pull at her thin, dark-haired arms that were now bound suffocatingly tight around him. The ride seemed to have terrified her. She climbed off. He could see her short legs trembling. She was his possession. A girl. He felt the warmth of her body still on his back. He smelled the acid smell of her body. But there was nothing he could do or could consider doing. He couldn't take her with him. He couldn't have her and then send her back. He wouldn't do anything, he corrected himself. He was a gentleman and so forth. He took hold of her, however, and hugged her, his nose in one small ear, holding her tightly enough that he could feel her small breasts against him, the strong length of her body pressed against his. He felt it and let go, pushing her away again. He pointed at the motor-cycle and said, 'It won't ride.' She stared. He made large x-shaped gestures to tell her that it wasn't working. He said again, 'It will not go. It will not go.' She gave no sign of understanding. 'Home,' he said. 'You go home.' Still she didn't move. He pointed back up the hill and shooed her away. Finally he took hold of her shoulders, turned her around, put one hand on her left buttock and pushed. She understood. She ran and didn't look back.

In the villa that night, Will indulged himself and masturbated. He knew that he'd done the right thing but now he imagined himself throwing her down onto that stony track, pulling the clothing from the helpless girl and fucking her there and then.

13

It was a pleasure the following day to sit in the office and type up his report. Cigarette, coffee, the hammering of the typewriter keys loud in the bare, high-ceilinged room. Briefly, he stood up and walked to the window and looked down at the harbour that was seething with brown uniforms of newly arrived men and the turning cranes lifting crates and machines. Returning to the desk he continued describing his singular exploit. The account was dryly factual, understated in what Will imagined was the best Whitehall style; nevertheless the image of his success shone out, not gaudily painted but emerging from the essential substance like a profile on a coin.

And it seemed that word had already spread. In the afternoon an Arab arrived at the office and asked specifically to speak to Mr Walker. Will was called out to meet a small, unhappy, very tidily dressed man who shook him by the hand and said, 'I understand you are a friend of the Arab people.'

'I am,' Will answered. 'I mean, I'm here in a sense representing the Allies. We're here for every . . .'

'Yes. That's good. Do you smoke?'

'Thank you, yes.' Will accepted the proffered cigarette.

'I can bring you many boxes. Good American

tobacco, if you like it. So. As a friend I ask you, go to the French prison and ask to see the fish pool.'

'The fish pond?'

'Yes, the fish pond. Where you keep fish in a garden.'

'And what is it?'

'You will see.' The man's small brown eyes were urgent, his mouth set. 'Go and ask like that and you will surprise them and they will think you know everything already and they will show you.'

'But I don't know anything because you're not telling me.'

'It's better not to know. You'll find out when you get there. Then you will know what to do. Goodbye now, friend.'

'What? I beg your pardon, but what are you saying?'

'I'm saying I go now. Thank you again. The fish pond.'

14

It was all happening. That night after a good meal accompanied by the oily aromatic local wine the sky began to vibrate. Captain Draycott knitted his hands and leaned forwards over his plate. He said, 'Oh dear.'

'Is that . . .'

'I fear it is. Yes. Christ. There it is.' Anti-aircraft guns began hacking from their positions around the port. An air raid siren started it, its long loops of panic rising and falling and rising again. The men sat still and thoughtful.

'Should we not . . .?'

'What?' Henderson asked, challenging them.

'Go somewhere. Downstairs. There's a cellar, isn't there? I haven't looked.'

'You haven't looked? You're Field Security and you haven't looked?'

'Yes,' Captain Draycott answered, 'that might be a sensible prec—' The rest of the word was lost inside the loud detonation of a bomb.

'That was close.'

Three of them got up and headed for the door.

'Don't shit yourselves, boys,' Henderson shouted through the noise. He was lighting his pipe, slowly applying the flame to the circle of tobacco.

Draycott was pale, staring. He breathed noisily through his teeth.

'It's like being back in London,' Samuels said.

Will grinned at him. 'Is it?'

'Yes. Night after night of this.'

'Fine old time,' Henderson said. 'Grabbing handfuls of fanny in the Underground shelters.'

'Not exactly.'

Planes were now directly overhead, shaking the room. The chandelier jumped and skipped on the end of its chain. The guns were going mad. Draycott leaned forward and vomited then got up and tried to walk out. He stumbled. Someone was in his path, lying under the table saying, 'Please, Mother. Oh, Mother. Oh, shit shit shit shit.' Draycott looked down, bewildered, then hurried out.

Samuels shouted, 'Seems sensible!' Another bomb fell and its light flashed at the window.

Seeing Samuels about to go, Will leaned forward and grabbed his wrist, holding him there. Samuels looked back at him, confusion in his eyes, apparently trying to hear what Will was saying and then realising, trying to twist his arm free. Will held him and held him, and then let go. Samuels swore at him as he turned but Will couldn't hear through the engine noise, the firing and explosions.

Will's body felt very light and thrilled, like he wanted to dance. He got up from the table and rushed out onto the terrace from where he could see the swinging diagonals of the searchlights, one catching the sea as a bomb dropped into it and cast up a brief tower of black water. The light of the guns stuttered. Fires were taking hold in parts of the city. From a gun position behind him, anti-aircraft fire was dropping red-hot shrapnel onto the terrace. Will could hear it tinkling as it hit. A bomb fell so close that he felt the hot wind on the side of his face, stinging with masonry grit. Still he felt invulnerable, exalted, charged and powerful and really there. He was haloed in his own safety. He was with his father in courage. He was in his presence. It was like they were brothers.

15

The prison was a square building with a central courtyard. A bomb had smashed one corner to a heap of rubble. Rather poetically, from the exposed walls above, twisted iron bars had been blown back like a curtain in a breeze. Apparently three men had been killed. Will could see others, unhoused, chained together, waiting in the courtyard.

Perhaps this confusion might be to Will's advantage. The clerk or whoever he was behind the desk was evidently without sleep, blinking dry eyes, holding a cigarette in slightly trembling fingers.

'I'm here from Allied Field Security,' Will informed him.

'Name.'

'I beg your pardon.'

'Your name.'

'My name is Walker. I'm here from Field Security. This is my pass and I'm here to see the fish pond.'

The man blinked and took the card from Will. *The holder of this card is engaged in SECURITY duties, in the performance of which he is authorised to be in any place, at any time, and in any dress. All authorities subject to Military Law are enjoined to give him every assistance in their power, and others are requested to extend him all facilities for carrying out his duties.* The man looked up at Will and back down at the pass.

Will said, 'I'm not going anywhere until I have been shown the fish pond.'

'Please wait.' The man flapped his hand in the direction of a wooden chair then left the room.

Panic. The ants' nest had been disturbed. Will sat and smiled to himself. The smile faded as he was kept waiting. Repeatedly, he checked his watch against the clock on the wall that filled the room with a *chip-chip-chip* sound. After fifteen minutes he decided he certainly would not stand for any French nonsense and called out, 'I say!' Nothing. He called out again and got up and smacked the desk with the flat of his hand. Noises behind the door and then the man appeared holding it open for someone who was evidently his superior, a slow, fat man with a face composed of heavy circles, dark orbits round his eyes, hanging cheeks, a drooping moustache.

'Yes, you are here?' he said.

'Yes, I am here. I am here to see the fish pond.'

'For any reason in particular?'

'At this point,' Will answered, 'that is no concern of yours.'

'Very well.' The senior man shrugged.

'What is your name?' Will asked him.

'Marchand. Look, I will show you but I don't understand it can be interesting to you. It's just the usual dirt.'

'Nevertheless.'

'Okay. Okay. You follow.' Marchand hummed as he led Will out of the room, down a corridor and out into the courtyard. Behind them his junior scurried.

Will looked over the prisoners chained together. All of them Arabs, they weren't saying anything. They looked at Will. Carefully, they did not look at the other two.

Marchand gestured and the junior bent down and inserted a key into a large manhole cover. The key turned, he pulled up a handle and dragged clear the heavy lid. Rolling up from the darkness below came a stench that made Will recoil.

'What is it? A sewer? The usual dirt?'

Marchand looked at him with sorrow or contempt, it was hard to tell quite what that dark, slumped expression was. 'It's the fish pond,' he said.

Will stepped forward, his hand over his face as his digestive tract bucked, returning the flavour of coffee to the back of his mouth. He looked down into the darkness. There were noises. Wounded by the sudden chute of light, cowering, streaked with filth, were naked Arab men, bearded, cringing. Slowly one stood up on weakened legs and turned his face upwards with closed eyes to breathe the fresh air.

16

This was the worst ever. It couldn't get worse than this. The noise, emplaced guns, planes ripping over, guns, single shots, bursts, everything. From different heights. The ground surging up ahead, sinking away behind. Ray saw Randall fall just ahead of him. He ran over, crouching, holding his rifle in one hand. In the heavy fire Randall had gone down softly, crumpling into the foetal position. Randall's eyes were shut. Both hands were closed around the barrel of his rifle the way a mouse holds onto the stem of grass with its little white hands in the picture on the cereal packet. There was a sore on his face but that was old, crusted dry around the edges. Ray yanked his arm. 'Hey!' He couldn't see any blood. 'Where are you hurt? Where are you hurt?' Three yards to the right the ground stuttered with impacts. Ray could see Randall's mouth saying quietly 'What?' then he sort of settled his lips together, swallowing. He pulled his rifle a little closer. He was sleeping. 'Holy shit, Randall! Wake up!' Ray slapped down hard onto Randall's face. 'Wake up! Wake the fuck up!' He dragged his shoulder and got some movement out of him and then ran. Fire was coming in. He ran up around a corner of ground, tufted with growth. The path was a grease of trodden mud. He glanced behind. Randall was with him. A mortar thumped the place where they'd been.

They sheltered in a slit trench, someone else's. Whoever had dug it was gone. Now Ray and three others were there. Above them was a bush charred black on one side. On the side closest to them it was green, its leaves dry and warped with heat. The earth of the trench was striped, layered, with stones in it and fine tangling yellow-white hairs of roots, the colour of under ground, of seeing no light, exposed now, like wiring ripped out of a wall. Once Ray had seen a building going up in his neighbourhood. The old one, condemned, had been pulled down in an enjoyably violent, almost festive demolition. He'd seen the new building constructed in stages, bricks and cavities, pipes, laths and plaster, toilets. It shocked him. He'd thought homes were as solidly consistent as prisms, definite places full of families, family odours, meals and arguments and objects. But they weren't. They were fabricated out of layers of materials. They weren't really anything. Artillery showed this to be true of the whole world. Life was a skin: it could be peeled away like strips of wallpaper with its coherent pattern. The soil wasn't that deep. A shell gored it and there was rock beneath. Plants burned, uprooted. It could all be scraped off easily.

A curving arm up ahead. A voice calling. They had to get out and run. They were getting higher. This was good. They were getting up onto higher ground, safer ground. Where was George? Was he firing? Was he safe? There he was. They shivered, shouting to themselves. They ran.

17

All the cloud cover had blown away. The sky was empty. The planes seemed to race through it faster, towards the sun. The mountains were difficult now with light and shadow. Their eyes couldn't adjust quickly enough from one to the other. It was blind darkness or blazing saturation. Not that they wanted to move from where they were. They'd watched other men run past to be slapped onto their sides by a sniper across the valley. They were safe. They had cover. Alice bounced up and down on his bent legs. He said, 'Nng. Nng God. Nah. Hmm.' Below them down in the pass the fighting had gotten insane. All the American boys had to get through the same narrow throat of the mountain where Randall's brain had given out and fallen asleep. The Germans had artillery positions now above it. The guns were pounding and pounding. Men were stuck there, among rocks, being mixed with the rocks. Stone bowl of his ma – what was it called? – a pestle. Garlic and salt in it. Smash. Her strong round dimpled hand on the stick thing. Smash. Molecules. The fragrance coming out.

Okay, fuck. That was something new now. A crater to their left from a new position throwing up a crown of dirt as it appeared. They couldn't stay. George was fumbling at his fly. He was pissing himself and trying to get his penis out, spraying his hands and weapon before he could angle the stream clear.

'We have to run! We have to run!'

'What?'

'Run!'

Ray held the brim of his helmet, stooped and ran. Rough ground rising and falling underfoot. Through wet matter, a soldier spread open, daubed across the rocks. Shit from everywhere, from overhead and the sides, the whole world lethal, folding over them and around, swallowing them. A bigger blast. Ray threw himself down. Film this. Take a camera and throw it. Put it on a rope and swing it. See everybody die. Another blast so close it hit him like a punch in the head and his whole body jumped an inch off the shuddering ground. He landed with grit of shattered earth burning him. Got up again and ran. His footsteps sounded strange. Strange that he could hear them, inside his body. His head was light, altered. He felt his face for blood. A high thin tone was ringing in his head. Beneath that there was a crackling, a sifting of something pulverised and shifting about. Voices, the explosions were quiet as though distant. There was blood on his cheek where stones had hit him. He found with his finger that there was blood in the hole of his right ear.

A hand on him. George pulling him. They had all turned to run in different directions but he hadn't heard them say where.

18

Floating now   weightless without sound

                                                         fear

Fear so great it had washed him empty

                 Up through his bones his foot beats
                 told him he was

                             running

Two thumps of explosion, mud splash, fire in it

small shots pecking the ground in several places

People lying on the ground like what are they?

                         Running, burn of ankle twist over

Like people, shaped like people?

                   over rocks. Behind rocks, a piece of sky,
                                 towards that

                         Like dolls! Dropped.

Everything dead already.
Dead piece by piece

>a man lying
>with one arm already dead
>the rest of him thrashing

>Dead and running, fast as he could. Dropping
>to hide flat with the others and wait and
>his shoulder against the hip of a man in front
>solid bone, rapid trembling

Over there a man trying
to dig a foxhole with his helmet
metal pranging off the rocks

>Just in front, something moving, effort to focus
>to see, before it was too late, but
>it was so close, a bug, nothing, moving in a
>small circle
>on its disturbed patch, jointed feelers dabbling
>the ground.
>Smart black. Crumb of sand on it.

Planes screaming over.

All matter just matter, jerking with life, some of it.
Just jumping a little bit, tearing against itself, fraying,
frittering, bleeding, lying still, scattered.

Whizz of eighty-eight. Just short. Throwing stuff in
his face.

Pushing himself flatter against the earth. Nothing underneath. Earth darkness. Up.

Running.

Low ridge to get behind and settle and up.
He had to join in now, pulling his trigger at those shapes over there. The crack of his gun faint by his ear.

George! Was George doing the same? Or was he lying, dropped?

Couldn't see him anywhere.

Smoke rolling across from something.

Up again, into blasts from all directions
that he couldn't survive.

running

19

Several days after seeing the prison, when Will finally cornered Draycott and told him his story, Draycott listened, wincing and shaking his head, and was no help at all. His gaze kept flickering past Will or over him; that reminded Will of their difference in stature. He complained relevantly at the bloody filthy behaviour of the French and affirmed that in no way could they be trusted. When pressed for support for action, he offered none. Will argued his position – something should be done just for decency's sake and think of the advantage to Anglo-Arab relations here. Draycott, holding the door jamb, looking at Will's dusty shoes, countered that they should be very wary of upsetting the local balance of power. Perhaps Will could gather intelligence and write something up. Draycott glanced again over the top of Will's head, stepped backwards into his office and, without saying anything further, closed the door.

Since the nights of heavy bombing, Draycott had been behaving strangely. At breakfast the other morning, spooning trembling scrambled eggs onto his plate, he'd told Will that, from now on, whenever they were in a public place, Will should refer to him as Lieutenant Bryce loudly enough for people to hear. 'Price?' Will had asked. 'No,' Captain Draycott looked aghast, his plan about to be compromised. 'No, "Bryce", with a "b" and a "y".' Samuels had told Will that later that same day he'd walked in on Draycott and found him carefully repositioning every object in his office, dragging his desk to the other wall and changing the left–right order of all the items on it.

It was alone, with no concrete plan to offer, that Will went to meet again the man who had sent him to see the fish pond. He'd left a card days earlier: Dr Zakaria, a physician. In a small Arabic café he explained that he had patients only among the Arabs. He made less money but he didn't want to risk intimate contact with the French or their idle, dangerous wives. Dr Zakaria sipped from a tiny cup of thick aromatic coffee, an iridescent sheen on its surface. Such contact, he went on, can lead to a bullet in the head or a convenient road accident. He set his cup back on its saucer and rotated it thoughtfully. 'The prison,' he said. 'So now you have seen what it means to be Arab in this place.'

Will wanted to be precise, to resist any theatrics from this little man. 'I have seen what happens in one part of the prison.'

'All of this country is a prison.'

'Dr Zakaria, if I might intrude a note of circumspection, you sent me to the prison, not anywhere else, and the people I saw would therefore be criminals.'

Dr Zakaria laughed, a short blast through the dark tufts of his nostrils. He tilted his head on one side, smiling, his eyes still on his coffee cup. 'If only life were so logical. They were arrested. They were thrown into a sewer to rot to death. This is all true. But did they commit a crime? Have you any evidence that they did? I don't. Perhaps there isn't any. Perhaps they committed no crime. Perhaps they annoyed a Frenchman or the police needed to make up numbers.'

'Of course I realise that's possible.'

'I am telling you as someone who understands that this is in fact the case. There is no justice here. This is not England.'

'I do understand. You understand I have to ask questions.'

'Of course.'

'I do hope there's something I can do.'

'A man on his own cannot do anything.'

'I think that depends on who the man is and what he does.'

Zakaria smiled again. 'You are either an optimist or vainglorious. Either way, the prison is a small matter – no? Simple to use your authority and make a little bit of change there.'

'Arguably it would be a small matter. Bureaucracy among us is rather Byzantine, I'm afraid. I have to pursue esoteric lines of inquiry.'

A crashing brilliance of noise outside the café. Trumpets and a rattling drum. Will and Zakaria looked at the doorway. As the band passed, the sound lurched even more loudly into the café. Senegalese soldiers, the man in front whirling a cane at chest height. Behind him, trumpeters blew and threw their trumpets spinning up into the air, caught them and blew again. Their scissoring strides cast rhythmical triangles of shadow across the café floor. At the back were the drummers, two of them, who produced an intricate, thrilling racket despite seeming merely to lay their sticks motionless over the tilted surfaces of the drums with their soft dark hands. Somehow from this languid action their sticks blurred and they generated a terrific battery of sound that was shockingly, almost embarrassingly loud as they crossed the open doorway. As the music receded along the street, Will turned smiling, mildly elated, to Dr Zakaria but Dr Zakaria did not smile back.

'Our country,' he said, 'is not our own.'

Will swallowed, sobering his expression. 'I understand. It must be horribly frustrating.'

'Yes. That is one word you could use. It is frustrating. It is frustrating to have your goods stolen, to be killed, to be thrown to die into a pit full of shit for no reason, to have your own land filled with strangers, strange thieves, unclean people. That is all frustrating.' He sipped his coffee once again then removed his spectacles. He polished the lenses with the edge of the tablecloth and returned them to his nose. He looked at something on the table then something else, checking their clarity.

When he spoke again he was calmer. 'Of course we are told that Arabs are not fit to run their own countries. We are . . . what are we? I don't remember. Are we feckless? I think feckless and also chaotic, and tribal and dirty and lazy. Perhaps you think this also?'

'I don't,' Will said, wondering if there wasn't a grain of truth there, if allowing them to run their own affairs might not end in a mess.

Another sound from outside: the long tapering wail

of the call to prayer. Will loved that sound, so passion-
ately forsaken and faithful. There was emptiness in the
sound, empty space that the soul had traversed, a
nomad sound. Will also liked the way that people
accepted it, registered it without amazement, ignored
it, going about their business, or stirred themselves
towards the mosque. That outflung spiritual grandeur
was natural to them; they lived half in that dimension
all the time.

'I have to go to the masjid,' Dr Zakaria said. 'As
you can hear, it is time.'

'Can I come with you?'

Dr Zakaria looked at Will, revising his opinion again,
Will thought, elevating it. 'If you wish. No one will
stop you.'

Will walked with the smaller man through the streets
to a little square. By a line of taps, the worshippers
crouched, washing themselves like cats, looped inside
their fluid gestures, rinsing hands, feet and heads,
breathing water into their nostrils and blasting it out.

At the entrance, Will removed his shoes. He was
noticed by the faithful but they made no comment
nor seemed to care, strolling towards their more
important business. They found squares of the carpet
patterned with these geometric cells on which to
place themselves. Again Will felt that rich, assuaging
sensation of carpet underfoot, the opposite of desert
harshness, a great relief. With no pews or screens to
baffle the view, the space was wide. Above was a dome
that rested on a ring of small windows. Perhaps, if he
could have chosen, Will wouldn't have included those
great brass circles of lamps hanging down on such

long chains. They were the one thing that slightly impaired the open effect. Will faded to the back of the mosque and watched as prayers got underway. He watched the men stand and hug themselves and look left and right and read from the book of their empty hands. He watched them kneel, all at once sinking down to the carpet and bending forwards, the vulnerable, human soles of their feet all peeling up towards him.

Will turned away from the worshippers, leaving them to finish their business. He walked quietly along the back wall, admiring the beautiful patterning of the tiles, regular, mathematical but sinuously growing out in all directions from any point so that the eye raced and rested, raced and rested. It was very cleverly done. Will felt he understood its endless elaboration. Its meaning was divine.

20

Ray was kept from George, travelling in a caravan of the half destroyed. At the back of the advance while the delicate membrane of his hearing healed, Ray got used to medical smells, of bandages and alcohol, sometimes also the smell of burning flesh that could be surprisingly similar to the smell of bacon. There were psychological cases also, the shell-shocked, staring and shaking, repeating precise gestures or clawing at themselves. At night he could see them struggling in their dreams but, being deaf, he couldn't always hear their cries. Deafness made things distant. They looked like figures struggling underwater.

George was distant. Ray yearned towards him, to protect him. Surely he wouldn't survive on his own, a secret pacifist in the middle of a war, in the damned infantry for Christ's sake. Ray wrote letters to him in his head, arguing with him. *My friend*, they began, *my friend*. Ray would assert how important this war was and how the killing was necessary, the lesser of two evils in the world. George didn't realise how valuable his own life was, so valuable compared to some useless Nazi. His life was precious and he should defend it. Ray imagined these letters – that he never wrote or sent – convincing George on the night before a decisive battle and saving him. At the same time, Ray imagined George protected by his goodness, a slight shimmer in the air around him, coming through the battle unharmed. George could be the hero of a new kind of war movie, about a man whose goodness triumphed.

All of these thoughts were repeatedly burned up and destroyed in the sudden certainty that George had just been or was just about to be killed, in that moment just gone or coming right now. Confirmation of this came with each new wounded or maddened soldier brought in from the fury of battle to be dragged along behind with Ray, drugged and repaired enough to be returned and properly killed next time.

At night, Ray cried out towards George, his own voice through his deafness high and weightless and weak.

21

'Is it possible, do you think,' Will asked Dr Zakaria, 'that Alloula is a French informant?' It was a mischievous question, a little flashing out of the excitement that Will felt at these meetings, the dense buzzing in his belly as he leaned forwards, smoking, listening. He asked the question with a hint of a smile.

'No,' Dr Zakaria answered, eyebrows raised and eyelids drooping, an expression of serene disdain. 'Not only do I know Alloula thoroughly but you make the mistake of assuming that the French are interested in us. They aren't. They don't think we are capable of anything. We are invisible as far as they are concerned. The Bey is a pet. No one else has any authority.'

'But now that I'm here and I've been meeting with you, their interest might have been piqued.'

Zakaria shook his head. 'Because you are here, all of you British and others, the French withdraw entirely. They are on vacation. They are waiting for you to go away again and then life will return to normal.'

Alloula was the first of the others to arrive. Tall and sloping, his long heavy belly abbreviated by a tight belt, he looked, as ever, tired. His eyes were vague with worry. He flattened his thick black hair to his head and with the same hand summoned the waiter.

He sat and before he'd made eye contact with Will

or Zakaria, he said, 'My wife is very unhappy about me coming here.'

'I see,' Zakaria answered. 'She likes the French too much.'

Will rose slightly in his seat as he considered attempting a joke about a French lover but decided against it and sank back.

'No,' Alloula answered. 'But she thinks it might be dangerous, that the French are watching us.'

'That's precisely what I was just saying,' Will said.

'Not precisely,' Zakaria corrected. 'They aren't,' he went on. 'They like different kinds of gossip and they're too busy considering their positions when the Allies go. The Free French supporters will want to take control. As far as they are concerned, we'll still be their niggers.'

'Until you commit your first outrage. Anyway, you're repeating yourself.'

'To someone else. Repetition. Perseverance. Doing the same thing again and again before it gives way. It's boring, trying to change things. Boring and difficult.'

'I'm not bored.'

'Until you do something, until we all do something, my good friend, you are still a spectator.'

Mr Ammar arrived next, sudden through the hanging beads at the door, shaking hands with his right hand, holding a match flame to a cigarette with his left. Ammar was angry. Ammar was always angry. He had weapons in his cellar. He abused waiters, clenched and unclenched his fists during conversation. He was a powerful man, compact and raging. Will liked observing him, feeling him seethe. Ammar was trivially powerful at the moment, powerful conversationally, personally, but Will could see how as events changed he might darkly blossom. He was the one. He could be a great force at the right moment.

Will sat beglamoured in the company of the conspirators who talked about some Italian armaments that could be bought. Several more arrived, argued and departed before the evening was done, faces hovering in the light of match flames and lighters. Dark hands held his forearms as ideas were elaborated. He listened. It was intelligence, pure intelligence.

22

Back at the villa, Samuels was still awake, sitting in a clean cone of lamplight, his hands spidery with shadows as he stripped and fixed the wiring of their telephone. Humming along to some dance music on the wireless, with tools spread out and litter of Bakelite pieces, Will thought he looked as idiotically happy as a child in a sand pit.

'Evening.'

Samuels looked up, mouth open, and down again at his task. 'Out with the rebels again?' he asked.

'Something along those lines.'

'Need a drink, I imagine, after all that boozeless Mohammedan plotting. There's Scotch in that window seat for some reason. Don't know whose it is.'

'Excellent idea. Draycott's probably. According to Travis he's now hiding things. Travis found one of the maps under the rug. That's why when you knock on the door he tells you to hang on and there's a lot of fuss and thumping about before he lets you come in.'

'There's a mug on the table as well.'

'A mug. Ideal.'

Will poured himself a sincere measure of about three fingers and sat with the mug resting on his belt buckle. He tilted his head back and sighed.

'Aaah. Hmmm. There's quite a lot I need to remember, actually. I should make a few notes.'

'I see. They seducing you to their side?'

'No. What a fatuous thing to say. I'm not being seduced by anyone. You make it sound . . .'

'Oops. Sorry if I hit a nerve.'

'You haven't hit anything because you don't know anything.'

'I don't see that that follows logically. Anyway, I'm not wrong. You're sympathetic to their side.'

'Samuels, I think you're straying out of your area of expertise. You don't know the language here. Your brethren are a little north and east of here, aren't they, somewhere in Palestine?'

Samuels said nothing, then, 'They're in London and on the Continent.'

'Muttering to yourself like an old woman.'

'Snippety snip. Somebody's very tetchy.'

'No idea what the situation is in this country.'

'Doing my job. Minding my own bleeding business. Not blessed, you see, your excellency, with your understanding of the great game here. I does what I can in me humble way. For example, this telephone now works. You go on and win the war for us, sir.'

'Oh, for crying out loud. I'm going to bed.'

23

Sergeant Major Henderson stood with his thick, freckled arms folded high across his pristine shirt, his eyes half closed with sceptical curiosity. 'So who was that fucker with the sharp stick up his arse?'

Will examined the card the man had given him. Tilting it so that the swirling curlicues of black ink caught the light and shone. 'He works for the Bey. Says here he's an adviser, a courtier.'

'Works for the what's that?'

'The Bey. Local royalty. As I understand it, he hasn't had much to do since the French took over. He lives in a palace and he wants to talk to me. A car will collect me tomorrow evening.'

'Arab johnny?'

'Yes.'

'Probably dressed up like the bleedin' haberdashery department. Don't tell him anything, will you.'

'I'm not planning to tell him anything. I'll tell him that we're going to win the war and I'm wondering what he has got to tell me.'

'We are going to win the war.'

'I know we are.'

'And what does he want you for anyway?'

'His adviser, his courtier, tells me that he wishes to make contact with his British friends.'

'Wants a nice white arse then. And don't go stealing anything.'

'I wasn't planning to.'

'I know it's tempting. Some fat Arab with more money than sense. He'll have a lot of knick-knacks, I reckon.'

24

The car that collected Will was certainly beautiful but he thought that the tyres needed air. They had a rather glutinous grip on the road, stones pinging under the rubber as the car snaked its way along the coast road and Will slid to and fro across the leather upholstery. He held onto the handle above the window to preserve his dignity and looked out at the lilac sea, the landscape pitted with shadows. He looked at the back of the driver's slender neck that emerged from a wide starched circle of collar; his uniform looked big on him. On top of his head he wore a dove-grey chauffeur's cap. His gloved hands rotated and Will gripped the handle as the car turned uphill, inland, through orange orchards towards the palace. Will recognised them as orange orchards despite the absence of fruit. The trees were regularly spaced, the leaves waxy dark green. In the dusk, without fruit or blossom, they were dowdy as cattle. Will regretted that it was the least romantic time of the year to see them.

The car slowed to a squidgy halt and the driver sprang out to open Will's door. Will stood up, ignoring the man, and walked to the palace gate where a guard stood who looked more at home in his uniform. An enormous African, his skin mauve in the evening light, his chest pressed smooth the dark blue cloth of his jacket, tasselled with gold braid. On his head he wore a red fez. In his right hand he held a bared scimitar, its blade shining blue. He pulled open the gate and waited for Will to pass through, his eyes dead ahead. Behind Will, the car rumblingly withdrew.

Another guard or functionary approached wearing a different uniform, a red sash around his waist, and led Will up through a rose arbour to the palace garden. The building itself appeared, large, its many windows mostly unlit, clean cut against the early stars.

And then the man who Will thought must be the Bey appeared in white, smooth-faced, floating towards him. 'So good of you to come. Welcome.' He had a neat, subdued moustache and a beard that ran only along his jawline, framing large, plush, shaven cheeks.

'Your highness.' Will bowed very slightly from the waist.

The Bey stood still a moment, examining Will or expecting him to say something further. Either way, he was completely motionless, a mannequin standing there, his hands by his sides. Just as Will was about to say something, he jerked back to life. 'Come. Come and join me.'

He gestured for Will to walk ahead to a table topped with ceramic tiles with a lamp on it beneath an arch of greenery. Will sat and twisted round in his chair when he heard a dry, flustered noise that turned out to be a bird in a large metalwork cage. The bird bounced from perch to perch. A servant approached and placed on the table before them two cups of mint tea, the gold patterning on the glass shining in the lamplight.

'So,' the Bey began. 'Where did you school?'

Will's school would have been unknown to the Bey. He pretended to misunderstand him. 'I was at Oxford.'

'Ah. How excellent. So was I. At Exeter College. Do you miss it? I do, in my maudlin moments. I miss the climate from time to time, would you believe it. Also here there really is nowhere to play golf.'

'I do miss it I suppose,' Will said without really meaning it. 'I'm happy to be out, though. Oxford is where I learned my Arabic.'

Another servant appeared with a silver platter on which were arranged squares of folded cloth. Having sipped his tea, the Bey picked one up with his finger-tips, patted his lips with it and let it drop to the floor. When the tray was proffered, Will did the same and discovered that the linens were chilled and scented with rose water. Just dropping it onto the ground was a strange, slightly dreamlike thing to do.

'Yes, I've heard that you speak Arabic. Do you mind, old thing, if we stick to English? It's such a pleasure for me to speak it.'

'Not at all, your highness. You speak it so well.'

The Bey tutted at the formulaic compliment and closed his eyes briefly.

'The reason you were invited here was because the world is at an interesting moment. Things are in flux, wouldn't you agree?'

'I would.'

'Of course. Wars. Empires.' He gestured with a ringed hand. 'We've had rather a lot of them in this part of the world. It seems that one empire is passing so it is time to consider the future, hopefully without barbarians or dark ages.'

'I see. I've met – I think you know I've met – countrymen of yours who are preoccupied with the same questions. They are devising some answers.'

'So I gather. But are they the barbarians, perhaps? It is an interesting question. Perhaps there are other more time-tested forms of authority that could emerge. Once the ghastly French have gone back to Rouen and Dieppe or wherever, their boulevards and puffy old mistresses, as I see it this country will head in one of two ways.'

'Chaos or . . .'

'No, not that. I mean two kinds of state: either a socialist republic or a stable royalist state. I think the gentlemen you have been meeting in déclassé cafés are rather militating for the former but I think that is really in nobody's interest. Their activities could be useful in creating the latter but I'm hoping for a way in which such things wouldn't be necessary at all.'

'Either way, an independent state.'

The bird started jumping again, half opening its wings.

'Of course. There are Sicilians here contending for the same choices. Did you know that? They're here, apparently, because they believe or know that once your lot have swept through here, Sicily will be next, and then up across the Continent, and they wish to free Sicily from Italy.'

'I didn't know that. I haven't seen them if they are here.'

'Possibly you have without realising. I'm told that because of Norman and Moorish invasions, a Sicilian will look either like a Frenchman or like an Arab. That is very convenient here, evidently.'

'That would be.'

The Bey sipped his tea again, again the servant stooped forward with his platter. The Bey patted his mouth and dropped the cloth.

'But we're getting off the topic there,' the Bey said. 'I fear that you've leaped to a conclusion there with the notion of an independent state. A fledgling state would be a delicate thing. Complete independence might be too much for it. It should be protected, let's say, helped into the world. Why you are here is because I'd like to put to you a proposition to take away and discuss with others and quietly to set in motion. I would like us to become here, once the French have finally buggered off or been pushed out, rather, I'd like us to become a part of the British Empire.'

25

Before Will knocked on Captain Draycott's door, he could hear him at his activities on the other side, in particular the twanging sound of things thrown into his metal waste-paper basket. Will rapped hard, thinking again of the necessity of circumventing his useless superior. The reins were in Will's hand. He was riding the horse of the world. He could steer the course of this part of North Africa. Draycott opened the door and said, 'Ah, Walker, come on in.' His cheeks were flecked with hectic pink, he was slightly breathless, but Will immediately thought that he no longer looked mad. His face was clarified, sober. Draycott's eyes were meeting his.

'Captain, I have some news of a very interesting, very interesting, development, possibly actually very significant for British interests here, I mean really significant. I'd need time and further work but it seems, well, I have contacts with senior royals in this area and they have made submissions to me that they are minded to join the British Empire, to become part of the British Empire here once the war is over. Sir, is everything all right?'

Draycott was emptying the entire contents of one of his desk drawers into the bin. Perhaps his sanity had been fleeting, a lucid moment only.

'The war is over here, Walker,' he said.

'Sir?'

'That all sounds very interesting. Top work on your part, awfully exemplary intelligence work, I imagine. It's not really my area beyond needs must. We'll have to find a way for you to pass it on to someone.'

'Sir, what are you talking about?'

'Oh yes. I haven't informed you all yet although I think everyone's got the gist from the rumour mill. There's a terrible joke there that I can't quite think of about gist to the mill.'

'What gist?'

'We're leaving. The war has headed east and we're heading with it. It's the lookout of the Free French round here now. There's a handover being organised, so I'm not really sure how your new colony can be brought into the Empire. Fearfully complicated, I imagine.'

'But we can't.'

Draycott laughed, actually laughed at him. 'I'm sorry, old boy, but we do just have to get up and go. It's not down to us to decide. You can put it all in a report.'

'Yes and toss it into the void of complete army incompetence. I've made this. Don't you see? I've done important work here and all you can bloody well say is put it in a report and flush it down the lavatory.'

'Now that isn't really fair. I didn't say that.'

'More or less. You don't care is the problem. You're just as bloody idle and indifferent as the rest of them.'

'Look here, Walker, I'd rather you weren't, you know, insubordinate in a way that made difficulties between us.'

'Oh, fuck difficulties. Do you see what I've done? I've won England a part of the world.'

'That definitely is insubordinate. There are penalties for that, Walker.'

'I would be being insubordinate if I were your inferior. But I'm not. I'm your superior in every way so logically I cannot be insubordinate.'

'In every way except rank so piss off out of this room before you put us both in an awkward situation. Don't you see what this means? You ask me if I do. This means we're winning the war. We're winning it!'

'Some of us are.'

26

The long, tediously detailed labour of evacuation was housewife's work, a porter's work. Every action of it pained Will.

Moving, the sea ran always on their left-hand side. Turning a corner there'd be a shove of wind and the sea would flash and then disappear as the convoy wound through schematic, insignificant towns that could have been won as sleepy corners of the British Empire. Now they were just lagging behind action, not taking it. When they caught up to the battlefield Will saw in one place long lines of stretchers leaning against a wall in the sun, the canvas smudged with quiet shapes of drying blood.

27

Returned to his unit, racing, finding them among the others. All the men looked different and alike. They were pared down by battle, gaunt, in faded uniforms, unshaven. Seeing him, seeing that George wasn't dead, that he was alive, thin and weary, sliding his pack down from his back, Ray ran to him and caught him, shocking the taller man who didn't recognise him at first and then did. Ray grabbed the sides of George's head, the dry prickles of his hair, and kissed him, pressed his mouth to George's and held it there. George squirmed backwards, his lips wriggling to form words of complaint and then, just for a fraction of a second, before he put his hands on Ray's chest and shoved him away, he kissed back, an answering pressure in his lips. George flung him off. Ray let himself fall to the ground, laughing. He looked up. He was floating. He was mixed with the enormous sky. He saw George scowling down at him and laughed some more.

With his long straight fingers, George kept whisking particles of dust or lint from his clothes. His face lengthened with the effort of looking down at himself. He said that Dunphy was dead. And Randall was dead. And Carlson. They had all died at the same moment, or two moments, two big shells landing one after the other. Coyne was killed later. George was right beside him when it happened. A sniper blew off Coyne's jaw and it landed on George's forearm. George flicked at his clothes, remembering the sensation of this thing, this object, warm and light as a teacup. Coyne had drowned in his bubbling holes.

'I picked the jaw up, with all of the teeth in there, and held onto it in case it was going to be useful but it wasn't. He died. I balanced it back on his face so he could be buried with it and we ran.'

Ray and George stood together in the evening air, a soothing moisture in it, a substance in the distances. No sound of fighting, only voices and more men arriving.

George was different now. Sometimes, in flashes, Ray could get his old self out of him, but in the silences George's face hardened and he disappeared.

Ray asked finally, 'Did you shoot? Remember what you said that time that had me worried all the time, did you stick to it?'

George opened his mouth and inhaled looking up at the sky. He closed his eyes and Ray understood. But knowing that George had been doing exactly what Ray had prayed he was doing and had defended himself brought Ray no relief or peace of mind. Instead it made Ray sad, awfully sad, to think of gentle George being forced to do that and maybe killing people, to think that they were all forced to do that. Ray stood next to his friend enclosed in this sadness, knowing he would never be outside it again. This had happened to them all. This was for ever.

28

They were done with Africa now. That was the news, the reason for celebration. The men played in the sea. Despite the fact that Ray's hearing was now crisp, finished and sensitive, he was not permitted to join them. He sat on the beach, pouring handfuls of sand over the gaunt bones of his feet, and looked at the men splashing and laughing in the brilliance of the sun-struck water, the light sliding about their shoulders, over their heads and backs. Feet kicked up and disappeared. George was not among them, as far as Ray could see. Ray had to let go of that, of George, and to try not to panic. He had to care about himself instead. His return to his unit had been short-lived. Ray had been called out to form part of a special division of men, men with Italian names – all the Rossos and Rizzos and Romanos – who would be last to arrive in the invasion of Sicily that was to follow. They were to stay there and secure the peace.

One man rose up in the sea, eyes closed, his hands on his head, water pouring down his face and lips and Ray felt the cool of that over his own head, the relief.

Ray's head burned often, with memories, with fear. But now he would miss the battle. In Sicily he would not really be a soldier any more. He would be part of the peace. George would have liked that for himself but George was not an Italian. Ray had to forget about George now, to let him go. Perhaps it would be better for him to think of him as dead already. Ray twitched at a memory: in the mess of action once he'd had that thought, that everything was dead already, only some of it moved and lived. That wasn't really going to help. He just had to hang on until it was over. That was all. He had George's address back home. If they ever got back home, he would get on a bus and use it.

Part Two
Sicily

1

The Princess liked to outpace her guards, to kick up and canter as far from them as she could, making them chase, but here in the motor car there was nowhere to go. One guard sat beside her. He breathed through his nostrils as loudly as a farm animal and bit at the corner of his moustache as he stared out of the window, a pistol on his hip. When she was a little girl there were always more of them, men on the other side of the windows, crouching on the running boards with rifles across their backs. As a child she'd envied them: she wanted to ride on the outside of the car. Now the threat was much diminished but still her father wouldn't let her travel without at least one to protect her.

In front, the driver in his cap paddled his feet, jerked his levers and turned the wheel. Outside the windows the landscape changed. The bricks and avenues of Palermo gave way to the countryside, the landscape hollowing, rising up into rigid, incessant hills. She was not sad to be leaving the city. It would be good to be out again on horseback with the wind striking her. For a while. This was the task of Luisa's life: evading boredom in one of two places. She did this by moving arrhythmically between them, taking her friends by surprise in Palermo, going among the feathers and ballrooms and knowing eyes and then suddenly substituting them with the sun and emptiness, the peasants and her father's travails. There she was free to ride within a certain range, as long as she was accompanied and kept away from the malevolent edge of the country that was always there, encircling. She sensed it looking out of the motor car. The landscape was vigilant. It knew things. It could see her.

In a walled garden in Palermo, by a pond in which large goldfish slowly twisted, rising and fading, a Fascist mayor had told Princess Luisa that there was absolutely nothing to be worried about, that the party had smashed those backward rural criminals. He had jutted out his chin in a ridiculous imitation of the Duce. All the Fascists these days strutted and posed like him even as a light sheen of panic appeared on their faces. At parties aristocrats from the old families caught each other's eyes and shared this observation. They themselves felt confident, monumental, historically vindicated, while the Fascists struck attitudes and drank and spoke too much. The effect of events in North Africa on Luisa's own pet Fascist, Mauro, a Tuscan of refined, not to say pretty, features, was to make him more ardent. He wanted to marry her.

Mauro Vecchio was the prefect of Sant'Attilio, a part of the island he confided in her that he found squalid and incomprehensible. The best of Sicily was the east, where the Greeks had been. The half-Arab peasants of the west could not be made political. It wouldn't take, any more than you could teach pigs to speak Latin. You could move the feeding trough, make them trot in a different direction, and that was as far as it went. Luisa's father disliked him for these opinions, the Prince having a peculiar, dimly Tolstoyan reverence for the tough local people that somehow survived his dealings with them. Mauro and her father liked to argue it out in the persons of The Future and The Old Wisdom. Now, it seemed her father had won the argument. Mauro had retreated to Palermo and Luisa suspected he would never return, although as he drove with her to the city in his official car, he had promised her that he would, no matter what happened.

The conversation on the bouncing back seat of the car was a long coda to the conversation in the garden. Sitting on the pedestal of one of the statues, Mauro had looked up squinting against the light and asked Luisa to marry him. The answer, of course, was no, although Luisa could not have said why the 'of course' was so immediate and definitive. She liked Mauro. He was always entertaining in his silk shirts and boots, declaring things. He was ardent, about her, about Italy. But there was something she was sure she should have felt that she didn't. It was a kind of terror that she wanted to feel, her solitude broken open, a fiery golden tearing into the centre of her by the man who would then have the right to marry her, and that she had never felt.

In Palermo, Mauro had sent messages to the apartment in the palace where she stayed with her cousins (the Prince having long since rented out his Palermo residence to his nephews). She had replied only insincerely, with jokes and exhortations to courage. She had met the usual people and done the usual things in an atmosphere now effervescent with the closeness of war. Until, that is, being there had bored her and she'd left.

Arriving home, the driver got out, trotted around and opened the door for Luisa. The guard waited and walked behind. Luisa saw Angilù walking from the main door towards the wing of estate management rooms. He stopped where he was and lifted his hat, almost as though he was showing her his balding head, a little surprise he kept for her. Angilù wouldn't have understood this comical thought, he was always so serious and hard-working. The Princess waved at him, allowing him to walk away.

Into the lion's mouth, the echoing hallway where the dogs came out to greet her, claws scrabbling on the tiles. She rummaged briefly among their furry necks and sides, their warm, damp breath, before walking through to her father's study. Presumably Angilù had just come from there. The image of him standing outside, subordinate, his hat uplifted, stuck in her mind for some reason. She found him a frustrating man. He'd been working with her father, around the house, for almost twenty years and he always kept such a pious distance from her. Only once, when she was a girl, she remembered, he'd treated her like one of his own children. Luisa used to follow him around, pursuing him at his work. She was playing outside with some kind of seeds that he needed, tossing them onto the ground, and he'd grabbed hold of her, handling her roughly, and scolded her. She had been so shocked and outraged at this unprecedented behaviour that she had wailed with scarlet anger. She could still see the fear that had appeared in his eyes, the

154

desperate effort to placate her before anyone else saw. After that assertion of her will, Angilù had kept away. When she followed him, he ignored her respectfully. Luisa felt at odd moments abandoned by him still, his veneration of her a kind of denial. She would have liked to talk to him sometimes, she imagined he knew interesting things, but he was mute. She could have asked him questions and he would have been forced to answer, but it was not the same.

Her father was sitting in his red armchair with the wireless on, his gaze resting in midair, a slightly foolish look of cogitation on his face. Cigarette smoke was rising slowly along his arm and up from his head. It rolled with turbulence when he saw her and moved. 'Ah, my dear.' He stood up. 'One moment.' He went over to the wireless, a waist-high cabinet elaborate with honey-coloured grilles, and switched it off.

The Princess approached and kissed the Prince's proffered cheek.

'Well,' he asked, sitting back down on his armchair, the leather cushions huffing and crackling. 'What news on the Rialto?'

'They're scared, Father. They think Sicily is next and that the Germans are about to arrive in force. Rumours. I think Mauro might be making plans to escape.'

'Doesn't that rather suggest he won't marry you?'

Luisa laughed quickly, dismissively. 'I wouldn't have married him.' Mauro appeared to her mind's eye the way he always did, his pretty features like an illustration in a children's book, a simple, impertinent face.

'That's a relief. A few years ago I suppose you might

have got away with it, when things were different for them. Now I would certainly forbid it.'

'Yes, Father. But there's no need. I've already forbidden it.'

'Good.'

'I'm going to change. I want to ride before dinner. Any news here?'

'I just had Angilù in here.'

'Yes, I saw him.'

'There's a lot of news coming back from cousins in America. Certain people who left a long time ago are apparently helping the Americans. Which suggests that the news in Palermo may be correct. I don't know. I don't know what's going to happen.'

'Nobody does.' The Princess thought her father looked very old in his chair, the way his long, narrow thighs jutted out and converged weakly at the knees, his bony hands on the armrests. He had worked very hard for the estate. Prince Adriano was a rare eccentric: a Sicilian landowner who liked the land.

2

Walking home, Angilù caught sight of the witch of Montebianco in the distance. Perhaps she'd been visiting someone in the house, the servant Graziana maybe. Short, dark, she moved with a rapid skimming walk, a small bag hanging from her right hand. Angilù wondered what she knew. For himself, he preferred the church now and again. He should go soon to get a blessing. He pictured the holy sparkle of it descending on him, protecting him.

He walked up through the whispering avenue of olive trees and into his home, into the blue shadows of his whitewashed hallway with its smooth, cool smell of plaster dust and paint. For two years, Albanese's widow had remained in this place. After two years, she had moved back in with her mother in Sant'Attilio and later, when she'd married again, into Silvio's house. The Prince had invited Angilù and Rosaria, then pregnant with their first daughter, to move in. The house frightened both of them at first. It was so large and quiet and still. And Albanese had lived there. His presence remained. The families in Sant'Attilio who were friends of the Albaneses, those of them who remained, watched Angilù as he passed in the street. Angilù had the house blessed. Holy water flashed into every corner. And then the baby was born, a new blossoming of loud life, and Angilù forgot; the place became their house.

He could hear Rosaria in the kitchen, the melody of her talk to Mariuzza, their youngest daughter. Walking in, he found Mariuzza sitting on the counter, kicking her soft legs. Rosaria was pouring olive oil into the bottom of a smoking pot. Beside her were heaps of sliced vegetables. Angilù put his hand on the back of her neck, a strong, thick neck, a mother's neck. Always that distance he crossed in himself to reach out and touch her, still at heart a shepherd and far from everything. He kissed the ticklish damp hair on her nape as she picked up a handful of silvery onions and dropped them into the pan. 'Hello, little bird,' he said through the sudden noise of frying.

'Yes, yes. You need to move.'

Angilù caught hold of one of Mariuzza's swinging feet. He held it, straightening the girl's leg, and bent to kiss the dimpled knee.

3

Graziana had unpacked Luisa's things by the time she went upstairs. She put on a riding dress and stepped out to fetch a field guard from their office to accompany her. The first flames of evening were in the sky. Luisa chose to ride Ezio, sharp-boned and volatile, a horse that tended to fidget and sidestep and yank at the reins. The guard subdued him in the stables then bent down to offer his hands to Luisa. She stepped up into the saddle. The field guards were always so strong – the man's knitted fingers felt like a stone step. In the courtyard, Ezio tried whirling on the spot. Luisa sat on the beast, imposing herself. She spoke at him and patted his neck. Ezio calmed, stalled finally under her, breathing and thinking. Luisa kicked. She rode out. The guard followed after.

Ezio didn't like going downhill. He fended away at the slope with his forelegs, trying to tread back upright, but Luisa leaned in, persuaded him down. His hooves scraped. Small stones slithered after. And that was the last of Ezio's resistance for the day. They rode together, a strong headwind cutting away at Luisa, cleansing and purifying. Ezio's long eyelashes flickered against the onrushing air. Their wills fused – that was Luisa's sensation. Ezio understood what Luisa intended and stretched his legs, gathering the ground behind them.

Luisa was freed in the loosened movement. They walked for a while, Luisa resting her gaze in the distances, creases of shadows in the hills, clouds turning scarlet in the sky. At this pace she saw the birds hopping and people labouring among straight rows of vines. She turned in the saddle to see the guard trotting after. When she stopped, he did, keeping the distance she'd demanded. He sat waiting, his hands on the pommel, his thick legs stuck out. Luisa turned Ezio with a swipe of the reins and kicked. His head and shaking mane crested in front of her. They galloped down past the guard and back towards the house.

4

Connecting the swirling lines of the maps with the reality of the old country was difficult. Maps and memories were so different. Standing over them, the colonel patiently waiting, Cirò thoughtfully rubbed his nose between his thumb and his forefinger. His part of the island had many concentric rings of contour lines that looked like knots in wood. Those were the hills he remembered. He followed one road with his finger. If Portella Corvi was there and Sant'Attilio was there . . . then he knew where he was. That hill, he could see its surly shape again in his mind, the near side always shadowed. Now he could put himself there and see the whole place unfold around him. He could say to the colonel that this was all Prince Adriano's land, that this belonged to the Santangelis, that there were wells here, here and here.

His route into that room was not one that Cirò would have chosen. It had been demeaning. Certain Italian and Sicilian men with influential American friends had been approached in a civilised manner, taken out to dinner, spoken to quietly in clubs and brothels. Or an unusually well-dressed stranger had appeared at their prison cells and led them out. Cirò, for all his American success, still belonged in a different category. Working his trade at the docks, he was no boss. He was collected in a mass arrest at a waterfront café. At least it had been a mass arrest. An individual arrest would really have worried him. Not that there was any evidence of the things he'd done. He hadn't used a gun. Docks were dangerous places. A cargo hook swings. A walkway is slippery. And that had been some time ago when he was establishing himself. They arrested everyone in the café. The officers sifted through them letting Poles and Norwegians and others go. They held onto the Sicilians.

The dumb cops had clearly been told to lay it on thick. A fat little police captain who for a long time had received tributes of money from some of the men in the room and had been taken to girls by others, barked out that they were cleaning up. Everybody would be in for a long stretch. Unless, that is, they were interested in cooperating. Given the rumours that were circulating (and more than rumours, good, hard facts passed along the line), no one was surprised when blue gave way to green and into this little theatrical production walked an army officer. He told them that they were all off the hook if they would step up and serve their country. The army wanted their help.

Like any of this was necessary. They could just have asked. Everybody in that room, even the ones who wanted to stay in America, wanted the Fascists off the island. They wanted back what was theirs.

After this rigmarole, excitement glittered among the sombre, determined men of Cirò's acquaintance. They met in cafés and bars, whorehouses and each other's homes and discussed the possibilities that lay ahead. It was a grand prospect. They were sharper, now, harder and cleverer. They weren't just stealing sheep and squeezing mill owners and collecting tributes and making sure they got certain leases. They were American businessmen who had kept up their interests against all kinds of competition, Poles, Italians, Jews, Chinese. They'd killed and they'd negotiated. They ran numbers and nightclubs and girls. They imported morphine and booze, Cirò's special area of interest, and they received tributes from all sorts of people in all sorts of places. They'd negotiated with the authorities and got them on side. They'd become political. These conversations made them sentimental about all that America had given them and all the work they'd done, the people lost on the way. And now it was time to go home. Now it was time for revenge.

New York was home now, too, of course. Cirò loved taking his money up into the canyons of Manhattan, striding towards the narrow blade of sky that forever retreated up the avenues. He saw the millionaires with their tiny dogs and fur collars, the women with foxes looped around their necks. He saw the taxis and doormen. You couldn't have invented the place. More meat than you ever dreamed of eating. A place that answered to his appetites.

Sicily was home, though. Sicily was mother. It was his olive trees and sunshine flavoured with herbs and the smell of hot earth. It was the hard-won property and Teresa.

And he would see Teresa again. In America, he'd had news of her, brought by new arrivals or people who had visited home, arriving in the hills in their suits and showering gifts on the shoeless children.

Teresa had thought what she was supposed to think, that he had been taken, destroyed, a death that disappeared, his body never found. Or she had acted as though she thought he'd been shot with the white shotgun. Maybe she guessed otherwise, what with so many men of respect escaping away. And couldn't she still feel him, the force of him alive, no matter that he was across an ocean? Whatever, she had become a widow. In those early days, the thought of Teresa alone in an empty bed, wearing black, had closed Albanese's mind with pain. Years later, he'd heard the news of her remarriage to that peasant Silvio. He remembered exactly where he was when he heard. Ginu had been almost too frightened to tell him. Cirò was halfway through a meal, his mouth was grainy with ground beef and tomato sauce. He pushed away the plate. The food in his stomach turned instantly heavy and poisonous.

Now he would return to reclaim her.

In his own way, Cirò had been faithful to her, for twenty years consorting only with mistresses and whores. Apart, that is, from one woman.

Cathy was an Irish girl, a typist in a small glass-sided office inside one of the warehouses. He would glimpse her in there, her red hair, a bird in a cage. She took her lunch on a bench that looked out over the water. Cirò noticed this. Other men shouted and whistled at her as they went past. Cirò was silent. She looked so nice, sitting there. It was something about the shape of her shoulders inside her coat and her smart polished shoes side by side beneath her. Cirò had the café fill his thermos with coffee and took it and sat beside her. She was someone he wanted to be next to, delicate and contained, small and beautiful in the rough winds of the docks. He asked if she minded. She said she didn't. They looked at the water together.

Each day he went back and found her there at the same time. She told him she liked the sea, had grown up seeing it. Later on, she accepted his invitation to go out somewhere fancy for dinner. He thought she guessed what kind of a man he was but decided not to know. The restaurant thrilled her, so smart and lively, and Cirò was greeted by all the staff. He ordered the best wine, a beautiful Barolo. When she tasted it, he saw her shoulders droop. She looked sad. He asked, 'What's the matter? Isn't it good?' 'No,' she answered. 'It's delicious.' Cirò knew that she was uncertain now, that she was losing a clear sense of the limits of her world. 'Why don't you have a cocktail? Cocktails are more fun. We can save the wine for later.' Cathy allowed him to order and drank, her face half eclipsed by the wide circle of the glass. Later they went home together and made love.

They lived like lovers. Cirò bought her gifts of jewellery that she never wore but put away in the bank. She didn't know what to do with him. Part of her was frightened. Cirò was often telling her not to be silly. She clung to him. Whatever it was she'd left behind in Ireland meant she was alone here too, in her rented room. She was nervous and loved the size of Cirò, his bulk. She patted his belly, kneaded with her small fingers the meat of his shoulders.

Cirò going off to war felt like the end of everything but it also pleased her in some way; it conferred an average kind of nobility on him. It cleaned him morally. They were part of the crowd. Greedily, he ate what he could of her before he left. The rosy translucency of her stockings drying in front of the fire. The bead necklaces she wore hanging over a corner of her dressing-table mirror. The piles of picture magazines she kept. Her Christ on a cross on the wall, his small silver body as jointed and slim as a wasp. The dumpy old mattress that took on the warmth of their bodies. Cathy's hair was gold at her temples and waved out to a faded red. Over her unbelievably fair skin, her face and forehead, her shoulders and the tops of her arms, was a strange scattering of colour, her freckles, multiple. They swirled like money.

She was so strange to him. She was not Sicilian. She was not his wife. He left a large roll of cash under her pillow when he left. He said he would be back before she knew it, like all the brave soldiers did, and left, he assumed, for ever.

Cirò Albanese was returning to Sicily with all the power of America, all the money and metal and giant scale. The invasion fleet was immense. You could look across the ocean on either side and see it stretching away. It was a city on water, Manhattan armed and loosed, grinding forward under a bright half-moon. Down avenues of green-black water raced corvettes and lighter craft. In the sky above the Allies roared towards home.

Later, hearing the guns, the bombs, every detonation was for him, was a visitation of his will upon his enemies. The light of dawn spread across the water. Aircraft raced back and forth. Cirò was being held, ready. He was important to the Americans. Imagine that. He would be part of the new order on the island. Dense smoke, full of the pollution of random burning, rolled back elegantly over the surface of the cold sea. Cirò inhaled.

5

Ray could feel it already, even before it started, the dryness in his throat. Out there, his mouth would be so dry that his inner cheeks, his tongue and gums would feel like rough external surfaces. His teeth would be grainy pegs of bone. He'd be unable to swallow. Ray was exempt from this battle but his body was returning him to it whether he would or not. His body was stiff with memory, muscles rigid while his bowels began to bubble and slide.

His boots were laced. He had his pack and gun, grenades and a helmet, none of which he should need. That was what he was told. Ray and his unit were arriving along with many reinforcements several days after the first landings. They were there to make peace, specially selected Italian-Americans who could speak with the natives. Meanwhile, they sat in the boat and listened to the chaos and killing. Hours later, he was once again splashing through heavy water. It was a long shallow approach. The sea sucked at his legs. The sand in strange sensations shrank and twisted under his boots. There was no need to be scared. The beach had been secured. They were just landing, just coming ashore. No one would fire on them from those pill-boxes. The debris was harmless.

Hundreds of men were having their orders shouted

at them. They were moving out. As the fighting men were marched or driven away, the Allied Military Government units gathered together. Someone slapped Ray on the back. It was Tony Geminiano, a boy from Queens who everyone called 'Gem' and who hadn't been in battle before. He was joining the war here, now, at this point. He looked strangely exultant. Holding his gun in both hands, he inhaled sharply into his nose. 'Ooh, mamma,' he said. 'We're here. The boys are here.' Ray slowly understood what he was saying and nodded.

The first problem the AMGOT teams faced was a lack of transportation. The fighting units had taken every vehicle and so they spent all morning on the beach watching the traffic moving out and the small waves shifting back and forth at the edge of the sand with a thin shine. The sun grew taller. The men's voices quietened in the heat.

After some time, Ray's legs relaxed and he sat down. They were told to eat and they all did, washing down bread, cheese and chocolate with tepid water from their cans. Political men, US brass and Sicilian advisers, kept apart, each one standing with the bearing of a general, occasionally looking presumptuously round at the troops. It reminded Ray of the way his brother and his friends sometimes stood about, surveying everything, assuming command, keeping their secrets. When they smiled it was for each other or themselves and it meant *we're better than you little people*. They thought they were big men. But these were the big men, Ray realised. These were the boys grown up and they were in charge.

Eventually there were trucks and Ray was inside one looking out of the open back, staring at that bright changing screen. He thought of the men far away now in the fighting, each of them locked in the limited square of their perception. That was what it was like in battle: things happened very far away or lethally close. The only place you could move was a small cell, your hands, your weapons, the space of a few steps, people either side of you. In that cell you lived and died.

White dust closed the view. It blew away to reveal a phalanx of marching men white with that dust sinking backwards into the distance. The truck swerved and more men could be seen, smaller, further away, moving across country. One of them jumped in a red cloud. As the sound of the explosion reached the truck, two other men could be seen lying on the ground and around them men cringed, stopping still. They all froze in a moment's image that vanished as the truck turned again and they were out of sight. Ray felt himself covered in sweat. He panted. He tried not to but he couldn't stop himself, he had to, he flung himself forward and vomited out of the back of the truck, his loose fluids whipping back and disappearing onto the speeding ground. When he was done he got up again. He was handed a canteen of water.

6

Will lingered over a sentence in the *Invasion Handbook*.

*The women are sometimes charming, petulant, witty
and gay, with more than a soupçon of orientalism, very
feminine, rather helpless and appealing.*

He saw dark eyes, smiling lips, a long neck, a cloud
of crinolines. She was smiling as she gave way beneath
him. In his imagination, he wasn't in contact with her
exactly. It was not so much physical as a dreamy
enacting of the word 'yielding'. She yielded before
him, sinking backwards, smiling.

Will found this pleasant to consider. Nothing else
to do with Sicily was particularly attractive. The
Invasion Handbook warned of 'the pushing business
man, the more pushing middle-class loafer, all gloves
and cane and collar and tie, a vulgarian if ever there
was one. He is from every point of view appalling,
and there are many of him.' These did sound repellent
but it struck Will that the same attitude might appraise
him as a pushing, middle-class man and Will felt a
stab of dislike for the anonymous author and his
officer-class hauteur. The handbook went on to taxon-
omise the aristocracy and warned of city crime and
rural vendettas.

The language had been easy enough to acquire. In the classes given to the AMGOT servicemen, Will found Italian to be Latin pronounced with the exaggerated swooping accent of an ice-cream seller.

Will had shared those classes with some Americans. They were all to work together to build peace on the island after the invasion. Will found the Americans slovenly and overconfident and horribly well fed. Also on some level he didn't quite believe in them. Their accents sounded put on, as though they were pretending to be 'Yanks', imitating the people in the Hollywood pictures. He had the thought that on their own, speaking honestly, they would sound quite different. This seemed to be particularly true of the Italian-Americans among them. They were immigrants and their American-ness came and went. All Americans were immigrants, more or less. They were all pretending to be American.

Will lay back on his bunk with the *Invasion Handbook* on his chest, one finger keeping his place. The sea sank beneath the ship, tilting his feet up and his head down. Over the water the invasion was happening, the Americans unleashing their unbelievable masses of firepower. The ship floated upwards and dipped. Beneath him a Sicilian coquette smiled and yielded, again and again.

7

Cirò was not home. He didn't know this place. He'd never seen this part of the island before, with sulphur mines, sore and yellow openings in the ground. There were foreign soldiers in large numbers. In New York he'd occasionally had nightmares in which he returned to Sicily. In them, he felt the motion of the boat urging forwards, the sun on the water, the breeze. Then he went through the door of his home, his heart beating in his chest like the wings of a dove. He ran to find Teresa. Her round back was turned to him. He spun her around. She looked at him with fear and without recognition. She was old. Sometimes she had the clouded eyes of a blind woman, sometimes a witch's penetrating stare of judgement.

Along the coast he could hear the dull, crumpling sound of German shells. Cirò and his people were heading away from them, through areas the war had cleared days before. They passed a Fascist truck lying on its side, its tyres exploded. There were bodies not yet cleared away, blackening and bloating, some also exploded.

They drove that day though a world that outstripped his imagination and his urge for revenge. He forgot how much he wanted it, seeing those sights. He even pitied the bodies. It was the Fascists' fault. These poor boys had been duped by the Fascists, tricked into death for nothing. The sun swung from side to side overhead as the road snaked. They passed bodies, smashed rocks, burned equipment. They drove up into mountains.

That night they requisitioned a house at the edge of the village, a large brick house that seemed to be stumbling up the slope. They made a fire in the hearth and cooked their rations, soldiers running around doing women's work. Aircraft flew overhead on sorties, dragging sheets of sound.

Cirò elected to sleep downstairs on the shelf of the hearth, keen to show the military boys that he was as tough as they were – tougher, in fact, a native. He set his pistol down beside his head. Still the planes went over. It was like the air was a flat surface and they were grinding it, like the slow scrape of a millstone. He lay for a long time staring up at the ghostly shape of the ceiling, thinking about things. He thought about Cathy pale as milk in her bed, lonely again without him, the little bird in the glass-cage office. He thought about Teresa and what she might look like, and what he might do with the peasant Silvio. Muffled voices could be heard upstairs. Why would anyone still be up and talking? He listened, pushing himself up off the couch so both ears were unobstructed. The voices weren't coming from above. And they were speaking Italian. As quietly as he could, he pulled out his gun, lowered his feet onto the floor and stood up. He went upstairs and knocked on Major Kelly's door. The major's expression didn't change while Cirò explained that there were people hiding in the cellar. 'Okay,' he said. 'Let's go winkle them out.' He gathered his spectacles from the bedside table and put them on, winding the steel arms behind his ears.

Two more soldiers were collected. With a flashlight, they found a small wooden door that seemed likely to be the way into the cellar. Against stifled protests, Cirò pressed his head to the wood. He could feel them in there, their shifting animal presence. He nodded.

Major Kelly was not a coward. He arranged himself in front of the door, lifted the latch and gently pulled it open. With the flashlight in his left hand and his pistol in the right, he stepped in and down. After a few steps, the others heard him say. 'Okay, you two, get up and move or I shoot.'

Cirò shouted the phrase in Italian and heard them move. Some bumping and scraping and two men now climbed the steps ahead of Kelly. An old man held up his arms as though to ward off blows. One of the soldiers grabbed his collar and yanked him out. The other was a boy of fighting age. He grabbed the lapels of one of the soldiers and started pleading. The soldier pushed him off.

'Please, please, please don't. We're innocent. We're just peasants. We're not . . .'

'What's he saying?'

'He's saying they're innocent.'

'Yes, yes. Innocent.'

The old man bowed rapidly, affirming this. He reached out and put his hands on Cirò's shoulder, large, dirty hands, the fingers knotted and kinked by years of labour. Cirò didn't move. He looked the old man in the eye and said quietly, 'Don't touch me.' The old man started backwards. He looked at Cirò then looked carefully away, his mouth open. Cirò smiled. He was a man of respect. They still knew. Cirò was home.

'Don't worry about it,' he told the major. 'They're not going to be trouble. They live here.'

8

North Africa had been like a sports field for war, a baseball diamond for the movements of tanks and planes and eighty-eights. At night it was floodlit with flares. Sicily was terrible, so crowded. There were refugees on most of the roads. Having been dispossessed of their truck by an artillery unit, Ray's group resorted to appropriating a couple of carts and mules from some fleeing peasants. Brightly painted with figures and scenes, the carts looked like something from the funfair. Their owners stood on the side of the road with their luggage round their feet and new packets of cigarettes and chewing gum in their hands. Ray and the AMGOT officers now pursued their course at the sway-backed, breathing, ancient pace of farm animals. Geminiano had taken the reins on Ray's cart. He whipped them up and down, shouted 'Giddeyup!' and pretended to spit like a cowboy, 'Hwit-ding!' Ray shouted up at him, 'Hey, this is Italy, remember. Don't you know your own country?'

'Not mine. This is Sicily. Come on, horsey.'

'Not mine either.'

The whole place was ancient, just like his parents had said. Passing through the liberated towns, the doorways were full of hungry children who came out to beg for food and cheer them. Their clothes and faces – they looked exactly like the children in the family photographs in the dresser in the hall, stiff cardboard images of rigid Pugliese families, dark eyes, moustaches and oiled hair, heavy beaded dresses, hands immobile forever on knees and solemn children standing in knickerbockers, thick socks and polished boots. Most of these clothes, his mother explained, would have been hired for the occasion. Here these children were now, famished in the middle of a war. On the walls behind them, already defaced, were posters of Mussolini. They shouted at Ray in his parents' language. *Believe! Obey! Fight!*

9

The peace was colliding with the war. AMGOT Civilian Affairs Officer William Walker had run into the thick of it. There was shellfire, minefields, wreckage, prisoners sitting on the side of the road with their hands on their heads. There were people and parts of people around stains of burning. The force of it was insane, the excess of it. It came out of nowhere, out of the air, out of the ground. It was what everybody here was supposed to do. People ran with stretchers.

They were stuck now, delayed. Ahead of them was a battle over a bridge, Germans on one side, Allies on the other, like a game you would play with lead soldiers or the war Will's father fought in. The battle was stubborn and grinding. It had two jaws. It was eating men. Vehicles raced towards it. Samuels suggested playing cards while they waited.

They waited for two days. The sounds were terrible. Will was increasingly angry. The lassitude, he thought, was making him sensitive. He could feel his heart pumping in his chest, the sweat forming on his skin. He looked at his hands, the fingers in three parts, curling towards him. He heard the men being killed. Ambulances raced. It was horrifying, horrifying and boring. Maybe this was what produced his father's heroism: boredom, all those hours in the dugout, in the mould and damp hearing the weapons and doing nothing, going out of your mind. In the end you were bound to break out. Will fancied that he could have done the same, rushed out and taken a machine-gun nest on his own. He clenched his molars together hard, stifling a yawn.

Will walked around. He spoke to people. He smoked cigarette after cigarette, his pulse becoming light and fast.

The fighting changed in intensity. A spastic firing dropped away almost to silence, a quiet spattered with light gunfire followed by some bursting shells then quiet again. Will heard that on the third night they had stopped fighting and through some negotiation agreed to let each other come forward and collect their dead. He was told this by a soldier who couldn't stand still. In the darkness his cigarette brightened and faded as he pulled on it. He thanked Samuels for the booze and swallowed it. He said that the men had walked past each other in silence, ignored each other, picked up the dead and the larger parts of the dead by torchlight and carried them away. They did this for a few hours. Afterwards, in the widening light of dawn, they began firing again.

Eventually, somehow, the Allies pushed through. The Germans were outkilled. The bridge was repaired by engineers and the weight of the stalled invasion rolled slowly forwards. Will didn't look at the place as they drove through. He didn't want to see it. It ought to be private in some way or concealed. It was obscene and degrading what had happened there. It felt possibly contagious. Will didn't want to breathe in until they were through to the other side, in clearer air, picking up speed.

10

Luisa hurried through the house and out onto the terrace to see what it was she was hearing, matching the glinting aircraft with the throbbing sound. She saw their wings flash as they banked, saw them sprinkle tiny bombs that fell all the way down and sprouted as grey cabbages of smoke. A few instants later the noises of the explosions arrived one by one. The sound was like someone bumping down the servants' wooden stairs.

The war was getting closer. The servants were all terrified. Prince Adriano pretended not to be, striding back and forth with his hands behind his back and the wireless on, proud and useless, like a chicken in a peasant's yard.

Luisa watched as much as she could. It thrilled her. It filled her body. She came in breathless, with her teeth chattering. At night she could see the pulses of red tracer fire, she could see fires in the darkness.

Retreating Germans gathered near the palace for a while. Luisa could see them from one window at the top of the house. The Prince was terrified that they would requisition the place but they never did. A few of them came to ask for some water. Afterwards, Graziana was hysterical. When she'd opened the door, she said, she thought that there were ghosts standing

182

there. Their hair was completely white. Their eyes were as pale as the sky, their skin cracked and falling off.

At dinner that night the fighting was very close. They sat down at the walnut table to the accompaniment of crackling guns. Luisa's father's fear was so great that he could not show any sign of it at all. If he once flinched or moaned, he would have crumpled to the floor and crawled away to the cellarage. As it was, he walked in like someone balancing a book on his head and sat with his eyes very wide and unseeing. Luisa found his face very funny. Graziana was also amusing her – her trembling, whimpering progress around the table with the soup tureen. When she started whispering prayers to herself as she ladled out stuttering quantities of soup, Luisa openly laughed.

'I find it rather sinister,' the Prince said once Graziana had withdrawn, 'the way you seem to be enjoying this warfare so much.'

Luisa didn't say anything.

'Particularly,' the Prince went on, 'given how many friends you have among the Fascists.'

'I have none. I know some Fascists. That's a different thing. I'm pleased things are changing. I want the Germans gone.'

The Prince paused with his spoon halfway to his lips and closed his eyes at the sound of artillery shells. 'But consider how they are changing. I'm not sure if you understand that this is quite real.'

'That is precisely what I like about it.'

11

It had taken longer than expected but the British had taken the east of the island and were heading west. Cirò Albanese was with the Americans who were racing to get there first, led by General Patton. They did. In Palermo people came out and cheered. Children stood on piles of rubble shouting and waving. They ran up to the jeeps and trucks. Cirò smiled and waved at them. Like the others, he threw out cigarettes and coins and gum and the children dived for them.

12

Any fool would have realised that the Strait of Messina had to be cut off but no fool had and the Nazis simply poured north out of the top of the island and up into Italy. They'd be waiting for the next invasion coming after them.

So the fighting was done in Sicily. Ruins and corpses. An apparently grateful population in a state of chaos it was now Will's duty to calm and clarify. The Allied Military Government was hastening into position and Will was with several others in the wrong place. Deploying the extraordinary powers of their identity cards, they got themselves transport to Palermo.

Having identified the headquarters, Will decided to delay a little longer and go for a stroll. He walked out among the American soldiers and the sunshine, the locals who were silent and stared and the beggars who approached. He looked around for the oriental beauty and the repellent pushing middle classes but he didn't see them.

Palermo looked like a grand old opera set of a place. There were avenues interrupted with massive piles of rubble where bombs had fallen. Pigeons sputtered from one balcony to another. There was a huge bomb crater near the encrusted cathedral. Hundreds had died there apparently. People in Palermo were used to crowding together. Backstage, so to speak, behind the tall façades, Will discovered a sordid network of streets infested with people watching him go by or calling out to him. Voices shouted from windows overhead. People beckoned and begged. He turned a corner and a small boy ran out to him, fleeing his raging father, a thin man in an undershirt with muscles jumping in his arms as he gesticulated and swore. The boy clung to Will, hiding behind him, pulling at his hand, squirming, while the man shouted. Others were watching. Embarrassed, Will tried to calm the man with an authoritatively raised voice and good Italian but he was too wild. He lunged forwards, bumping Will as he tried to grab hold of the boy who now ran. Will saw him escape, his light bare feet striking the dirty ground. The man, giving up, walked away with his hands in his pockets. It was only later, back in the AMGOT building, that Will discovered his wallet was missing and pieced together what had happened. He was furious and could do nothing.

The thieves had better spend the money quickly. When the new temporary currency was issued, it wouldn't be worth anything. A couple of Americans lent Will some cash. They went out together to drink and found a hot, wood-panelled place with sour red wine and, annoyingly, an accordionist. Afterwards, the two Americans, who had been in Palermo for a few days, led Will to a kind of courtyard which might partly have been a gap created by a bomb; certainly there was a heap of rubble on one side. The place was gloomy. Light came from the late evening sky and a few candles in glass jars. Little groups of glowing cigarettes hovered and circled together like flies. Women were standing by small piles of tinned foods. The smokers were soldiers. The atmosphere was quiet and serious, disrupted now and again by outbreaks of laughter or grunts and sighs. The Americans Will was with watched his face as he decoded the scene and noticed the figures on the ground. The soldiers were bringing food in exchange for sex. Some had the sex standing up, the soldiers crumpling into the women as though blown helplessly by a gale or bending the women over and shagging them from behind, some even swigging from bottles at the same time as they thrust back and forth. Some lay on the ground and struggled. There was a particularly large group waiting for one woman who proved to be an astonishingly beautiful girl of about eighteen, improbably beautiful, a freak of nature, rich hair around her shoulders, large, soft lips, long-lashed, suffering eyes. 'Well, her family will be all right,' Will commented as another soldier put a can on her pile and she wiped her mouth with her wrist then lifted her skirt. The Americans said nothing. They just watched.

No one was stopping this. Will felt himself alone among these animals, alone with his intellect and bitter thoughts. The drink in him made his inner monologue loud and polemical. He was excoriating this depravity to some senior ranking figure, and arrogating the responsibility for dealing with it. Meanwhile, he remembered for some reason the shipload of prosthetic limbs, pilfered from, in the wrong place. Battle was the same. No rules, no limits. Just acting. Just animals. And this was the whole thing. You killed people with

187

guns and machines, smashed homes to bits, and in the ruins you fucked hungry survivors in exchange for tins of meat. Will's anger and disgust made him drunk. Everything was floating, everything was sliding apart. Then, catching his breath, he dwindled back into himself and felt very bleak. Order would have to be imposed. He would have to do it.

'I'm going,' he announced suddenly and walked away. The night air sobered him, as did the concentration required to find his way back. He thought he saw rats running in the darkness. He felt a mawkish solidarity with a starved-looking cat he saw stepping carefully over rubbish.

Back in his room, his bedside table presented him with a choice between *De Rerum Natura* and *The Wind in the Willows*. Will had had enough of random collisions and thoughtless matter. He stretched the sheet over his knees and tucked it under his waist and as high up his chest as he could manage so that he was tightly cinched to the bed. He'd done this as a child. It made him feel neat and prepared. His copy of *The Wind in the Willows* was nice to handle, a humble edition with covers of stiff blue board that were rounded at the corners with use. The paper was soft, golden, mothy. The book smelled of wood. Will lit a cigarette and looked around for a section to read.

Late in the evening, tired and happy and miles from home, they drew up on a remote common far from habitations, turned the horse loose to graze, and ate their simple supper sitting on the grass by the side of the cart. Toad talked big about all he was going to do in the days to come, while stars grew fuller and larger around them, and a yellow moon,

appearing suddenly and silently from nowhere in particular,
came to keep them company and listen to their talk. At last
they turned into their little bunks in the cart; and Toad,
kicking out his legs, sleepily said, 'Well, good night, you
fellows! This is the real life for a gentleman! Talk about
your old river!'

Will's eyes were heavy. The book was wilting towards him. He righted it again. The words began to slide and repeat *tired and happy and miles from home suddenly and silently Talk about your old river!*

13

Ray had said that he didn't want to go looking for a
girl. He didn't want the feeling afterwards. A sweet
girl to hold him and kiss: that was one thought, a
persistent fantasy, astonishing and delighting, that
flooded his chest until he wanted to cry. He remembered his story about the office girl on the bench, her
wide hopeful eyes, the small turn of her head. That
buzzing, swarming feeling. But that was not what he
would find. Instead, the girls were sick and poor and
hungry. Talking to some of the locals, he learned that
their parents sent out these girls. They needed the
money or gifts to survive.

Instead, Ray sat on his bed and looked at his old
movie magazine. He looked at the face of Claire
Trevor, the pale smooth skin of her cheek, and imagined the cool soapy smell of it. Or perhaps she wore
perfume. You would get close and inhale flowers. Her
face was perfectly still. Bam, just that one instant.
Her hair and make-up and her face in that precise
expression. Her small breasts pushed out the white
fabric of her jersey. Ray looked closer, bringing
the page to his face. Her breasts were defined by
gradations in colour, the white turning to blue underneath and between them. The colours were made by
the tiniest dots of ink. The white dots turned blue.

Up higher, the dots were pink and yellow to make her neck, red for her lips. Tiny white dots were separated by narrow channels of blue and black dots and they made her teeth. Ray panicked suddenly. Claire Trevor wasn't there any more. She was sinking away from him like water into sand, the way men died, just pouring away.

Ray crushed his eyes shut. He shook his head. This wasn't good. His mind kept doing this. It was like missing a stair. He kept falling. He reached out for George. He said his name out loud, 'George. George, if you're alive or dead.'

14

Everything was the same and different. The streets were the same but the scale was wrong or more right than Cirò could remember. There was a slow, strenuous reconciling of his memories with the real world of Sant'Attilio that felt almost physical, his mind compressed here, released there. As soon as they had arrived, Cirò wanted to be rid of his Americans so as to concentrate on this process of arriving. He looked for people he recognised but the young boys on the streets were of a generation that would have heard of him, probably, but would never have seen him. They didn't see him. He'd left in a coffin and come back invisible, a ghost returned to haunt them.

Finally he saw a familiar face, Jaconi Battista standing in the doorway of his little shop. It was definitely him although the intervening years had done what they could to disguise him, blurring his face, tearing his hair in handfuls from his head. And Cirò saw Jaconi seeing him. He saw him straighten up and step back a little. Cirò shouted to the driver to let him down. 'I need to speak to someone.'

Major Kelly said to him, 'You know where this town hall is?'

'Sure I do. I'll see you there.'

He stepped with his own feet onto the ground of Sant'Attilio.

Jaconi was gone. Cirò went after him through the door of the shop. Still the same. Sacks of rice and lentils, a few tins of food, some flaking dry vegetables. No meat. The trays were empty. Cirò couldn't smell the cold metallic smell of puddled blood and flesh that he remembered. Jaconi stood behind the counter, biting a fingernail. Cirò asked him, 'What's the matter, no meat?'

'Nothing. I have nothing.'

'How can that be true? No animals on the hills? What's going on here? Anyway, don't worry. That's going to change now.'

Jaconi laughed. 'Sicilians won't be poor any more? You forget what it's like here when you were in America?'

Cirò stared at him until the laughter had drained out of Jaconi's face completely. He decided to play with him, demanding from him what he already knew. 'Where's Teresa?' he asked.

'Cirò, it's been so many years.'

'I know how many years it's been. I counted every day.'

'We all thought you were dead.'

'Where is she?'

'So much changed. It was so long.'

'Where is she?'

Jaconi covered his face with both hands then dropped them, sighing. 'You remember Silvio who lives up from the church?'

Cirò didn't respond. He himself stood very still.

He'd meant to frighten Jaconi, to torture him, but he was having trouble standing upright. Cirò hadn't thought that hearing these words from someone who had been in Sant'Attilio all the time he was away would actually wound him so much. Jaconi couldn't look at him. He hung his head and said at the floor, 'After four years she . . .'

'Shut up! Shut your filthy fucking mouth!'

'Cirò, we thought you were dead.'

'I'm not dead. I'm not the one who's dead.'

Walking up to the square and past the church, Cirò saw that blind Tinu was still in the doorway. That was unbelievable. He'd been an old man when he'd left. His beard was pure white now, his cheeks sunken. Shimmying in their sockets, his upturned eyes were the same milky blue. Mother Mary must be caring for him. His open mouth mumbled as though talking with her. His limbs were withered as a thorn bush but he was still there.

Children were playing in the little street. One of the older boys, a lad of fifteen or so who wasn't playing, stood watching with his arms folded. Surely he looked like Teresa. Over a faint first moustache, he had her sleepy, curled snail shell of a nose. And the flat hairline across his forehead. This was like a dream. Cirò walked up to him. The boy backed away but not quickly enough and Cirò grabbed his wrists.

'Who's your mother?'

'What?'

Those were her eyelashes, fluttering with terror. 'Her name. What's your mother's name?'

'Teresa Santangeli. You're hurting my arms.' The boy was stronger than Cirò would admit, twisting and complicating his grasp.

'And who's your father?'

'Silvio . . .'

'No.' Cirò interrupted him. 'No. Wrong. He isn't.' Cirò pushed him away.

Out of the brightness of the street, Cirò shoved into the darkness of the little house. As he blinked he heard Teresa shout, 'So, did they have any rice?'

'I don't know,' he shouted back.

He heard footsteps. Teresa entered the room slowly, a hand over her mouth, her eyes wide. 'You,' she said. 'Jesus Christ. Sweet Jesus Christ and Mary. It's you.'

She looked shorter than he remembered, perhaps because of the weight she had gained. She looked like a solid little Sicilian woman, a wife and mother.

'Yes, it's me.'

Teresa held the sides of her face.

'I'm back.'

'I see. I see that.'

'I'm back now so things will go back to the way they were before.'

'Cirò, I have children with this man. I have two children who are dead, even. It's been a long time. I was a widow.'

'How can you be a widow, Teresa, when your husband is still alive?'

'But you weren't alive, Cirò.'

'I was always alive. Do you think I should stand for this, for the shame you're bringing on me? People will know that I'm back now.'

'After how long? Twenty years?'

'And now I'm here and things are going to be how they were and you are still my wife.'

'But . . . but . . . You can't, Cirò. The children. He didn't know.'

'The children will have a father.'

'You can't.'

'Teresa, you are my wife. You married me in a church with God looking at us. You know what that means.' He walked over to her, caught hold of the back of her head as she swayed backwards and kissed her sweating forehead. 'Make sure he's here on Friday evening. That's all.'

15

Will decided to linger another day. There was a reason for this but it couldn't be admitted, even to himself. He kept the reason as deep and invisible as a river current, known only by the darkly streaming weed or turning froth. He walked out into the streets of Palermo.

He walked among buildings and ruins and intermittent churches. In places, sunshine reflected from liquid filth moving sluggishly in the drains. After his pickpocketing, Will was wary of the quick, skinny children and the watching adults. There was too much movement, too many people here. Much as he'd tried to convince himself otherwise, Will had never liked London for the same reason. He turned a corner and saw a man aiming a gun up at a window. Will started to intervene. 'I say!' The man fired and a pigeon tumbled down. It bounced then lay there, swatting its wings against the paving stones as it died. A man brushed past Will's back on a bicycle.

Will took refuge in a café. On the small circular table in front of him, he placed his Lucretius to refresh his Italian. He opened the book to read of the strength in the frenzy of Venus which was not what he wanted to think about presently. Instead, he sat like a spy and observed. At a certain hour the place filled with Sicilians. Sicilian men: no women entered. Perhaps to be a woman in such a place was to put your reputation in as much jeopardy as a lone woman in a pub back home. The men were short and intimate. They touched and held each other. They clambered over each other like bees, collecting coffees from the bar, their voices overlapping. There was a repertoire of gestures that were foreign, flicks, pinchings of the air, touches to the face. Their facial expressions were proud, indifferent, righteous, resigned, intent, philosophical.

At the table next to him, several men were mingling their cigarette smoke over a game of cards. They slapped cards down and grabbed them and flipped them across to each other without speaking very much. Occasionally they commented with pure vowels, 'ooo' or 'eee'. If they were playing for money, Will didn't see it, and he didn't know what game they were playing.

Hours to pass. Will smoked cigarettes. The thought occurred to him that he might have written in a journal if he'd had one. He should have been keeping a diary all this time, although in all likelihood he would have failed to do so. He'd never managed to before. Better to compose his narrative at some point in the future, when he could look back and see it all clearly and discern the significant shape. It would be easier then to strip away the tedium, the triviality and error, those endless hours guarding the port, Samuels such an uninteresting man.

Will needed to find a tin of food. He walked out

into the afternoon and wandered. They needed to do something about rubbish collection. Heaps of filth could be seen everywhere. With a sickening start he saw that one was alive: a whiteness of moving maggots. So repulsive, that naked writhing, the pulsing and probing of their feeding bodies. Will's digestive tract jerked. He spat into the gutter. For cleaner air, he walked down to the sea. There were barriers everywhere to keep people from the ships but his pass was effective and he walked through, beyond the boats and the men.

Violet water, sombre and low. The darkness of evening was gathering on it. Soothingly inhuman and ancient. *The sea, the sea.* A deep vista to a horizon, clear air above it. Lucretius argued that the universe had no limit or centre. A thought, a random thought from his reading with which Will did nothing. His mind uttered it as he looked at the sea. He turned around and into the business of the night. He needed to find a tin of food.

That beautiful girl was like something from a painting. It was the kind of beauty that enslaved poets – the lustrous hair, the vulnerable mouth and deep, sad eyes – and anyone with a can of food could possess her. Will had a tin now, tightly clasped in his right hand, a ridiculous emblem of the need that was driving him. He wanted to possess her. He wanted to be there first, to be the first to have her. As he found his way back to the place, into the narrow backstreets, young boys called out to him, offering to lead him to other women, but he ignored them as if disgusted, shaking his head.

Wrong turnings were frustrating. He felt he was being baffled and prevented. He was losing time. The story of his life. Always confusion and delay when he wanted to be swift in action. Several soldiers also carrying tins of food indicated that he was on the right road at last. He hurried ahead of them and found himself at the rubbled space. Already there were soldiers and women gathered but Will couldn't see her. Perhaps she would come later. Meantime he had to stand and seem not to watch as the women received their payments and accepted what followed. Hotly ashamed at first, Will found that as he waited the clamouring self-disgust in him slowly quietened. Everyone was there willingly. No one was getting hurt. It was usual for soldiers in a war or for gentlemen at various times and places to avail themselves of the comfort of women. This was the getting of experience. This was being a man.

But still she did not appear. Perhaps she'd got all she needed the night before and would not return. Will gave her ten more minutes.

No. She would not appear. Or perhaps a little later she would. While he waited he might as well join the queue for the next best girl there. He shifted towards her as each of the men ahead of him had their turn and departed. Still she didn't arrive. In exchange for a tin of mackerel, he lost his virginity to someone else. Afterwards she patted him on the back of his head. Will caught her hand by the wrist and pulled it away. He rushed back to his billet to wash himself thoroughly in case of disease.

16

Teresa had visited the Montebianco witch a little while into the dark time after Cirò's disappearance. Alone, in her hot widow's clothes, she had walked the miles to Montebianco and had arrived at the witch's door just as Alvaro Zuffo stepped through it. He recognised Teresa and put a hand on her shoulder and said kind words. He reached into his breast pocket, feeling along the slope of his fat chest, and pulled out his wallet. He gave her several notes and tears came to her eyes. She kissed his hand and thanked him. Kinder than Cirò's own brother, he was. Zuffo let her lean in and moan against him. He patted the top of her head and disengaged himself, stepping away to a motor car. 'When we know what happened . . .' he said, wagging a finger, his voice full of promises. He was driven away. Teresa dried her face on her shawl and knocked on the witch's door.

The witch caught hold of Teresa's hands and led her to a chair. She asked why she had come and listened in that way that nobody else had, so intent the air around her sparkled. She was alert, this woman, she saw things. Everything that Teresa had ever told her she seemed to know already. 'Yes, yes, of course,' she interrupted. 'Would you like coffee? Just a moment.'

She hurried over to the stove and set some coffee

boiling. Teresa looked at the saints and symbols and objects on the walls. The saints had been Teresa's first port of call. They always were. Teresa believed in the Church above all else but the saints never spoke back the way the witch did. The saints never gave you answers or, if they did, they gave them in hints and signs that you could easily get wrong. When you wanted to hear something, the witch was better. A good woman, she cured people of all sorts too. She knew how to drive out worms and cure the fevers caused by ticks and how to guarantee sons.

Today, the witch didn't take out cards or a diagram or use any stones. She didn't make a prayer. She said simply, 'Your husband will be put in his coffin twice. I know this for sure. The first time he will not be dead. He will climb out of that coffin alive.' She stopped, sitting back and pursing her lips in the way that indicated her revelation was over. Teresa said, 'Thank you.' Always such a tingling in the air in that room. You wouldn't want the witch as an enemy. Teresa reached into her pocket, awkwardly holding her coffee cup, and, as she tried to pull out a coin, she dislodged one of Zuffo's banknotes. It fell onto the dirt floor. She couldn't pick it up and give the witch something smaller now, so she reached down and collected it and handed it over. The note had arrived and now it went. It had fallen out like that so it was obviously fated to happen.

17

Jaconi raised pleading hands. 'Why me? Cirò, please.'

'Because you saw me first. Friday night. I'll be by old Luca's place.'

'But, Cirò, please.'

'Nothing's going to happen. Nothing's going to happen to you. Friday at nine o'clock.'

18

Silvio couldn't understand why Teresa was so angry with him, finding fault in every little thing he did. He whistled at the table and he shouldn't whistle. Why didn't he ever wear his good shirt? Her movements were quick and stabbing and clumsy. She burned herself. A red mark on her wrist the size of a coin that would turn brown and then a wrinkled silver. She blinked tears onto her round cheeks and swiped them away with her apron.

There was a knock at the door. Teresa said, 'Who would come knocking at this time?' She opened the door to the shopowner, Jaconi, who said, 'Silvio, come with me. They're giving out cigarettes at the town hall.'

'Really?'

'Yeah. Who knows why but they're doing it. Look.' He held up a new packet of Chesterfields. 'I'll show you.'

Mattia, the eldest boy, got up to go with them too but his mother stopped him. 'Stay here. I don't want you mixing with the foreigners.'

As Silvio walked out, he felt Teresa touch him on the shoulder. That was strange. He turned around, surprised, but the door was shutting.

'Here, have one of these,' Jaconi said. 'I'll get more.'

'No, it's all right.'

'No, go on. Here.' Jaconi took a cigarette out of the pack and handed it to Silvio who shrugged, put it betweens his lips, and waited while Jaconi lit a match. Silvio puffed the cigarette alight. Jaconi shook the match until the flame went out and tossed it away.

'Nice, isn't it?'

'Sure.' Silvio held the cigarette up and looked at it as he exhaled. 'It's good.'

They walked on. Before they got to the town hall, a voice called out to them. The man, who was leaning against a wall, pushed himself upright and said. 'Good evening. I know you two. Jaconi, I saw you the other day. And . . . Silvio. Remember me?'

Jaconi shook the man's hand. Silvio offered his. 'You're . . .'

'I'm Cirò Albanese. Remember now?'

Cirò kept hold of his hand, wouldn't let it go. 'Thank you, Jaconi,' he said.

Jaconi didn't say anything. He dropped his head and walked quickly away, back the way they'd come.

'Cirò, please . . .' Silvio tried to pull his hand away.

'Sshh. Quiet now, Silvio. You know what's going to happen.'

'Please.'

'Come on. Let's not waste time.' Cirò still had hold of his hand. He pulled Silvio and turned so that Silvio was in front of him. 'Just walk straight ahead. I'll tell you where to go. Don't whimper like that. I hate that sound. Pray if you want to but don't moan like an old woman.'

Cirò directed Silvio down and out of the town, out into the fields.

'The Germans were all around here,' he told Silvio. 'And the Fascists. We killed them all. I came back with the Americans.'

They crossed one field and carried on down a little way into the valley. 'Here.'

Silvio swallowed twice and said, 'What are you going to do?'

'Don't worry. It'll be fine. It'll be very quick.'

'Tell my mother . . .'

'I know. I'll tell her. There are mines in front of you, about twenty yards away. Walk around and find one. Accidents happen. Go on. Walk in a straight line away and then back. I've got a gun so don't run. It'll be better than the other way, believe me. Quicker.'

'Please, Cirò.'

'Go on.'

Silvio started walking, his hands outspread on either side of him as if to catch hold of something for balance. 'Please, God,' he said. 'Please, God.'

He walked for thirty metres. Cirò whistled and shouted, 'Turn left.' Silvio did as he was told. 'Now walk back towards me.'

Nothing.

Cirò directed him again to the left and sent him away and then back. The walk seemed to take hours. Still nothing. He did it again. When Silvio reached him this time, Cirò was laughing. 'You're the luckiest man in the world. How are you not dead yet? We'll have to do something else.'

Cirò walked up to Silvio and put his hands around Silvio's throat. The man's neck was slippery with sweat. Cirò could smell shit in his trousers. He started to squeeze. Silvio caught hold of his wrists, his eyes wide with surprise. 'Shoot,' he said.

'I know. But it's better this way. Ow. Stop pulling at my hands. It won't help.'

Silvio stared at Cirò, his eyes thickening and fading. He stumbled, his legs giving way. Cirò kept up the pressure despite a cramp in his right hand. It was a good thing he was just strangling him until he passed out, not to death. Silvio became soft and heavy in his grip and Cirò let him drop to the ground. Silvio lay face down, one hand by his head, the other arm underneath his body. Cirò took a grenade from his jacket pocket. He pulled the pin, placed it gently on the back of Silvio's neck, and started to run.

It seemed to take ages. He was a long way back up the hill before he saw light flash on the ground in front of him and his own thrown shadow and heard the explosion. He turned around as earth and small stones pattered back down. In the darkness he saw a hole. He couldn't see Silvio.

The Civilian Affairs Office that Will, Samuels and others were now stationed at had charge of three towns, Montebianco, Portella Corvi and Sant'Attilio, in the mountains south-west of Palermo at the far western edge of British territory. There weren't many villages or smaller settlements in the hills. The peasants didn't seem to like them. Instead, those that worked walked long miles out to the fields and the vines and came back again each night, clustering in their stony habitations like bats in caves. Most didn't work. The rest of the men and boys skulked in the towns. The women went unseen. When Will did spot them, they were receding into the front doors of their homes or they were between those doors and the sculpted fragrant darkness of the churches. One of the first things Will did, in Grand Tour fashion, was to enter the big church on the square in Sant'Attilio. Inside, headscarfed women were on their knees or hunched in the pews. Rosaries clicked, circling slowly in their fingers. Will looked at the building. After the spacious, mathematical elegance of the mosques, the church looked cluttered, superstitious, Hindu. There were dolls everywhere, in every recess. Doves and clouds, lambs, gold, and the executed Christ, starved and agonised, pouring down his blood. Dark and ugly, full of magic and death, a religion for the ignorant.

One of the first things they needed to do was to get the sappers in and the minefields cleared. Only yesterday one poor peasant had blown himself up just outside Sant'Attilio. But the whole island was mined. It might be days before they arrived.

AMGOT's main task was what they were referring to as defascistification. The former rulers were rounded up and imprisoned, in part to prevent communication with the mainland, but many were disappearing into the crowds, burning their uniforms and becoming ordinary. Posters were put up calling for information and denunciations. Interviews with locals were arranged. Many denunciations arrived at the town hall handwritten and anonymous. Will and the others were told to find a certain individual who 'has the eyes of a hypocrite'. Someone else could be identified because 'he has a mortal fear of cats'. The local police forces were to remain in place, subserving the Allies, because there wasn't time to replace them. They announced themselves loyal to the new government and thankful to be liberated from the Fascists – but who knew? They would have to be watched too. 'The eyes of a hypocrite' was a phrase that lodged itself in Will's mind. He thought of it often, seeing them everywhere.

20

Cirò Albanese would not have recognised Alvaro Zuffo if he hadn't been told it was him. Because he did know, however, he looked and slowly saw on the thin face of the old man the features of the person who had, enthroned in his heavy flesh, ruled over so much. Alvaro Zuffo had saved Cirò's life but he himself had not left Sicily. He had refused to. Instead, he organised and exerted his power in any way he could. People were paid huge amounts of money. Others never woke up again. And all for nothing. The Fascists were not reasonable. They were fanatics with no business instinct. Alvaro Zuffo was arrested for nothing, for rumours and reputation, and he had spent years on a prison island. Cirò was not the only person who had told the Americans that he was one of the most important anti-Fascists they needed to release. Now Zuffo sat in an armchair in a suite in a Palermo hotel, smiling and shaking hands with old friends.

Cirò stared at him. Zuffo seemed surrounded by the ghost of his former flesh. Cirò's memory kept adding it to the figure in front of him. Zuffo's neck looked weak. His head trembled, his lips dark and loose. He kept them clamped together, a diagonal line across his face. He patted them with a handkerchief after he had spoken.

'I never liked the sea,' he said. 'And I had to listen to it for years.' He sipped from a small glass of red wine. 'The things they did to me in there. Every day. Every day. They tie me to a box on the ground then one fits a gas mask over my head. It has a tube attached to a thing this other guy is holding full of sea water. He squeezes, the mask fills up. I'm drowning, I'm swallowing. I have to. Then they stop. One kicks me in the belly again and again and I puke up all the brine. I piss blood. I shit blood. When I find them . . .'

'We'll find them.'

'And every night I could hear the fucking sea with it still stinking in my eyes and nose. Now I want to eat swordfish, I want to eat tuna. I want to eat every fucking fish and fuck the sea.'

Everybody laughed. Zuffo waved with his handkerchief and wiped his mouth.

Zuffo was a rich man again. American money had arrived with these men. They all brought tributes and tomorrow he would be a fine figure again, beautifully dressed. Some of the men Cirò had known in New York and New Jersey. Others were fellow prisoners. A few had escaped from a prison the other week when it was hit by a bomb. They described kicking through cracked and buckling walls and just walking out into a heavy air raid. 'To me it was like rain in springtime,' one of them said. 'I was so happy.'

For once these men lost all reserve and spoke not in the old arcane figures of speech, and in hints and ellipses. Instead they chattered like schoolgirls about the possibilities ahead. The new currency that was coming in. The prostitution boom. The morphine market. Food shipments, transportation, the threat of Communism among the peasants, what they were telling the Americans, where certain Fascists had been spotted. They established where they all would be and who would speak to whom. There was much that they would do together. That was the talk in the room. The feeling was something different. Strange and wild, there was a feeling like love between them.

21

Walking through Palermo the following morning, through shouts and sunlight and strangers towards the docks to do some business, Cirò reflected that those men were better than family. They gave you more. And you knew how much you couldn't trust them.

Having dealt with Silvio, Cirò had walked to his brother's house in Sant'Attilio. They were all there. Cirò endured the explosion of recognition, of surprise and delight, sensing something else in the silences of each person who stopped talking and stepped back to allow another to come forward and embrace him. Unknown children ran around him. Some bare-arsed babies were carried in the arms of his nephews' wives, his nephews who were men now. All this that he didn't have – another thing that had been stolen from him. The grief of this as bitter as sea water. A glass of red wine was put in his hand.

Cirò's brother was old now. He was still lean, still agile, but he also still had the same muddled, anxious look in his eyes. There was a fog inside. He was stupid and to compensate he made sudden, clumsy moves. He was a man who made mistakes. He took Cirò outside to smoke and said, 'My boys, they haven't been brought up in the old ways.'

'Probably they're too old to start now. Maybe they should go to America.'

Cirò's brother tutted. 'They can't leave their families.'

'Lots do. And send money back. I did. I had to. I did.'

Cirò's brother nodded while ignoring this comment, thinking of something else, thinking of himself. 'You could at least start teaching them how it all works.'

'How what works? There's nothing. I've only just got back.'

Cirò had no intention of giving anything to them. With their families they would make larger and larger claims for things they hadn't earned. Cirò just needed a son of his own. He had often imagined one: handsome, taciturn, fearless, reliable.

Cirò turned a corner and saw at the end of the street a dazzle of sea light. That sight, it meant different things now. When he had left it had looked terminal, alien, the end of what he knew. It was where his world collapsed and dissolved. Now it looked familiar. It looked like work and stirred with possibility, particularly if he could be the first to negotiate this area of interest with Zuffo. The business would pay more than enough to give Zuffo his tribute. It would be something for Cirò to get in on this Palermo action but he could do it. The waterfront was busy with naval troops and was guarded. Cirò had to show his papers at a sawhorse barrier – military eyes on him, the card, on him again and waving him through – before he could go on to find two particular men who knew which ships were delivering the medical supplies.

22

In the chaos of the invasion, as it split and fissured across the island, Ray and Gem had somehow ended up separated from the others a long way east, and now they were a couple of days late for their destination.

They had lost the others in a small town that had rushed out, cheering, to greet the Americans. Sicilian men slapped their chests and declared, 'My cousin – Chicago!' Or 'America best! Is best!' And if one of the soldiers spoke a word of Italian to them, they threw their hands in the air with delight.

Ray was walking with Gem. Gem had close-set brown eyes, a prominent knob to his chin. When he sweated, his hair separated into little black spikes. He was not very military in his bearing. His uniform hung off a skinny body. His helmet looked on him like something picked up from a fancy dress store. When he saw something he liked, he looked around to share it with someone, beckoning them over with a scoop of his whole hand. He did this now, calling out to Ray, 'Hey, Ray! Ray! Come and look at this!'

Gem stood at the end of a narrow side street. He disappeared into it and Ray followed. He found Gem staring upwards, mouth open.

Ray looked up and saw a row of wrought-iron

balconies, all with birdcages and little yellow birds hopping about in them.

There was a blazing stripe of brickwork and cornice above the shadow cast by the buildings on the other side of the street. Above that was blue sky, deep hyacinth blue. One of the birds starting to sing, trilling loudly. This set off another. Suddenly the whole alley was ringing with birdsong.

Ray smiled. He thought that this would be a memory, this would be victory in Sicily and how happy the people were.

When they went back to the main street, they'd lost the rest of the unit.

They hitched a lift from a man who drove a small, snarling three-wheeled truck. They mixed their Italian and Sicilian and thought they understood each other. It was only when Ray felt the mellow heat of the sunset on the back of his neck that he realised they were heading in the wrong direction. They were useless soldiers. It was comical. They climbed out of the truck in the next village and knocked on a door. They slept that night on the owner's mattress, stuffed with what felt like straw and horsehair. However they positioned themselves, it poked and irritated. Fibrous tufts scratched at their faces and stuck into their bellies. They writhed and swore.

In the morning they looked around for a ride but couldn't find one. They received a number of instructions about where to go and to wait for someone called Beppe who might appear. He did not appear. Ray watched the skulking cats, the men who sat with arms folded and muttered. After a couple of hours, they started walking west.

Gem stopped to pick up coloured stones. He ran to catch insects. He brought his closed hands up to Ray's ear so he could hear the dry buzzing inside.

He was new, Gem. He'd hardly seen anything. He wanted to know about Africa. The questions made Ray feel sick. He couldn't answer. The closest he came was saying that you sure made good friends in those situations. He tried telling Gem about George but found he couldn't conjure up what was so good about him. He said, 'He was just a great guy. The best, you know. A pal, for sure. I got his address from him. When we get back I'll write. All the time we were invading I was thinking of him ahead of us, where he was, you know. I hope he's doing okay. I'm sure he is. Sometimes when I'm down I fear the worst and it's like he's not there any more. Then, when I'm feeling okay, I know he is.'

'I'm sure he is,' Gem echoed. But you couldn't say that and it didn't help, pure corny sentiment. Ray wiped his sweating palms on his pants and kept walking.

'That stuff,' he said. 'It's better if you don't ask.'

'Okay. Whatever you say.'

'I don't want to crack up,' Ray interrupted him. 'You've seen those guys. How it gets.'

'Yeah, no. Fuck that. That's no good for anybody. Look, how far do you think I can throw this stone? You reckon I could hit that tree?'

That night they ate from the hospitality of one of the locals, a thin minestrone with hardly anything floating in its flavoured water.

Gem told the black-clad woman, 'Just like my mamma makes.'

Ray said, 'I think we should go to Palermo and start again from there. Otherwise we'll be lost for ever.'

'Could be worse.'

'Or we don't go back at all, how about that?'

'Become deserters, you mean?'

'That's the way. Blend in. Disappear. Just watch it all happen.'

'Become Sicilians. This old girl's gotta have some daughters.'

The following day they were starting to get into the higher country. They passed between the flaking, bullet-pecked walls of a village and out into hills.

'They look sorta soft, don't they?' Ray liked Gem enough now to share thoughts like this with him, odd, vulnerable thoughts that took some understanding. 'The way they're crumpled up, I mean.'

'Yeah.'

Ray thought they looked like heaped cloths with long folds of shadow. 'You could make a cowboy picture here. They've even got those cactuses.'

'Prickly pears. And we got guns. Just need some Indians.'

'Indians all ran away, thank Christ.'

'Look up ahead. One of their trucks.'

'Indians didn't have no trucks.'

On the road about a hundred yards ahead of them was a burned-out truck, its green paint blistered by fire, its canvas gone but for charred shreds. As they approached it, Gem started to jog ahead to have a look. Always eager. Ray saw him jump up into the air and

219

apart in pieces. That was a strange thing for him to do. Ray felt a powerful hot wave overwhelm him. He saw one of Gem's lower legs, the boot and the shin, whirling towards him, right at his face.

23

Ray woke up and opened his eyes. The immense, painful light of the sky dropped onto him. His mouth was full. He wrenched himself over onto his stomach and coughed, hawking hard to dislodge a gritty paste at the back of his tongue. He stood up and started walking, falling forwards and catching himself with each stride. He walked past the small crater and the remains, the colours strong in the sunlight, and past the truck, its shreds of canvas flickering madly, rasping in the breeze. He walked straight into that area so that he too would jump and disappear. But he didn't. The world wouldn't take him. He had to carry on hobbling over its hard surface, over rocks and into the wind.

He walked for some time, well clear of the area. His feet kept hitting the ground and he didn't fall over. There were little itchy patches on his face and body. When he touched them, they were wet, loose or sticky. He walked over a hill and down to the right. The apparition of a large building. He walked towards it.

The building grew. It had three sides. No one stopped him as he approached. He went in through the door into a hallway as big as a museum. Overhead the ceiling swarmed with clouds and angels. In front of him, stone steps, round at the edges. They poured towards him.

He started walking up them. He wanted help, he supposed, but he didn't call out for it. The silence was nicer. It was nice to be inside where it was quiet.

Corridors and furniture, gold-framed paintings leaning forwards off the walls like they wanted to look at him or tell him something. There were rooms to the sides of the corridor, widely spaced. The third of them had an open door. It was a lady's bedroom. There was a dressing-table with a mirror and brushes and little bottles. Soft colours, patterns. So gentle and floral, he stepped inside. A bed. A chair, books. He reached out to touch a book and saw his fingers leave blood marks. He caught sight of his headless body in the dressing-table mirror. His uniform was stained. This made him want to cry.

The bed was extraordinary. An ornate silver frame had doves resting in curlicues of branches. The cover was of dark silver satin. He lifted it up, slippery between his fingers, and climbed in. The thick pillows slowly gave way under his head. He drew his knees up to his chest, pulled the cover over him and closed his eyes.

When he opened them again, a young woman was sitting on the end of the bed, staring at him.

He tried to speak but his voice cracked. He coughed and tried again. 'Don't make me go back. I'm not going back. Don't make me.'

24

'You are American,' she said.

Who are you? What is this place? Don't make me go back.'

The young woman was smiling. Her skin was pale yellow. Her eyes were dark and glittering. She was breathing intensely through her smile, through her teeth. He said again, 'Don't make me go back.'

'You are American soldier.'

'That's right.'

'You are young.'

Some kind of shock went through his body, tightening every muscle. His feet pushed down, his hands gripped the cover. When the spasm let go of him, he sank back down, soft and weak. 'Don't make me go back. I ain't going back.'

'There is a place,' she said. 'Do you speak French? French is better.'

'I don't speak no French. Are you French?'

'You put blood everywhere,' she said. 'The servant will want to know. But it is fine.' She stood up from the bed and went over to the dressing table.

'What?' His head, as he raised it from the pillow, felt heavy and unstable. She had a small pair of scissors in her hand. Its little silver beak was open.

'It is fine,' she said and dashed the scissors against

her arm. She looked, unsatisfied, at the result. She did it again. 'There,' she said. 'What an accident.' She did it one last time and swore, throwing the scissors onto the floor. She held out her left arm and Ray could see blood tapering down to the ends of her fingers, hanging in red droplets. 'See. Accident, look.' She shook drops of blood onto the dressing table then walked over to the bed and wiped her hand on the covers and the pillow.

'There is a place,' she said in a whisper, leaning over him. 'But you must make no sound. Why do you cry?'

'Don't,' he said, holding the covers up to his chin. 'Don't hurt yourself.'

25

The Americans arrived from Palermo in a jeep. A message from their superiors in Messina had alerted the British in Sant'Attilio that they were coming.

Samuels led in three men, Major Kelly, his subordinate and the local contact. Kelly removed his hat to wipe his forehead and revealed dark red hair, the colour, Will thought, of a red setter's. This made Will think of dogs and the black Lab, Teddy. How was he getting on back home? Major Kelly said, 'Good afternoon, gentlemen.' He wore round spectacles. His skin was pale and blotched by the heat. Despite his American baritone, Major Kelly was clearly an Irishman, his parents or grandparents had been immigrants. Another American pretending to be an American. As an Englishman, Will could see what he was underneath. The underling was of the neat and healthy American type, square-headed with fair eyebrows and blue eyes watching the major to anticipate his needs. The third man was the local, a heavy, middle-aged man with large hands, slow and economical in his movements.

'Shall we?' Will said and led on to the room where a table was prepared with glasses, paper, ashtrays, and where the local police chief sat waiting with Sergeant Whelan of the Metropolitan Police Force.

The Sicilian absorbed his surroundings, raising his eyebrows. He reached out and touched the painted walls and felt the doorknob.

'I won't keep you long,' said Major Kelly as he sat down. 'Gentlemen.' He nodded at the policemen. 'I'm sure we've all got plenty to do getting Sicily back on her feet. I'm here to introduce you to Mr Albanese who is returning to Sant'Attilio after a long time. His anti-Fascist stance meant he had to flee to the land of freedom some twenty years ago.'

'How do you do?' said Will.

Major Kelly glanced up, surprised at the interruption. 'Good, good. Get to know each other,' he said and went on, 'Mr Albanese has been of great aid to us, providing a good deal of useful information. He's well connected here, of course, his family and so forth, and despite his long absence will be able to help you in the business of defascistification.' Major Kelly whistled. 'That's a hell of a word. A man ought to be allowed a drink before he attempts it.'

'Quite,' Will said, thinking that of course Kelly, being an Irishman, would welcome that arrangement.

Albanese spoke suddenly. 'Hey. You got a cigarette?'

'Oh, surely.' Will patted his pockets. 'I've got some somewhere.'

'Here.' Samuels leaned across the table and offered his open packet, cigarettes steepled towards Albanese.

'Thanks.' The Sicilian then accepted a light offered by Kelly's subordinate. 'You Italian?' Albanese asked.

'Me?' Samuels pointed at himself. 'No. No, I'm from London.'

'You look like you could be Italian.'

'He's a Jew,' Will explained.

'Is that right?'

Samuels nodded.

'I knew Jews in New York. Smart guys. You got people there?'

'Some, I think. My mother's brother went there. We don't hear very much from them.'

'You should go over and find him. Family, you know. And maybe you'll like it.'

'Perhaps one day I will. The rest of them, who aren't in England, are in Poland. I'd like to go and find them too.'

'So,' Will interrupted, 'you live here? In Sant'Attilio?' But Albanese hadn't finished.

'It was a Jewish guy made this suit.'

Will smirked at that. 'It's a beautiful suit.'

'The best.'

'So you live here in Sant'Attilio?' Will repeated.

'That's right. My wife. My family.'

'So, you'll be on hand.' Albanese said nothing. 'You'll be nearby.'

Albanese exhaled smoke and shaped the tip of his cigarette against the glass of the ashtray.

'Whatever you need. A lot of these Fascists, they'll act like they've done nothing. And you won't know who they are, who's innocent, who's guilty. But I can help you. I can show you around, make friends for you, make you at home.'

'Allow me to introduce you . . .'

'I allow you. You're allowed.' Albanese interrupted and turned his smiling face around the company, looking for amusement at his joke.

'This is Sergeant Whelan. He's come from the

Metropolitan Police in London to help with the re-establishment of law and order here.'

'And this is Captain Michele Greco of the local police. Did you two ever meet?'

'No. I don't think we did.'

'No, we haven't met.' Greco wriggled upright in his seat. Albanese said something to him in Italian and the two men exchanged words too rapidly for Will to understand. The up and down melody of the language threw up quick crenellations of sound. Afterwards, Albanese said in English. 'We are going to work great together. Greco here understands me. He knows I am a man of respect.' Albanese translated that phrase into Italian and Greco, frowning, confirmed this with an inclination of his head.

'That sounds like what I wanted to hear,' announced Major Kelly. 'And with that, I shall return to Palermo. Gentlemen.'

Outside, Cirò detained the Americans with questions to which he already knew the answers, long enough for people to see them together. He wore his new hat. He shook their hands and gave them advice. He patted the younger one on the shoulder. On the other side of the road, three young boys sat with their arms folded.

While the jeep bounced away, Cirò beckoned the boys over. They sauntered across, loose and casual, not too interested, but Cirò could see the dissembled haste, the urgency: they were coming like cats at feeding time.

'Here, ever seen these?' Cirò pulled out of his pockets some American coins. 'They're from America, the US. You want them? You can have them. I've got plenty more.'

Cirò walked away, up to the square and past the church, past Tinu, and up the narrow street under lines of laundry hung in careful mirroring patterns – socks, underwear, vests, shirts, nightshirts, shirts again, vests, underwear and socks – to the house where he now lived.

He found Teresa and kissed her on the back of the neck. She sank heavily in his arms. 'You can't wear black for much longer. One more week. People will understand. It's different because I'm back.'

Teresa didn't say anything.

'You remember our wedding day?' he said.

'Yes. Of course.'

He looked over the top of her head, remembering.

'Where is the photograph? You still have it?'

'I have it. It's put away.'

'Well, get it out. We'll put it up. I'll get a new frame. You don't know what it means to me. You don't know how happy I am to be back even if we're only halfway there. Things are going to be like they were before.'

'You look young when you're happy,' Teresa said. 'You look like you used to.'

'I feel like I used to. Where's Mattia? I want to talk to him.'

'I don't know. In their room, maybe.'

Cirò climbed the narrow staircase and opened the door to the room with two mattresses on the floor and three half-naked children, forbidden to play outside so soon after the death of their father. They were fighting, tussling, a litter.

'Where's Mattia?'

The eldest, a boy of about nine, said, 'I don't know.'

'You do know.'

'I don't.'

'Where is he?' Cirò took one pace towards the boy.

'He went out.'

'So you do know. Go out and get him for me. Go on.'

The boy wriggled past him and pattered down the stairs on his bare feet.

Cirò looked at the two who were left. 'Who wants a coin?'

'Me!'

'Me!'

Cirò produced one from his pocket and flipped it spinning into the air. He left them fighting for it.

A youth in the doorway of the house. Sullen, waiting, one arm up on the door frame.

'Look at you,' Cirò said. 'You're strong. Look at those arms. Like Jack Dempsey. Shall I call you Jack?'

'Don't care.'

'What should I call you?'

'Don't call me anything. I don't care.'

'Really? What about Shit-the-bed? What about Little Dog? You don't care, you don't care. I'll call you what I want.'

'Doesn't matter to me. What do you want me for?'

Cirò walked over to the boy and took hold of his shoulder. He gripped until Mattia looked up. Mattia said, 'I know what you are.'

'You don't know anything, Jack. You're a kid. I'm

your mother's husband. That's who I am. I'm your father. I want to help you.'

Cirò let go and Mattia went and sat on the stool by the hearth.

'I'm sorry about what happened to your father.' Cirò received a flash of the boy's dark eyes, fierce through their pretty lashes. 'You know, even though he died in an accident, it's like really he died in the war. That's how you should think of it. He was killed by the bastard Fascists.'

'I know what killed him.'

'I know you do. He was a war hero. He died for Sicily. You should be very proud of him.'

Mattia sat hunched forwards, his hands under his thighs.

'To die for Sicily. Things will be better now. That's what we all want. My friends and me, we want better things for Sicily. You don't know this yet. We weren't allowed to be here for so long. It's a life, Mattia, a way to make a living. You could have it. Actually, you know what you could have?'

'What?'

'Something I got for you in Palermo.'

'For me?'

'Sure.'

Cirò left the room. He returned with an object on his upturned palm: an unopened bar of American chocolate. The brown paper and silver foil were pristine. 'Here.'

Mattia took it from him and looked down at it. 'The whole thing?'

'The whole thing. I can get plenty more.'

'When?'

'What do you mean, when? Whenever you want. If you want some, eat it.'

'Now?'

'Jesus, if you want it. What's the matter with you?'

Mattia carefully opened the paper envelope, breaking the contact of its adhesive without tearing, then tore the foil wrapping and snapped off three squares and put them in his mouth. Lushness of sweet flavour, a slow melting into a thick fudge that coated his teeth and tongue. His eyes closed and opened again. He chewed, folding the wrapper tightly shut, keeping it all as neat as a pressed shirt.

'Why don't you give that to your mother? She can hide it from the little rats. Then come with me. There's something you should see.'

Mattia nodded, swallowing like a bird, ducking his head and rising.

They stepped outside into early dusk, the walls of the buildings glowing, a drift of pink in the sky and swifts screaming in rapid circles over the church. Cirò led the boy down to the left, out of Sant'Attilio, past the others on the street. Albanese greeted an old uncle of the Battista family. The old man looked at him wonderingly, hopefully. Cirò passed on. The Battistas had been friends of the Albaneses. He must have been wondering if what he'd heard was right, that it was all coming back.

Mattia felt very awake after the chocolate. The evening breeze vibrated over his skin. He wanted to run but instead walked beside this inescapable man.

They walked in the direction of the Prince's house. When they got to Angilù Cassini's house, Cirò said, 'Wait.'

'Yes?'

'Sshh. You see this house?'

'Yes.'

'You know who lives here?'

'Angilù Cassini.'

'Angilù Cassini? Angilù? He was just a little shepherd when I left, out fucking his goats in the mountains. Angilù Cassini?'

'Yes. He works for the Prince, on the estate. He does everything.'

'Does he? You're a good boy. You should work for me, you know. Work together. Two leaves of the artichoke. You want that?'

They were both quiet. Cirò looked up the avenue of olive trees to the front door. It was a strange feeling for Mattia, spying like this. It felt like something was going to happen. The quieter they got, the more it felt like that. Eventually, Albanese said, 'He has children?'

'Three daughters.'

'No sons? Doesn't surprise me. Probably none of them are his. You know the girls?'

'Sure.'

'Hey, you haven't? Jack, don't tell me you have . . . already? Those innocent girls.' Cirò laughed, looking at Mattia's pained frown. 'I'm only kidding. You know who used to live here?'

'Who?'

'Me. Me and your mother. This is where we lived

when we got married. I was the landlord of the estate. You didn't know that? Big, isn't it?'

'It's big.'

'These trees. I used to make the oil from these olives. My house. My house until the Fascists. Our house. You want to live here? A room to yourself?'

'It's big.'

'And when I'm gone meeting Jesus somewhere, it would be your house. You're the oldest. You and your wife.'

26

Something outside made the dog bark. Cesare always barked in threes with short, absolute silences between. Cesare set off Sal's dog two hundred yards away. It answered with its hoarse single responses, like fright-ened coughs. Together they roused several other dogs at different distances, a cacophony of paranoia and display that went on until they tired and relaxed slowly back into silence. Angilù didn't like to hear it. It brought the night to bear, made him feel the space outside, when he just wanted to sit with his family and eat his soup, all of them in the single circle of lamplight. Angilù had too much to think about.

The end of the war was worse than the fighting had been. You could hide from that and you knew it would end. Now, Cirò Albanese was back. This was definite. Everybody knew. And if Albanese was back, Angilù could lose everything. Life on the estate was threatened. Angilù and the Prince had right on their side, they had goodness, good sense at least, but what was that against Albanese and his friends and the old, broken law? What he should do was to speak to the English as soon as possible and explain that he'd been living there for twenty years, that the Prince owned the property and he wanted Angilù there. It had taken Angilù some time to feel that he belonged there. At first the house was too big for him and his wife. They lodged in its corners. They huddled together. It was only when they had children, after long years of thinking they never would, that they began to inhabit the place. Anna was born and her yells filled the whole house and she survived and the place was theirs. It always had been theirs of course. The Prince had given it to them.

The English needed to understand how the whole system worked. He had to get to the Allies before the peasants also. No doubt some imaginative land claims would be made. The Santangelis were terrible for that.

In the morning, Angilù rode on a horse into Sant'Attilio, arriving at that prestigious height and dignity. When he was a boy, the only horses he saw were ridden by the Prince and his field guards. Those looming men in their liveries were the tallest beings in the world. Everyone else rode by on mules or jogged uncomfortably on donkeys, tensing their legs to keep their feet from touching the ground.

In Sant'Attilio, Angilù was recognised. Lifting his hat, looking down at people, he thought he saw a look in their eyes. Something they wanted to say but couldn't, some knowledge molesting them. That's what he thought he saw, but he was very agitated, jerking around in his saddle to look at everybody. He caught sight of Luca Battista and asked him where the Allies were. Luca told him they were in the town hall, of course.

At the town hall, Angilù dismounted, shooting down onto both feet. That hurt a little. He was getting older. Also, in his hurry, he hadn't placed his feet quite right and stumbled a couple of paces forward. He tied his horse to a railing and walked in.

A man in uniform seated at a desk looked up. Angilù took in his shiny, combed hair and, disconnected beneath the desk as though belonging to someone else, his bare pink knees. Like a child, the Englishman was wearing short trousers.

'Good morning, can I help you at all? If it's the medical officers you're after I'm afraid they won't be here for a day or two.'

Angilù answered in Italian. 'Do you not speak Italian? I don't speak English and I'm not going to be able to make you understand anything if you can't speak Italian.'

'I'm afraid you'll have to speak a good deal slower than that if I'm going to understand you.'

'I said, do you speak Italian? I need to talk about my house and the old landlord. I should have got the Prince to come with me.'

'Did you say "Prince"? There is a local prince, isn't there? Look, stay here, and I'll get someone who can help. I can read a newspaper perfectly well but you don't sound like what I'm reading. Stay here.'

Angilù watched the man get up and walk out on legs as red and bare as a hen's. When he came back, there was another man with him. When Angilù had repeated what he had to say, they led him into a room with a table. Their names were Treviss and Worka. Slowly, Angilù explained to them his situation. Each time they definitely understood, he said 'yes' and stamped the side of his fist on the table.

They asked him questions about Prince Adriano

and wrote down some of the things they said, pens circling on paper, small whirlpools of Angilù's thoughts now lost to him. He could understand numbers and recognised the shapes of some names but he couldn't read. When they were finished, they stood up and shook Angilù's hand and showed him to the door. They were interested in his horse and came out and patted its neck while he mounted. They waved at him as he rode away.

Will said to Travis, 'That was a little distasteful, didn't you think?'

'I'm not sure I trust anyone round here.'

'I mean, if he got his house when the former occupant was driven away by the Fascists, then isn't he the expropriator trying to hang onto his property? I mean, in a sense, he's just come in here and declared himself a Fascist.'

'Maybe. Though that's going a bit far.'

'Could be Albanese, of course. The person who was driven away.'

'Nice horse, though. Handsome animal.'

'Has this Cassini been mentioned in any of the denunciations? I'll ask Albanese and talk to the police. And I suppose I should go and visit this prince.'

27

Ray checked every inch of the attic on his hands and knees, peering down into the cracks between floorboards for any signs of wires or devices. The place was huge, the size of the whole floor of an apartment building, only with no interrupting walls. It was an enormous container of empty space. He felt the terror of that space around him. Always some part of it was so far away he wouldn't know. The search took him hours. Against one wall were a few boxes, some old paintings, a table and a rocking horse. He checked these first of all. They were the most frightening. Mouth hanging open as he crawled around them, sweat stinging his eyes. He reached his trembling hands inside the boxes and found only fabrics. The paintings were of old saints and landscapes. At one moment, he moaned, thinking it was all about to end but he realised that the wires in his hand were to hang the picture from.

Walls next. Shuffling around on his knees, he felt the plaster with his fingertips. There were cracks here and there. They didn't look deliberate. Along one side, Ray could feel the sun's warmth coming through, a slow pulse of heat transmitted through masonry and wood. At one spot along that side, something was happening. He heard scratching and leaned close. Silence. Then a snapping sound and a dry screaming started up. It was a bird's nest. He remembered that sound from home. Sometimes walking under a subway bridge, up in the grimy iron darkness, you heard the baby pigeons screaming for food. The adult bird flew away again and the screaming stopped.

There were two small windows. He was lying down, looking out of one at a geometric garden with spooky white statues standing in their postures, pointing upwards or lazily leaning, when he heard someone coming up the steps to the little door. He got up and ran to stand beside it. As the door opened, he reached through and caught hold of the person and threw them down. He got his forearm over their throat and shouted, 'Who the fuck are you? Who the fuck are you?' He saw beneath him a terrified woman, the same woman who'd cut herself in front of him and taken him to this place. She was twisting and jerking, trying to lift her head. When he let her go, she scooted backwards away from him on her heels and her hands.

'You are mad,' she said. 'Be quiet.' She laughed and winced and touched her mouth to see if it was bleeding. Her head was ringing. So shocking, the attack and contact of his body, the force of it. What it told her: he wanted to live.

Ray cursed like his father, calling on the saints to help him. Her eyes widened.

'You speak Italian. Are you American or Italian? If you are a hiding Fascist there will be a problem.'

'I'm not a Fascist. Jesus fucking Christ. That's the last thing I am. I'm an American.'

'You have to be quiet. It's a big house. But you have to stay here so no one hears you. You cannot go near the windows.'

'I have to check if it's safe.'

'Of course it's safe.'

'And don't come in without warning me.'

'How can I warn you? And why do you speak Italian?'

'I am Italian. I mean, my parents are Italian, from the south. I'm from Little Italy not big Italy.'

'I see.'

'Raimundo Marfione. But I'm Ray. Everybody calls me Ray.'

'Okay, Ray. Is it all right if I speak English and Italian also when I can't remember words?'

'Sure.'

'Good. Please will you stay on that side, where those boxes are? I'm going to go out for a while.'

She got up and smoothed her hair with trembling hands. She brushed the back of her dress. 'You've got me all dusty. If my father had seen you touch me like that, he'd have had you whipped.'

'What's that?'

She said in English, 'You know, hit. Like for a horse.'

'Oh, whipped. I'm sorry.'

'Just be quiet.'

She went out through the little wooden door and Ray fell back down where he sat. He could still feel her there, how she'd stirred the air around.

He looked up and saw timber rafters. How had he not thought of those? He needed to check all of them.

28

Descending back into the house, wondering about the secret violence and desperation she now had stored in the attic, Luisa turned into the corridor and saw Graziana. The old woman looked down.

'What do you know?' Luisa asked her.

'Beg pardon, miss?'

'What do you know?'

'I don't know what you mean.'

'I think you do.'

'I'm sorry, miss, I don't. There's lots I don't know, God help me.'

'That's good.'

'And I don't want to know it, either.'

'Even better.'

Luisa walked on past her. As a child, Luisa had thought of the large atrium with the marble staircase as a kind of huge mouth, like the jaws of a lion. When she went out, it spat her out. When she came in, it swallowed her. The lion was sneaky: it would pretend it wasn't there, that everything was normal, just a room and some stairs and a high, painted ceiling, but she knew it was there. She could feel it forming in the air around her.

She hadn't thought of the lion for a long time or perhaps unconsciously she always did and it was something she took for granted in the nature of the house. Today as she hurried out she noticed and remembered. Across the courtyard, her father leaned on his stick. He was smoking his pipe, his preferred form of outdoor smoking, and was deep in conversation with Angilù. She waved at them and whispered to herself, 'Just stay over there, don't ask me anything.' Her father raised his hand in lofty salute and rose to his full height as he saw her hurrying away.

In the stables, Luisa approached Ezio, soothing him with the palm of her hand and murmuring to him, carefully informing him of her presence. Ezio shifted sideways over his urinous straw. She fitted the saddle. From the bridle, Ezio reared and snickered, again and again. His neck was one long surge of muscle. He held his head high and disdainful. Minutes passed with Luisa attempting to ensnare him, her arms aching from being held up, her fingers losing their dexterity. But she would not give up and on one pass she caught the stupid horse and he knew he was beaten. Ezio allowed the bit between his long yellow teeth and jumping dark lips.

She led him out without a guard, without telling anyone. Unused to getting into the saddle without a guard's hands to step on, Luisa struggled for a while, cursing and flinging herself upward, pulling Ezio's head uncomfortably down to the side. Once she was up and had found both stirrups, she rode quickly away from this undignified tussle.

Her father met her at the door of the house.

'I know, I know,' she said pre-emptively. 'I was in a hurry. I needed to get out.'

'If you know then it won't happen again. Who knows who or what's out there at the moment. Do you understand? Luisa, I'm not often strict with you.'

Luisa pouted, looking at the ground.

'There's something else I wanted to ask. Do you know anything about an American soldier coming here? The gardener said he thought he'd seen one come to the house the other day.'

'No. I haven't seen anyone. Maybe he was lost. He must have wandered off again.'

Despite the convulsions of her heart, Luisa was pleased her father had asked this question. Now he had an answer and once people had a story they believed, they stopped looking for alternatives. The incredible reality was now the last thing her father would suspect. Just as he'd believed her about the accident with her scissors. She looked down at her hand and flexed her fingers. The bandaged wound was mute.

29

He slept in snatches, trying not to. The trench of Germans filled with blood. The blood overbrimmed and rolled along the ground towards him. If it touched him, he would die too. There were sudden explosions that blew him awake, threw him out of death there onto the floorboards checking around to see if he really was alive, if his body was still whole.

The dark was almost total. The two small windows could just about be discerned from their surroundings, a smoother, more liquid black. If he crawled to one of them maybe he would see stars or lights.

He didn't move. He lay there thinking about his mother and father, his brother and sister in the little apartment, not knowing about him. So far away. Like they were all in a tiny dark box in vast space. And there was George out there still. His brain went blank and switched on again. He listened for sounds of possible war.

Eventually, the dawn light hung blue in the big emptiness of the attic. Ray found himself staring at the rocking horse. It was made of carved wood. Its four carved hooves stood on two curved runners so that it rocked, so that a child could play on it. It was made to look like a real horse. Nostrils had been carved, and goofy teeth, and eyes and the shapes of some of the horse's muscles. The legs were realistic, particularly at the back: that big rounded section like a chicken's thigh. There was a saddle on it. Hours of work had gone into it. He could see that. Hands had worked for hours on that shape, scraping away with chisels and whatever they used to get that shape out of raw wood, a clear horse shape that stood in just the right place on its little runners so that it would rock back and forth and not tip over. Amazing effort had gone into it. A pattern of fur or hair or whatever the fuck you called it on a horse had been painted. The teeth were painted a different colour. So were the insides of the nostrils. All this effort to make this one pretend horse for a child to sit on and swoosh back and forth. A rocking horse. The name told you what it was. Nobody really needed it, but there it was for a child to pretend to be on a horse. Because horses were things children should know about. Children had to know about lots of things. They didn't know anything. They had to learn them one by one, one after the other, and horses were one of those things. Also, it was nice to rock back and forth, that movement was nice. It was a ride, a game. It felt good for the child to rock back and forth and so all those hours of carving and painting to make a little horse to ride. Ray felt himself on the horse as a child, tilting forward and back, falling forwards, sliding back, the weight of his dangling feet in laced shoes swinging his legs. It was wonderful. The rocking horse was made for this.

Ray closed his eyes, thinking about it, and lay back down. And the floorboards under his head were wood that had been cut. And the ceiling and the door. The whole world was made. People made it.

30

Two men had been killed in the square of Portella Corvi. They had died of shotgun wounds which were large and ragged. Shot, then, at close range. The presumption would be that they were ex-Fascists shot in reprisal. Nevertheless, this was very much the kind of chaos that could not be allowed to take hold. The local police were investigating under the newly arrived supervision of officers from the London Metropolitan Police, but, as a Civil Affairs Officer, Will took it upon himself to visit and ask a few questions.

An exhilarating, swooping motorcycle ride through the mountains left Will's body vibrating as he stood over the blood-stained paving stones and asked Sergeant Whelan what they'd found out. Apparently this was nothing. There were no witnesses.

'Isn't that a bit, you know, implausible, given that we're in the town square?'

'That had crossed my mind. I don't believe a word of it. Blank face after blank wop face. Their mother was taken ill. They were in church. They heard a noise but when they looked the assailants had scarpered.'

'The murderers.'

'The murderers.'

'Maybe it's true. How many people are there in this town? Not everywhere will be seen by someone at all times.'

'Maybe so but you get an instinct. They don't want to talk. Have you not noticed that generally? These people aren't at all how I'd imagined Italians, all mamma mia mamma mia and waving their arms about. They're surly bastards round here.'

'They are.' Will sighed through his nose, looking down at the blood dried in the sun. 'Will I get a report on this?'

'I think so. I can get it to you, if you like, try and expedite it to you.'

'Do. And the two men, Fascists?'

'No clear indication of that. I've sent a request to ask some of the prisoners about them. People I've spoken to here, some said yes, others devoutly of the other opinion.'

'I see. Well, I want someone banged up for this. We can't have this sort of thing going on under our noses. We're the authority here. The war is over.'

'I agree with all of that,' Whelan said. 'Can't have vendettas breaking out all over. In the end it's not England, though, and you have to take that into account.'

'We rule over a vast empire, sergeant. I think it's realistic for us to do so here as well.'

'Very good. Well, I'll keep you informed.'

Wheeling his motorcycle out of the square, Will saw a familiar face in the shadow of an awning. Albanese was sitting at a café table with an old, beaky-faced man, another man and a youth. They had in front of them the tiny cups from which they drank their fierce little coffees. Each was smoking a cigarette.

'Oh, hello,' Will said.

'Good afternoon, officer,' Albanese replied in his New York accent, sounding exactly like a gangster in an American film. 'You here because of what happened to those two men? It's terrible. I don't like to see it. The war is finished. I want justice not dirty business.'

'Couldn't agree more.'

'You know who this is, officer?' Cirò jerked a thumb at the old man. 'This is the new mayor of Montebianco. You get the message from Palermo yet?'

'No.' Will blinked. 'No. But it's probably waiting for me when I get back. So no doubt we will be meeting very soon.'

The old man didn't appear to understand. He leaned to Albanese who whispered in his ear. Then the old man raised a hand in greeting. He wore a quite enviably beautiful suit of brown pinstriped cloth and sharply sculpted shoes with a swirl and gleam in the leather that made them resemble polished wood. Glancing down at them, Will saw also his thin, knobby ankles filmed by fine yellow silk socks.

'And this is my son, Mattia.'

'Your son? From America?' Will didn't know that Albanese had brought a son with him.

Albanese smiled, saying nothing. He stayed that way long enough for it to be incumbent upon Will to speak again. Albanese did not introduce the third man and he did not look up. He kept his chin tucked down into his neck, a hand raised with his cigarette in front of his face, his fingertips resting on his temple. Will was left to guess who he was.

Finally, Will said, 'So, I'll see you back in Sant'Attilio.' He climbed, self-consciously, onto his motorcycle and kicked it awake. The engine hacked and rattled, blue smoke stuttered behind, and Will pushed himself away, lifting his feet.

Mattia envied the machine. When he was older he would have one of his own. He liked particularly the shape of the fuel tank at the front, a glinting teardrop or the thorax of a wasp. The machine had a look of agile power. He pictured himself with one that was black and highly polished. He would ride it wearing sunglasses and a wristwatch. People would hear him coming.

Alvaro Zuffo was telling them about seeing his witch for the first time in years. She had shown no surprise when he walked through the door. She said, 'I knew it would be today. You've been buried at the bottom of the sea all this time. Now you will breathe air again.'

'Mattia.'

'What?'

'Listen to what Mr Zuffo is saying. You know who this man is?'

'Cirò, it's okay.'

'He has to know. Mattia, you understand? You pay him respect.'

'I will. I do. I'm listening.'

'The boy understands, Cirò. He's learning. He's learned from the events here this morning, haven't you, boy? You understand.'

'Yes I do. I do. I understand.'

31

Ray awoke from a deep, black sleep that had been devoid of dreams. Every muscle in his body was completely relaxed. He was a dead weight pressing onto the floor, heavy as a rock. For this moment, Ray was free, completely hidden. A moment later, when he noticed this unusual state, he uncovered himself. He remembered all that he had forgotten. His thoughts began their marauding. His heart started up.

His body was too tired to jerk upright so he rolled onto his side to look around. Nothing had changed so he was probably still safe. From one of the windows, burning towards him across the floorboards, was the light of the sun. He looked into it, blinding himself, and crushed his eyes shut, a shape of hot molten metal floating inside.

Ray sat up, blinking. Still in this place. It was so large and a whole night had passed. Anything could have happened. He pulled off the blanket and got on all fours, crawling one way to check for signs. There was something in here, he remembered. Where was it? Oh, that. The rocking horse, poised, perfectly still on its painted hooves. He started towards it because he wanted to touch the choppy carving of its mane and the smooth swell of its flank. His long shadow stretched towards it. Every time he lifted his hand, the shadow fled up the wall. Every time he set it down, his hand and its shadow connected. But what was he thinking? He hadn't checked the place yet. He looked along the crack between the floorboards in front of him for any triggering devices.

There was a noise at the door. He kept his eyes shut and waited. Three. Two. One. Nothing. Three. Two.

'Good morning.' A woman's voice. 'What are you doing?'

It was the woman, the same one. Of course it was.

'Nothing. Nothing. I'm okay. No one's been up here, right?'

'No one's been up here. If someone came up here, you would know. There would be a big problem.'

Ray, still on all fours, hanging his head, looked at the woman through the gap of his armpit. Her feet were in the shooting sunlight: small shoes with shiny buckles.

'Okay,' he said. 'Okay.'

'Did you sleep well?' Luisa shook her head after that question, at the absurdity of inquiring after this man like a guest at a house party.

'I slept okay. I woke up.'

'Why don't you sit down?'

'Okay. Okay, I will.' Ray instructed his muscles to move, to let go. They wouldn't until suddenly, like an avalanche, they did. He arranged himself against the wall by the spot with the bird's nest, his knees drawn up. He rubbed his face with his hands, groaned, opened his eyes wide. 'So who are you?'

'Who am I? My name is Luisa.'

'Luisa. Luisa.' Ray mused on this for a moment. 'Okay, but that's just a name. I mean, who are you? I mean, where am I?'

'You're in my house, in my father's house, Prince Adriano.'

'Prince Adriano?'

'Yes.'

'Like, he's a prince?'

'Yes.'

'And what are you?'

'I'm a princess.'

'You're fucking with me. You're not serious.'

'No. I am serious. There are plenty of us in Sicily. Don't be too impressed.'

'It is a big house.'

'Yes, it is.'

'And only you two?'

'And servants and sometimes people who work on the land. It's a sad story. The house is very big. We get lonely. But my father prefers it to the city.'

'Cities aren't always nice.'

'You are from a city?'

'From New York.'

'The big city.'

'Yep, it's big.'

'My father will go out later. I can bring you down into the house and give you more food.'

'Okay. That would be good.'

'Did you use the pot?'

'What? Oh sure. Over there.'

'Okay, I will take it.' Luisa walked over and picked

up the chamber pot that Ray had covered with the napkin she had provided. Its weight slewed from side to side as she walked. 'I go now,' she said. As she descended the stairs, she caught the strong animal aroma of Ray's urine. Luisa never carried her own chamber pot. The sensation of holding a strange man's was extraordinary. She felt a calming abasement in her soul. She was a servant. She was performing one of the acts of the saints.

32

Mattia ran back with the news: the Prince's car had just pulled up at the town hall. Cirò left the house on the hunt for Angilù. Today the new currency was going to be distributed and Angilù would surely be coming on the Prince's behalf. The car was there but Angilù wasn't; he must have gone inside. Cirò couldn't see him in the small crowd. The place was busy. Stupidly, some of the people had brought things they hoped to sell in exchange for more currency. A man was being told at the door that his two chairs weren't wanted. A woman stood with a hen under her arm, its long red legs reaching out to steady itself on something, its talons closing around air. There were guards standing by the car, two of them, looking around with more of a display of vigilance than the action itself. A pair of pea-brained peacocks, twitching their heads from side to side. In America, those two would not have had those jobs. So stupid they were. It wouldn't take long to get them on side.

Cirò threw down his cigarette butt and walked over. He thought he'd play with the guards while he waited, ostentatiously admiring the car, tracing the swells of its bodywork with his fingertips, persisting until one of them complained.

'Oh, I'm sorry,' Cirò said. 'You're the chauffeur, yes? You're the chauffeur for a shepherd?'

When Angilù emerged and saw Cirò, the expression fell from his face. He had a child with him, one of his daughters. Cirò saw his hand tightening around hers. Angilù's other hand travelled to his breast pocket.

'Your wallet?' Cirò asked. 'You're worried about thieves? About people taking things that don't belong to you?'

Angilù said nothing for a moment. He dropped his hand and pointed to the car. 'I'm well protected.'

Cirò smiled. 'Is that your daughter? I hear you have three daughters, is that right?' He stepped forwards until he was close enough to drop his hand onto the hot, silky hair of the little girl. He felt her hair and skin shift as her skull tilted back and she looked up at her father. Her face full in the light, she narrowed her eyes. Long trembling lashes and glittering brown eyes with drops of sunlight in them.

'She's so beautiful,' Cirò said. 'She looks almost alive.'

33

The arrival of the new currency made this a good time to start visiting people. Fresh water and the bird will dip its beak. Neat and quick. He took Mattia with him, part of his education. Let him see what respect meant and how life could be for him.

Cirò started with Jaconi, poor Jaconi, arriving in the man's shop and waiting for the other customers to leave.

All Cirò had to do was glare at the little steel box he kept the money in and Jaconi understood.

Mattia was watching this silent exchange, not really understanding. Things were no clearer when Jaconi said, 'Oh no, I don't owe you anything. Not after what I did.'

Cirò said, 'I don't know what you're talking about.'

Jaconi was wiping his hands with a cloth. He looked at Mattia, hesitating.

Cirò shifted on his feet. Mattia watched him. He breathed in, widening his shoulders a little, and he lifted his chin. A mute display. Albanese just sent out the force of himself, his presence. He made visible his will and whatever decision the old shopkeeper was about to make, he changed. Jaconi's unformed words were reversed back down his throat. His shoulders drooped. His thick hands, trembling slightly, opened the cash box and pulled out one of the clean new notes. He held it out to Albanese who took it and put it in his pocket. Jaconi said, 'Here, Cirò. I'd like you to look out for my business, to make sure everything's okay.'

Albanese said, 'Whatever I can do.'

Turning his back to Jaconi, Albanese winked at Mattia. This sudden secret liveliness in the slow-moving Albanese made Mattia feel strange. The whole thing had been strange.

As they left, Jaconi called out after the boy, 'I'm sorry. I'm sorry for what happened to your father.'

Mattia didn't know what to say. He looked up at Albanese for guidance but the man's face was set. Mattia waved at Jaconi in helpless acknowledgement.

Outside, in the vertical heat of the sunshine, Albanese said to Mattia, 'You're learning. Soon you'll know so much it'll be too late. Don't worry. It's good. Everything will be good.'

34

Ray refused to leave the attic. He didn't think it was safe. Luisa sat on the floor, cross-legged, her hands fidgeting in the sling her skirt made between her thighs.

'What is New York like?'

'Busy. Dirty. Lots of people.' Ray pulled thoughtfully on one of the cigarettes she'd brought him. 'Here, apart from the war, everything's Italian, right?'

'Sicilian.'

'Sure, Sicilian. In New York, Italian is like a few streets. Sicilian is one street. And then it's something else. Jews over here. Chinese over there.'

'It sounds very interesting.'

'Sure it is. It's . . . everybody's there. It's crowded, crazy. I don't go too far, to be honest. You don't know what trouble you could get in. I mean my life is the Italian streets but I can see the other things. I go to the movies. I like the movies.'

'Oh, yes? I do not get to see them. In Palermo, the cinema is not a place a princess could go. Maybe in Palermo now it's different.'

Ray wasn't really listening. He asked, 'Is that rocking horse yours?'

'That what?'

'The horse. The wooden horse.'

'Oh, yes. From when I was a child, yes.'

'I thought so.'

'Now, I ride real horses.'

'You do? Like a cowboy.'

Luisa laughed. 'I don't think so. I like to ride, I like to be outside in the sun, and riding, moving.'

'But you can't do that now, right?'

'What?'

'It's dangerous out there, very dangerous. Lots of bombs. Don't go riding about on a big dumb horse for chrissake.'

'I am careful.'

'You have to be. It's very dangerous.'

Luisa paused. 'You didn't tell me, you didn't tell me what happened to you.'

Luisa's father caught her leaving this time so she was forced to take a guard with her. They rode out in the direction that Ray must have come from if he'd seen the house on his right as he approached. Wind. A hawk swinging overhead. Away to the left, a half-dozen goats on their hind legs stripped growth from a shrub with tough tearing sounds, their necks upstretched into the branches as though they were suckling.

When they met the road, they headed west and found the burned-out truck. Luisa rode up close and looked at the bubbled paint and exploded tyres. It was such a quiet thing it made a silence inside the noise of the wind. It was like something at the bottom of the sea. The crisis of gusting flames and fleeing men, the truck blown up and over, might have happened centuries ago when the Romans were fighting here or the Arabs or the Phoenicians. Ezio jerked his head away from the smell of the metal.

She struck him with her heels and he stepped forwards. A small crater twenty yards away. There were scattered things that she slowly understood, parts of a man spread out. A body full of incomprehensible space. There were long flutes of exposed bone and a torso with a small, burned, peevish head. Its eyes were empty. The noise of flies was the noise of the chaos in her head. Luisa's lungs couldn't take in air. She yanked the reins over and Ezio plunged around. She kicked and kicked.

Back home, she ran up to her room and emptied the pitcher of water on her washstand over her head, a crash of coldness on her crown that fell down her neck and around her forehead. She stared into the ewer and breathed. She caught sight of her own mouth wide open in the mirror. Her skin was tight and yellow. Her eyes were flat. She wouldn't meet them, wouldn't look into them. She smoothed her hair to her head and went up to the attic, checking for sounds of anyone else. She opened the door and found the American again on his hands and knees.

35

'God help us. It's like a wet weekend in Margate.'

Swatting his book against his thigh, Will stepped outside to where Samuels and Travis were playing cards at a rusty table. In the twilight, the little scratchy garden was violet and lemon-grey but it wouldn't be for long. The colours were changing, flaring and sinking.

'We can deal you in, if you like.'

'No, thank you.'

Will sat on a small stone bench by the wall. Behind him, the bricks released the stored heat of the day, a very comfortable fading of the sun into his neck and shoulders. He closed his eyes and relaxed.

The *thrip* of playing cards. Travis's voice. 'Ha-ha! Come to mother, little coins.'

The breeze was the perfect temperature and speed over Will's skin. He opened his eyes to see the glowing garden, a white butterfly tumbling around some purple flowers. A wonderful ease filled him. Something was happening, the heat, the light, the sound of voices. Everything was exquisite. Everything blended. And from this harmony something else seemed to emerge, to arrive. There was a completeness to the moment that felt like a presence. It was . . . what was it? It was kind, reassuring. It felt enduring. It felt like a refutation of Lucretius and his granulated universe crashing against itself. Will couldn't explain it. He was for that moment at ease and perfectly happy. He was cared for.

Too strange, though. He didn't have time for it. Will took out and lit a cigarette. 'It's nice out here,' he said.

'Then leave it out.'

'Very droll. We haven't met this prince yet, have we?'

'The big landowner.'

'No. His chap changed a lot of money, though. Same chap who came in ranting about his house.'

'Did you ask Albanese about that?'

'Not yet. Another denunciation of him came in today. Anonymous. He's a thief apparently.'

'But he's not a Fascist.'

'Fascists wouldn't have him.'

'Oh, that's useful.'

'What is?'

'The eight of clubs Travis just threw out.'

'I think I should go and talk to this prince.'

'Probably you should.'

Will blew smoke upwards into the sky. It was starting to darken. Travis said, 'What time is it?'

Samuels said to Will, 'He's got a woman in town, you know. They meet at night. I believe they discuss the progress of the war and read their favourite passages from the Bible to each other.'

'Have you been following us?'

'Just another poor girl who likes a soldier.'

'Excuse me, an intelligence officer,' Travis objected.

'My pass is access all areas. *All* areas.'

Will flicked away his cigarette end, a zooming light into the grey of the garden. 'Edifying as this is, I think I'm going to go and read.'

36

The attic was a tent of shadows suspended from the light of a single candle. When a draught pulled at the flame, all the shadows swayed. Outside was nothing, was night-time. Inside, their voices were small and secret and careful, crossing the air between them. Their faces were a golden blur.

'It shouldn't have still been there,' Luisa said. 'People here . . . someone must have seen it and yet no one did anything, no one ever does anything.'

'Him.'

'What?'

'Not "it". Him.'

Luisa clapped her hand to her mouth. 'Him. I'm sorry.'

'Or "it",' Ray said. 'It's an it now.'

Luisa didn't know what to say. She looked down at her fingers tangling together. A question occurred to her. 'Did you see . . .' but she stopped herself. There was something wrong in wanting to know, something greedy and obscene. But she did want to know, she wanted to touch the life that he had lived. 'Did you see many people killed?'

A breeze caught the candle flame. Ray stared as it streamed sideways with a bubbling sound then fluttered upright again.

'There is nothing after that I can see. I never saw any sign of it, no reason to believe it. It all stops. Just stops.'

Luisa nodded, waiting. Into the silence she said, 'People here are always killed but I never see it. Once when I was very small one of the peasants died outside in the courtyard. I have a memory, I don't know if I saw it or imagined it, this old man lying down like he's asleep. That's all.'

'It's not like sleep.'

'No.'

Luisa looked at the young American, at his soft inward eyes. His neck was so tense that his head trembled sometimes. Luisa could see the arcs of sinew inside rising out of his shoulders.

'You've seen some terrible things.'

Ray was tracing a pattern on the floor with his fingertip. His face opened in a laugh but he didn't look up. 'I've seen some terrible things. Yes, I have.' The smile went from his face again. He frowned down at his moving hand. 'Not a lot I can do about it. And you have too, now.' He looked up at her, his mouth hanging open in sorrow.

Luisa smiled at him, a new thought amusing her. 'I like you so much,' she said. 'I don't know why. I don't know you really. People I know very well I don't like the way I like you.'

It was the darkness that made these words possible, the night and their clandestine solitude. There was nothing familiar or ordinary there. They were alone. Luisa could have such thoughts and there was nothing to prevent her from saying them out loud. She was free.

'That's nice,' Ray said. 'You're very kind to me.'

'It's because I like you,' Luisa insisted. Mauro Vecchio, with all his power and position, saluted by people as he passed, didn't have what this American boy had. It was suffering, the authority of pain. His pain was the dark beautiful flower of the deepest experience.

'I like you so much,' Luisa went on, 'that if you wanted to I would let you kiss me.'

Ray looked up. 'You what?'

'I'd let you kiss me.'

Ray felt his heart sink down inside his chest. He looked at the Princess. She was smiling at him. She was glittering and fragile as new ice. The flaw was in her eyes, their gaze slightly fractured with fear. The moment was breakable. It was his responsibility to handle it with care. Ray said, 'I can't stay here for ever.'

The Princess was sitting very straight. Evidently she was waiting.

'Now?' he asked.

'Yes.'

Why not? Why shouldn't he? Only for some reason he hesitated. It was too much. But she was waiting. Ray moved onto his hands and knees and started crawling towards her.

Luisa watched him coming, prowling closer. His mouth was open. His eyebrows were knitted together in concentration. He looked passionate.

Ray reached her. Her face, gold-coloured in the candlelight, was in front of his, separating into its details: the light swimming in her eyes, her starry eyelashes, her lips and teeth and nostrils. She closed her eyes, composed herself for the event. Ray leaned forwards and pressed his mouth against hers. He felt the warm blasting exhalation from her nose against his cheek. He felt her teeth beyond the soft barrier of her lips. He felt nothing, emptiness, the collision of two bodies. He felt very alone.

37

Mattia didn't wake his little brothers. Two of them lay side by side, one with his arm around the other's shoulder like old men consoling each other.

Downstairs, Mattia found Albanese filling a bag in the darkness. He looked up sharply and the glimpse Mattia had of a man alone, absorbed in a task, vanished. Albanese had looked very different in that instant. He had looked relaxed and it made Mattia realise how vigilant the man was the rest of the time.

'What do you want?' Albanese asked.

'I heard a noise.'

'Huh.'

To Albanese, the boy looked soft and childish in his fatigue, his long feet inturned.

'Do you want something?'

'I just heard a noise.'

'Do you want to do something?'

'Sure.'

'Good. There's some coffee there. Drink it then put on some clothes. We're going out.'

Outside the stars were bright and rigid over the houses. The night wind, cold and direct, blew into Mattia's eyes. From the direction they turned, Mattia immediately knew where they were going. He thought perhaps he was wrong when Albanese turned another corner and headed towards the town hall. He stopped at a building beside it, opened it with a key and disappeared. When he returned, he had a jerrycan in his hand. 'Carry this,' he said.

Mattia took it. The fuel sloshing inside made it awkward to handle. It banged against his knees as they walked out of Sant'Attilio.

They stopped fifty yards from Angilù Cassini's house. Mattia set the can down and shook feeling back into his arms. 'We're not . . .' he whispered. 'While they're all asleep.'

'No, we're not. Be quiet.' Cirò put his hand on the boy's shoulder. Mattia couldn't really see his face. Cirò said, 'This is just a warning. People don't give you justice in this life, you know that? You have to go out and take it. Those are my trees. That oil, I had its taste in my mouth for twenty years knowing that someone else was stealing it. Now he won't have it. First thing, though: the dog.' Albanese produced a knife from the bag. It was a knife Mattia recognised from his mother's kitchen. It was a knife he'd fantasised about taking out into the street and using, a boy's violent fantasies, and now here it was outside in the night, the blade naked under the stars. Albanese handed it to him. Mattia gripped the handle. The weapon felt clever and agile in his hand. Albanese reached into his bag again and pulled out something white. Mattia could see its glow. Again Albanese handed it to him. 'It's meat, in the handkerchief. You remember where the dog is? On the left side of the garden. First thing is go in and cut its throat. It should be asleep. If it is awake, give it the meat and then cut its throat. Then put it on their doorstep. After that, we burn the trees. Will you be quieter with your sandals on or off?'

'On.'

'Okay. Go on then.'

'Okay.'

'Now. Go on. Be quick.'

'Okay.'

Mattia walked down the hill with the knife and the meat in his hands. As he reached the gate, he lifted his feet carefully, trying not to make the loose stones squeak beneath him. The house was in front of him, set back behind the trees, dark and sleeping. He went in. For long moments as he crept about, Mattia worried that he wouldn't even be able to see the dog in the darkness but then he perceived its round shape, curled on the ground. His sweat was cold in the wind. He stepped towards it, closer and closer, until he was near enough to drop onto it. He had his knees on its ribcage, one hand grabbing the muzzle that came awake, wet and sharp with teeth. He got his hand around it and crushed it shut. He reached under with the knife and pulled it up with a short tugging action, the way he'd seen men despatch sheep, and sure enough loose blood started pumping onto the ground while the animal whimpered and hissed, the air going out of it. Its body jerked in a seizure and lay still. He'd done it. He wiped his brow and caught the tang of the dog's blood on his hands. He cut the rope it was tethered with. That was hard work. It took minutes to saw through. The dog was heavy as earth when he picked it up, its spine pouring over his hands, hard to gather and control. To get it to the doorstep he had to adopt a bandy-legged, shuffling run. He laid it down. *Here you go, you thief. You see what happens? When you live in my house.*

When he got back to Albanese, the man was delighted. He put both his hands on Mattia's shoulders and shook him. 'Good boy. Good boy. Okay, now the next thing.'

Albanese led the way this time. Mattia followed him as he dashed kerosene around and up into the olive trees, starting with those nearest to the gate. When he reached the end, he flipped open a cigarette lighter and lit two sticks. He gave one to Mattia and side by side they walked down the avenue touching flames to the trees, watching fire appear in patches of beautiful liquid blue. It raced up into the oily leaves which started to crackle and burn with flames as sumptuously golden as church decoration. At the gate they dropped the sticks and walked quickly back up the hill.

Albanese was ecstatic. He put his arm around the boy and kissed his head. Mattia felt the man's strong lips push against his temple and the corner of his eye. Behind them, voices of panic could be heard.

Back at the house, Mattia washed the blood from his arms. Cirò gave him a glass of grappa which felt to Mattia like swallowing the same fire.

Upstairs, the drink, the smell of fire on his skin, the golden burning they'd made in the darkness, for some reason all filled Mattia with intense lust. In bed, he lay amorously on his front, his head full of images of women's stocking tops and the neat plump shape of cloth where their underwear fitted tight around their figs. He fell asleep pressing a fierce erection down into the bed.

38

There were footprints of blood in the hallway. Angilù had stumbled over the dog's soft body, kicked it away and then run back and forth through the puddle that shone black in the firelight.

He'd given up soon anyway. The trees hadn't properly caught from the hasty splashes of fuel so in the grey dawn light he saw only ugly and stupid damage, scabs of burned twists of shrivelled leaves. Olive trees were tough, used to fierce heat, and there would still be a harvest but that wasn't the point. This was bad. The dog was very bad. He remembered what it meant like something from his childhood, like a snatch of a song he hadn't heard for years. Angilù might have only days to live. Every step now was along a precipice.

Angilù dug a hole. It took effort. He felt up his arms every pang of his spade hitting a stone. He took Cesare, whose fur was matted and dull, whose lips were retracted in a snarl, whose tongue hung out, and dropped him in and shovelled over. Earth covering the fur, covering the face. He had to decide what to do. With the Allies here, even if Albanese was whispering into their ignorant ears, there was just a chance of justice. After they'd gone, there was no telling.

39

At breakfast, Albanese sat silent and ignorant. When Mattia tried to smile at him, he registered nothing. His face was heavy and soft, his eyes vague, his grey hair crinkled from the pillow. He fumbled with his coffee and cigarette.

Mattia tore at the dry bread with the teeth in the side of his mouth. Albanese leaned back in his chair, his lips pushed forward, his eyes half closed, somnolent and regal. Mattia asked, 'What's America like?' Across the kitchen he could see his mother's rounded back tense with attention, listening. Albanese brought his hand to his chin. He thought of the wintry docks and huge iron ships, running men, signals and operations, morphine arriving in olive oil barrels marked with a particular number. That particular line of business had been blessed. The city just wanted more and more and he was the obscure channel by which it flowed into dirty tenements, to clubs and high-class parties. Meanwhile, he himself was clean, a working man. He thought of himself in a thick coat and tweed cap, his breath steaming. He thought of thick meat sandwiches arriving in greasy paper. Around the work there was a dark penumbra of bosses and friends, number running, whores and horses, the nights, the necessary killings. And outside all of it was Cathy, her white skin and myriad freckles, her rosy nipples, humming as she brushed her hair.

'America was good,' he said, 'very good business. We learned a lot. Maybe I'll take you there one day. It's rich, America. You can do well. And I tell you there's better Sicilian food in New York than there is in Sicily. They have better meat there and good tomatoes from California. Olive oil you have to import. That was one thing I did. I was an importer. I'll be doing that here too.'

40

Will was pleased to get out onto his motorcycle. The morning with the medical officers had made him gloomy. There was something claustrophobic and hopeless about hearing about the diseases of poverty that they were seeing. It brought into focus what Will had only sensed, made it real and enclosing. Nutritional deficiencies, parasites, diseases and deformities going untreated. At least this part of the island wasn't malarial, nor were there the poisonings that happened round the sulphur mines. Ripping into the wind, downhill, released Will from this encounter. Probably it had not put him in the right frame of mind to meet a prince. Will was no socialist but the decaying feudalism of this part of the world was distasteful. Surely life could be better organised than princes and peasants? For all their rhetoric of machines and progress, the Fascists seemed to have left Sicily unchanged in this respect.

With the war pounding its way up into Italy, the liberation of mainland Europe underway, Will had started to think of what he might do when it was all over and, somewhat to his surprise, his thoughts had been turning to politics. With his experience, the diplomatic service would obviously have been the ideal fit but he strongly suspected that brown eyes and a middling stature would count against him there as much as in the army. The foreign service required a particular bearing born of a particular parentage, particular schools. Politics, though, was distinctly possible. He relished the slightly sordid associations of the word. He liked the verb form, also: politicking. Complexity, machination, agility, persuasion.

Finding the Prince's house did nothing to diminish Will's sense of the injustices of the place. The house was huge and, as the Prince soon explained, it was inhabited only by himself and his daughter. The other people Will could see were servants and estate workers. The house, then, with its many rooms, its decorated ceilings, ancient portraits and skulking dogs, was a vast store of empty privilege. The thought of a daughter, a single daughter, was intriguing. Will didn't meet her until later. First, he met the Prince.

Prince Adriano was relatively tall for a Sicilian and he spoke with a kind of delighted gaiety that Will had noticed in some educated foreigners when they were addressing Englishmen. They thrilled to converse with a representative of the Empire, Dickens, Pall Mall gentlemen's clubs and Sir Arthur Conan Doyle. Part of the pleasure seemed to lie in their acting English also, adapting their mannerisms, being clipped and reserved, and dissembling their enjoyment of the whole thing. The pleasure appeared in compacted smiles; it shone in their eyes.

The Prince was affable, meeting Will in a large vestibule. Behind him a large staircase climbed towards the light of a window. 'I'm very pleased we got the English,' he said. 'This is the last outpost, no? Everything west is American.'

'Even here too in some ways.'

'Oh, yes?'

'We work very closely with our allies and with our allies' allies.'

The Prince led Will into a large room where the light from the windows was doubled in an ornate, gold-framed mirror and a table and chairs were set on a rug in the middle of the tiled floor as though floating on a raft.

A servant bustled in with a tray. 'In your honour,' the Prince announced, 'I thought we'd have tea. Thank you, Graziana.'

The servant, a typical peasant woman, short with thick, strong arms, seemed alarmed at hearing her name among the English words. She set down the tray and hurried out.

'I shall be mother,' the Prince said, quietly smiling. He poured two cups of what turned out to be flavoured yellow water and dropped half-moons of lemon into them with silver tongs. Will thought he would have preferred Italian coffee.

The Prince sat back, nursing his cup and saucer at his chest. 'Well, let me tell you a little bit about this place,' he began. 'It has been in my family for a long time, since the Normans, although the building is newer than that, as you can tell. Mostly the princes have not been very interested in the estate, finding life to be more gay in Palermo or various other watering holes on the Continent. But I have always been interested in the land, the farming, and I've lived here for a long time. That is why I think the British will be far more sympathetic for us here. You understand the land very well, I think. Your relation with it is as long as ours. In America it all belonged to Red Indians until the day before yesterday and all they do is farm beef on those monstrous ranches or tend their crops, I am told, by aeroplane.'

Will obligingly smiled.

'Are you from the country?' the Prince asked. 'Or are you more of a man about town, Piccadilly and so forth?'

'No, I'm from the countryside. Very green and pleasant land where I'm from. I'm from the Midlands, Shakespeare's country.'

'Oh, wonderful. And do you farm?'

'Not really. My father was a schoolmaster.'

'I see. Very good.'

Will saw the wave of the Prince's interest break. The older man relaxed back in his chair. Will felt rejected. He pursued. 'We used to hunt.'

'Oh, very good. I've never been much of a huntsman myself. This isn't really the country for it.'

'That's a shame.'

'Possibly. Now then, what is it I can do for you?'

Will sipped his sour tea. 'I wanted to introduce myself and to meet you. You are plainly a significant personage in this area. And as you've been here, as you've said, for so long, you must be well acquainted with pretty much everyone. The process of identifying Fascists is rather tricky for us, trickier for us than it might be for you.'

'Yes. Well. That's a very complicated matter in some ways. Everyone had to deal with them. Sicily was Fascist.'

'But not everybody had to become one.'

The Prince gazed past Will's head, considering that formulation. 'Yes and no,' he said eventually. 'They were dangerous people, also they did bring some good changes.' He laughed. 'One of them wanted to marry my daughter. Can you imagine? That would have been going a bit far.'

'So, your daughter remains unmarried?'

'Oh, yes.'

'And you were never a Fascist?'

'Certainly not. None of the old Sicilian families were. A little enthusiasm here and there but no more than that. The Fascists came from the north. They were invaders, "polenta eaters" as we Sicilians call them. Some Sicilians joined them for advantage.'

'Not out of conviction, because they believed in it?'

'Oh, that. My dear fellow, you never know what a Sicilian believes other than that nothing can be done.'

Will disliked this glib, unhelpful remark delivered in such a relaxed tone. The urge came to him, the old mental tic, to hurl his tea into the Prince's face. Will cleared his throat.

'This makes it rather difficult for us. We're trying to establish leaders here, to create a new political class. It's our job, now the war is over, to make the peace. And it would be nice to know that the people getting involved were not . . . tainted. We have Cirò Albanese working with us and we know he was not.'

'Yes, I'd heard he was back.'

'And Alvaro Zuffo. Heard of him?'

'Just out of prison, I believe.'

'That's correct. What about you? Do you have any interest in politics?'

'Me? No. The less politics the better. It's when the peasants get hold of useless political ideas that I have problems. You should be on guard for Communism in this area.'

'Oh, we are. And would you have any idea who would be sending us denunciations of Cirò Albanese?'

The Prince shifted in his chair. 'Perhaps you'd like to stay for supper. My daughter will join us. She's forever disappearing these days. She loves to ride, that one. Do you ride?'

41

Luisa had become stealthy in her own house, a thief in the kitchen at night, returning to her room with food in her pockets and sleeves. She flitted between the movements of the servants. She breathed quietly, full of secrets. The American lived inside her just as he lived, unguessed at, unimagined, in the attic of the house.

She opened the door and saw him again on his hands and knees, peering into the cracks between the floorboards. Lost to her, he was barely a man at all in these moments. His mind was gone and his body had taken over. It was his body, overruling his thoughts, that was determined to survive. It used him indifferently so as to stay alive. He wouldn't even remember now that he had once kissed her. Perhaps that was better. A different madness of the night. Luisa couldn't imagine where that might have led, what the future with this man might be.

'Ray,' she said.

Ray's thin head swung around. A face patched with shadows, his beard darkening his cheeks.

'You look like Saint Onofrio.'

'What's that? Who?'

'Saint Onofrio.'

'No, you?'

'Ray, it's me.'

Ray reached one hand up and swiped across his forehead and eyes. 'Yes, it's you. I remember. I do.' He shivered. 'I'm gonna sit down,' he said.

'Yes. Sit.'

'Yes, I haven't finished but . . .'

'There's nothing here.'

'Yes.' Ray detached his hands from the floorboards and sat back. 'There's nothing here.'

'You have to remember that. There's nothing here.'

'I do. I will. I'll remember.'

42

A young woman entered and Will rose to his feet.

'Ah,' the Prince said. 'Here she is. This is my daughter, the Princess Luisa.'

Will bowed. The young woman seemed startled, breathless even.

'Excuse me. I did not know we had a guest.'

She touched her hair, pulled at her sleeves. She was fine-looking with a dignified strictness about the nose and mouth, but she wasn't lovely. Not like the girl in the dark in Palermo. The thought made Will twitch with shame. It was wrong to think of that in this place, wrong but exciting in its way. It made Will think of the warm blood in the Princess's body also. The Princess had dark, oriental eyes. Perhaps this was her, the Sicilian woman promised by the *Invasion Handbook*, complaisant and yielding.

'Is everything all right?' she asked.

'Yes, yes. Everything is quite all right. I'm just here to talk with the Prince. To make your acquaintance.'

'I see.' The Princess waited.

'Excuse me. I should introduce myself. My name is William Walker. I'm . . .'

'Walker. Please sit. And has father told you what things are like round here?'

'I'm sorry?'

'Why I am never allowed to ride my horse on my own?'

'And why is that?'

'Because of bandits, kidnaps.'

'Luisa, please. Do not exaggerate.'

'I'm not exaggerating at all.' She turned to Will. 'Do not talk is what he means.'

'I'm not sure I understand.'

The Prince attempted to explain. 'The war has been very difficult for us. It was very frightening. So the Princess has become agitated.'

'Ask Angilù,' Luisa said. 'Ask anyone. If they will tell you.'

'There was a problem here with criminals,' the Prince said. 'Very Sicilian. And now people are worried they will come back.'

Will looked at them both. 'I've met Angilù, I think. His name, it's like "casino".'

'Cassini, yes.'

'He came to me a little while ago. About his house, about owning his house, or rather that you owned it. And about how one of the returnees, Albanese, would claim it as his own.'

'He is very frightened,' the Princess said.

'He works for me for many years. A very good man, very decent. He was a simple shepherd boy when I met him.'

'Sounds like something out of a poem.'

'Yes, perhaps. In a way it is.' The Prince knitted his eyebrows. 'But it is also normal here. Where there are sheep, someone must be a shepherd.'

'Of course.'

'For twenty years we have run the estate together. In a way, he is like a son. He is a peasant, of course, but . . .'

'Earlier, you didn't answer me about Albanese. Angilù isn't the only one, I don't think, to have things to say about him.'

The Prince frowned, looking down into his lap. He fiddled with his cigarette lighter. He looked up again. 'Perhaps you would like to listen to the gramophone?'

'Possibly. But to stick to the subject.'

'You like opera? I can find out what we have.'

'You see, Mr Walker,' the Princess said. 'You see what I am saying.'

Prince Adriano twisted around in his chair to look at a clock. He said, 'Look, Angilù will be here in a little while. Perhaps it would be better to talk to him yourself.'

'That seems like a good idea.'

'Perhaps you would like to stay for dinner?' the Princess asked.

'That's very kind. I accept.'

'I'll let the cook know,' the Princess said. And then, compounding this peculiar atmosphere of languor and fear, of ease and morbidity, she said, 'An American was killed on the Montebianco road. By a mine or an unexploded shell. It happened some time ago but his body is still out there in pieces. It is disgusting. I found it when I was out riding.'

Beginning to describe his evening to Samuels, Will said, 'It was all rather strange.'

Samuels, in his pyjamas, joining Will for a nightcap, said, 'Go on.'

'It was difficult to make them talk. They didn't want to. Or they did and didn't. Other than the Princess, fiery little thing. She wanted to talk.'

'The Princess,' Samuels laughed. 'It's absurd.' He put on his thickest Cockney accent. 'Wait till I tells 'em back 'ome. What was she like?'

'Quite a pet. Very Mediterranean. Slender. Dark-eyed.' Will immediately felt that he was misdescribing Princess Luisa. There was a pang of shame at reducing her to this type. He could not find the words to convey her dry, dignified anger, so self-possessed and righteous that at times when she spoke she seemed to rise a few inches off the ground. And there was the quality of her silences too. When she wasn't speaking, the silence around her was very composed, full of what she was thinking and not saying. Will thought she had recognised his intelligence, saw him as an equal, and that a wordless acknowledgement had passed between them. Perhaps it was she, at last, the one he'd been imagining. 'Highly intelligent, though, I think.'

'And what about Cassini? Did he seem plausible?'

'He too was . . . circumspect at first. He's quite a big man, around the shoulders, but he looked small. He looked like he's not used to speaking to strangers. And his dialect is so thick I had to have bits translated. What he did say was pretty extraordinary. He said that Albanese had threatened his daughter, that he tried to burn down his olive trees and had killed his dog. Cut its throat and left it on his doorstep. Grotesque, isn't it? Can you imagine the savagery, to slit the throat of an innocent dog like that?'

'I'm sure the dog's the least of it.'

Will looked up. 'Not for the dog. And it's indicative. The things Cassini was saying. I think the man's paranoid. He was talking about a big conspiracy of criminals growing now in Sicily. And all this while we were eating this delicious dessert with flowers in it, actual fragrant flowers. I was eating flowers that had been collected from this enormous garden with paths and statuary.'

'Can we confront Albanese at this point?'

'I'm not sure what to do. I mean, if it's true, then this is very big news. The whole reconstruction effort, all of AMGOT, if it's being used . . . I mean the implication was very much that he's not the only one.'

'Hang on. If it was Albanese's property before the Fascists – which it was, wasn't it? – then hasn't he got a point? A valid claim?'

'I suppose it depends how he came by it but it is ambiguous.'

'Didn't he lease it from the Prince if it belongs to him? How do you get a lease against the owner's will?'

'How do you? Threats? Vandalism? We need to corroborate this stuff. I think I need to take action of some kind. Perhaps pre-emptively arrest Albanese and get some answers out of him.'

'Really? You should contact Messina, no?'

'That's a very feeble attitude.'

'No it isn't. That would be procedure, wouldn't it?'

'It might be but . . .'

'So you should. You don't want them coming back at you, or the Americans.'

'Oh, for God's sake.'

Samuels was so infuriating. Compact and logical, in his pragmatism (a man who liked electrical machines), he presented hard impervious surfaces. Will wanted to kick him and break him open. And just as Will was starting to think he wasn't so bad.

'You don't know the first of it, Samuels. You don't know how volatile and just barmy this place is. The weirdest thing Cassini said this evening was that there was a witch Albanese and his associates consulted and that she'd know everything.'

'A witch?'

'Precisely. Mad, isn't it? Should I try interrogating a witch?'

'If you're happy to take the risk of being turned into a frog.'

'I know. A witch! Where are we? They go to her for cures as well, apparently. I mean, everybody does. Perhaps I will try and track her down. Bound to be a diverting afternoon.'

'Meanwhile, in the real world, Messina.'

'But this is the real world. Frightened princes, criminal conspiracies, people slitting the throats of dogs, witches.'

'It's not my real world.'

'It is for now. We have to make sense of it.'

'We have to control it.'

'Precisely.'

43

To Angilù, his own family was so beautiful and strange. You live as a shepherd and you might as well be living on the surface of the moon. You sing songs, you make fires and keep yourself warm, but you're always alone. You live in the distance. You know that you are a fly on a wall, a tiny figure moving up the hillside surrounded by the coloured points of your animals, flowing and halting. You know that their bells can be heard from far away. To the person in town they'd be quieter than stones clicking underfoot or the noise of a grasshopper. There's so much space you can't come back from it, even after years, years of people.

Sometimes from across the table Angilù felt himself looking at his wife and daughters as if he were looking at Sant'Attilio from the hills. Staring at them now he felt that there was nothing he could do, that the empty air around their heads would be there after his death, offering no protection. There had to be something he could do.

He looked and couldn't think of anything. He wanted to escape. He had the urge to get up into the hills, to be in that place again. Maybe it would help.

There was a mule on the estate, a good one, four years old, that Angilù decided he would take.

The mule was a good mule, strong and intelligent.

He sat on it with his shotgun on his shoulder and started uphill, the reins pulling at his hands, the sun strong on his arms and shoulders, heating the air caught inside his hat.

In front of him the ground flinched now and again with jumping crickets. Around him they made their dense, wiry sound, the sound of heat and stones and dry plants.

He crossed into an area where the battle had been. This was new to him. The familiar land was altered, ulcerated with small craters. Something had happened here that didn't care about the land. It had been used. The atmosphere was strange. There was a large burned-out gun still standing. It looked like a humili-ated and foolish creature, its long nose blackened by flames. Angilù wondered at it. A place of fury, where men had run for their lives. A tinkling below him: the mule had dislodged rifle bullet casings and they rolled along the ground. Glinting gold pellets. As he moved, the light caught others and he saw them scattered around.

Angilù didn't know where he was going particularly. Up was his only thought as he followed a route he remembered, a path that was like travelling into his memories. Going hard uphill, the mule snorted and snaked its neck. Angilù saw a tuft of a particular kind of plant growing along a crack in a rock and stopped the animal. Swinging one foot over its skull he got down to strip a few leaves from the fibrous stalks and chew. Sharp lemon and a young green astringency, slightly dusty. It was just as he remembered. A flavour in the hills. Something waiting to happen inside him or whoever passed. Angilù felt sweat as a coolness trickling in his beard. He ran a hand around his chin, flapped the hot air into his face with his hat and then, groaning, remounted.

Riding on he saw that someone had been along there not too long before. Outside a little rock-shelf cave someone had left two snares for foxes. Nothing in them, they lay ready. A fox could be eaten if you really had to and killing them meant that it was more likely you would get to the rabbits or partridges before they did. He hadn't been up here for so long but it was all coming back to him. It returned him to an old unhappiness that was soothing in its simplicity.

He remembered that around the next height he would be able to look down at Sant'Attilio. And there it was. He dismounted by some low, woody bushes that would keep the mule there browsing. Angilù walked towards the view, his back hurting a little from the ride. Sitting down on the ground, he stared at the huddle of terracotta roofs, the stripe of road, the church tower, the little streets that seemed turned away from the main road for privacy, the houses whisperingly close to each other. Always interesting: to look down at Sant'Attilio and work out what was where, who was here and there. This distracted Angilù for a moment and he felt calm until his fears returned. They swarmed around him, getting closer, tighter.

The Englishman seemed like he would be no help. Angilù hadn't trusted the look on his face while he listened to him. And what had he said in reaction?

The Princess had translated for Angilù. 'It sounds like you're in a bit of trouble.' Something like that. A bit. He had no understanding at all.

And Angilù's fears were immediate and real and he had to do something, but what? In his pain he cried out loud. He dug his hands into the earth either side of him and pulled. He wouldn't go back down again until he knew what to do.

44

Teresa thought that the only thing you could trust was God, only the saints on the wall staring out of their gold, suffering and shedding light. The saints stared into a filthy world, where a husband vanishes, leaving a young wife alone with nothing, not even a child. The rites of mourning were terrible and weightless with no body to bury, with nothing to hold Teresa to the earth. Only God above. From that time on, Teresa's feelings, her pain or alarm, climbed upwards into the sky. Whenever she panicked, her eyes rolled upwards. She clasped her hands to her bosom and her soul called into the blue.

A strange mourning. There were those who didn't care about her grief and didn't try to hide it. She felt the curses active in their silences like cockroaches in the darkness when the lamps are out. Even Cirò's family were difficult with her, thinking she knew something they didn't. If only she had.

Years later a man without fear emerged and that was Silvio, of all people. And then life. Children.

Then a war comes that kills many in other places, that starves people, and brings the resurrection of Cirò Albanese. A miracle is hard to bear. It is terrifying. It changes everything. She knew how they felt, those women in the Bible, Samson's mother, the mother of our Lord, or the friends of Lazarus.

And then the end of Silvio. What can you do? Nothing. Claw at your own skin. You can't do anything. You live.

Teresa was not from one of those families, the Albaneses, the Zuffos, the Battistas, but when she married Cirò she knew what she was doing. She was joining the strong. She would eat. If you'd been hungry as a child you'd understand.

Mattia would not now be hungry. For as long as he lived, however long that was. Her heart raced up into the silence where there was stillness but no answers. When she was dead, finally the saints and angels would appear and speak.

45

'By it and with it and on it and in it,' said the Rat. *'It's brother and sister to me.'*

The book always fell open there at the beginning, flat as a table, the spine cracked, the white stitches of the binding loose and stretched. Will flipped on.

The Mole had long wanted to make the acquaintance of the Badger. He seemed, by all accounts, to be such an important personage and, though rarely visible, to make his unseen influence felt . . .

And again.

It was a cold still afternoon with a hard steely sky overhead, when he slipped out of the warm parlour into the open air.

That was the note he was after – warm parlour, those plush and modest and comfortable English words. Will wanted to climb into the book, to cover his mind with it. His day had been extremely annoying.

Will had sent a scrupulously composed message to Messina commissioning himself for action against Albanese. Neat. Decisive. Reasonable. Will was pleased with it and mentally was preparing himself for the next step and what he would say to Albanese when he apprehended him when the reply came. It was signed by Captain Draycott, of all people, and urged him to inaction, to avoid fuss or trouble. He was to remain a quiet and dutiful servant. Permission was not granted. For Will, this was intolerable. He wouldn't have Africa repeated. Showing no sign of it except a light sweat appearing on his forehead and a jiggling knee, Will was filled with rage.

He would do it. He would find a way.

46

The saddle and bridle were made from dark red leather. The stitching was strong yellow thread diving down and up through the material. Ray ran his finger over the taut stitches. He could see where the straps down to the stirrups had been folded around and sewn to the right width. He could imagine the pieces before they were sewn together, laid out on a table. They would be different shapes, flat and so much larger than the finished product. You wouldn't necessarily be able to guess what they would turn into. Ray's own father worked in leather. Ray remembered the shocking reek of his workshop, the bare lightbulb and dim walls with clock and calendar and cross. The piled leather had an acid tang. His pa sat there bent over the work. His hands were strong and skilful. They had to be to drive the thread through the tough skins. The spectacles on his nose caught the light in two half-moons. They were a concentration of focus. Sometimes he sang to himself. Ray would visit him occasionally to wheedle out of him small change to go to the movies. Afterwards, he would shut the door and leave him there, making things to sell, sewing skins into useful shapes, making a life for his family, alone in that room.

Ray heard the Princess's footsteps. He turned around and waited for the door to open. She came in, lit up with the secret urgency that surrounded her every time. She said, 'There are people now clearing away the mines. One of the peasants told me. Your friend. I'm so sorry.'

'Please don't. You don't have to say anything. Thank you.' He stroked his chin and felt his growing beard, the swarm of smooth fibres under his hand. Unsoldierly now. His body softening.

'I brought you water.'

The Princess had a bottle in her hand. Not a bottle. What was it called? One of those glass bottles that widened at the top. Some people he knew who worked in restaurants had them at home. A carafe.

'Thanks.'

Ray watched her walk over to him. She leaned down and he took the bottle from her. He glanced across at where his cup was sitting and she went over to fetch it for him.

She set the cup down and retreated a little way and sat. 'You like that little horse.'

'I guess. I like looking at it. It's a beautiful piece of work. Look at the painting on it.'

She smiled at him fondly, her head on one side. 'So strange. To meet a stranger. This is something that never happens. There are no strangers here. Usually I only meet the peasants, the aristocrats in Palermo. We play cards in the same rooms. There are balls, with dancing, all the floors polished. I could go away to see new things but for a woman. . . It means the end of certain things. A reputation.'

'That's a shame.'

'You know, in America the wild west always was

interesting to me. Since I was a little girl I always imagine it.'

'Yeah? Me too, I guess. The pictures anyways. I like those.'

'For me, what I read. Such a big place, big plains. And horses.'

Ray looked at her. She was smiling quietly, inwardly. She inhaled and Ray saw her taking in that imagined space and freedom. She was picturing it. 'Would you like to go to those places?' she asked him

'I don't know. I never thought about it, really. I just know those places in movies. I've only ever thought of them like that, in black and white. The whole of the country didn't really exist for me until the army when I met people from places other than New York or Italy. In the army you meet people from all over. I had a friend, George. I have a friend, George. I have his address.'

'Who is that?'

'Just this guy. A guy I knew in the army. He came from the Midwest not the far west.'

'I see. But you could go to those places. They're in your country and you are a man. You could go there.'

'I guess.'

'You seem better today.'

47

Angilù didn't often carry a shotgun any more and he'd never owned a pistol. He still had a shotgun in his house, its wooden stock worn gaunt over the years, a farmer's tool. But for this Angilù wanted a pistol. A shotgun could be misinterpreted. People would blame one of Albanese's natural enemies. A pistol: that might suggest something else had happened. There was a phrase Prince Adriano liked to say in French, a saying from one of the old wars – to encourage the others.

Angilù had a key to the field guards' room and went there early enough not to be disturbed, stars still bristling in the thick blue western sky, the east thinning out with streaky red. The bloom of lamplight revealed the room much as Angilù remembered it. A particular atmosphere of menace and relaxation and self-regard. Hair oil and clothes brushes and boot polish and oil for leather, hats, boots, a mirror, a Christ, a Saint Rosaria, chairs and ashtrays. Weapons were not visible. They were in a cupboard that the Prince called the armoury. (His own English shotguns were kept in an armoury in the house.) Angilù opened the door. Holsters and harnesses hung like bridles for horses. Long barrels of rifles pointed upwards. In a drawer Angilù found two pistols, holsters and bullets. He picked up a gun and weighed it in his palm. He spun the barrel and listened to its clicks. He pocketed it. No need for a holster.

The door opened. One of the guards, a tall, thick-featured man named Giuseppe with violet marks of sleeplessness under his eyes. Angilù saw them as their eyes met. Giuseppe hesitated, his mouth shaping to say something. After all, he knew about the burned trees, the dead dog. Everybody did. But all he said was 'Good morning'. And there it was, the silence that filled Angilù with rage. People in a trance, in a dream, blind with fear, silent even though they knew. Angilù would blow it all up but for now he said nothing. He picked up a cardboard packet and poured some bullets into his left hand. Golden and heavy, fat as bees. He dropped them into his other pocket, replaced the box, closed the cupboard and walked out of the room, out into the brightening day.

48

He was back at the coppiced wood. Beyond the straight trucks, out of reach, could be seen the slow, green glinting of the river. Will was trying to work out what he had to do. He could feel his father at a distance, a ferment of anger in the house. Will's father was dead, of course. Remembering that transferred Will into his father's presence. His father was at his desk in his study, turned away in his swivel chair. Paper and an open book were outspread before him. Will's father was dead. He turned around in the chair to speak to his son but he was too tired. He was pale, terribly weak, after the awful effort of dying. He had that ugly scratch by his nose.

Back in the wood, *The Wind in the Willows* was somehow involved. The animals weren't like they were in the book. They were disgusting, low to the ground, coarse-haired, fidgeting and shaking and suddenly scurrying away out of sight. Will needed to chase them. That part of the dream didn't last long. It gave way to a new task. The trees were information of some kind. Their pattern was like Morse code. In the wood somewhere was his younger brother who knew already, who understood. Will turned around looking for him and was blinded by sunlight, hot on his face. That was what woke him up. He was sweating.

The Wind in the Willows appearing in his dream was particularly ridiculous and shaming. He regretted having the book by his bedside. His thoughts would have been sharper, less confused had he been reading his father's Lucretius. Will felt smeared with shame at the dream, shame which intensified as he remembered another part: he was back at the fish pond. The cover was off. With a kind of tingling pleasure he was dropping tins of food down to the shivering prisoners below, naked in their filth. Anonymous soldiers waited and watched.

Through the shutters came blades of white light and the dry racket of insects and birds. Will kicked off his sheet and got up.

Water to wash his face and to organise his hair. Uniform on.

Samuels had some bad news. 'Just had one of the local police in. There's someone else been shot, in Montebianco this time. Funnily enough, no one saw anything. Shotgun wound. Close-range. Not a Fascist, though. Seemed sure about that. A Communist. But, you know, yesterday's Fascist . . .'

'If nobody saw it then nothing happened. It's the bloody tree falling in the forest with no one to hear. Bury the man and carry on.'

'Are you losing faith in the powers of justice?'

'I'll see. I'm off to Palermo to meet Major Kelly about the Albanese thing.'

'Had a message from Albanese yesterday. Said he was aware of some black market activity that we should look into.'

'I'm sure he is.'

49

Palermo had an air of Miss Havisham's madness about it, grandly baroque and broken up with sudden sky and heaps of rubble. The streets were sordid with people, untrustworthy people, lounging against walls, talking together, watching him pass. Markets seemed to have reopened and fishermen were clearly going out again. Will had to pilot his motorcycle on tiptoe through people ambling around trays of fish, bartering with sheets of the AMGOT money that was already smeared and stained. Revving his engine did nothing to hurry them. There were small red fish with large, simple eyes. There were normal-looking grey fish and on its own, upright on a table, the extraordinary head of a swordfish, like something from a natural history museum. Its long, lordly blade angled up into the air. Behind, its body was sliced, missing sections that had already been sold, gaps of absence.

Will kept twisting in his saddle, alert to every stranger. He was not going to let himself be pick-pocketed again. It was a relief to be out of this crowd and riding away.

Will had forgotten how glorious the building was in which AMGOT was headquartered. Stucco and gilt, marble and mosaics. Footsteps were repeated in quick echoes.

Will was shown in to see Major Kelly. He was seated at a large, lion-foot desk. Behind him on the wall, surrounded by an ornate frame, Saint Jerome contemplated his work of translation in rich oil paint. Major Kelly rose to shake Will's hand. He asked the man who had shown Will in to return with some coffee.

Will sat down and began explaining his concerns about Albanese, the anonymous denunciations and the testimony of Angilù Cassini and Prince Adriano. Will did so quickly and precisely. Major Kelly listened sitting back in his chair, so still that the reflections in his spectacles didn't move. When Will had finished, he leaned forwards and said that it was good Will had come to him with these anxieties.

The coffee arrived.

'"Anxieties" might not be quite the word,' Will said.

'Whatever you want to call it. Look, I know we picked up some pretty interesting characters to help us out with Operation Husky. Our Italian friends in America are a – what shall I say? – an enterprising group of people. I was always assured we were vetting them thoroughly. I don't know anything about Albanese in particular. He wasn't in gaol. Some of the guys came out of prison here. I guess you knew that.'

Kelly lifted a hand and plucked his spectacles from his face. The effect for Will was strangely disconcerting. He saw that Kelly looked quite different to how Will had thought he looked. Beneath his spectacles, his eyes were bigger. There was a greater distance between his nose and upper lip. His nude head, with large pink eyelids and smooth cheeks, was uncanny to look at. Will realised that the spectacles somehow summarised and finished Kelly's face, fronted for it. After he replaced his spectacles, hooking them around his ears again, Will was left to fit his appearance back together.

'I guess what I could do is get some questions asked and let you know. Is that the sort of thing you're after?'

'At least. I want more. I think I should step in and relieve Albanese of his powers until we know, frankly, who the hell he is.'

A smile lit up Kelly's face. 'I see. Action. Command. Good for you, kid. It's what this island needs if we're going to make a peace that will last. There's politics brewing in Palermo, I'm telling you. Separatists. Communists. It's all going to get messier before it gets clean.'

Will flew back on his motorcycle. *You see*, he thought to himself, *you see, it's possible.* The Allies were virtuous in their bringing of peace. There was suffering that didn't need to happen, violence that they could prevent. But it took someone of Will's acuity and daring to bring it about, to align insight and action and bloody well do something. He sped through the burning air rehearsing in his mind the words he would use when he apprehended Albanese. They were coolly understated and commanding. *I'm afraid that we're going to have to have a word or two . . . I'm sorry, Mr Albanese, but I'm going to have to . . . I wouldn't do that if I were you, Mr Albanese.*

50

The door was unpainted, the wood raw and dry. It looked like he could pick splinters out of it with his thumbnail. The surface of the door was subdivided into four sections, four rectangles separated by narrow raised sections. Ray wasn't sure why that was, maybe for reinforcement. He stood close enough to the door to listen beyond it.

The handle was high up on the left side. It was made of slender brass, notched along the edges, and curved in a rapid flourish like a line in someone's signature. The notches gave it a texture you would feel.

I won't die if I open the door. If I open the door I will not die.

Ray saw his hand reach out and hold the handle, four fingers and a thumb, the lines of bones under the skin, the frill of dark hairs at his wrist. He opened the door and on the other side the narrow staircase plunged down. It was as steep as a ladder. Ray stepped through, holding his breath, out onto the first stair and then the next, carefully clambering down into the rest of the world.

In the main house, perspectives travelled into depth through arches of doorways. No telling where Princess Luisa was in all that. He might miss her entirely.

Ray walked among paintings and curved, decorated furniture that stood up on the balls of its feet. Unharmed, unhindered, he found the large staircase and descended. In the large vestibule, under silent painted clouds, he looked right and left. He turned right and walked into a set of sunlit rooms.

In the third large room he came upon Luisa at a large table eating breakfast with an old man, presumably her father. There was a woman servant who looked at Ray then dropped her head, reddening. Luisa's eyes were wide and tried to communicate something – fear, a plea, a warning. Ray realised that he would not be able to say goodbye in the way he'd intended. Now the old man was standing up and addressing him. Ray interrupted him.

'I'm sorry to disturb you, sir. I got separated from my unit a while back in the fighting. I've been lost.'

'You've been lost a long time.'

'I've been lost a long time. Can you tell me the road for Palermo?'

'And how did you get in?'

He could feel Luisa's gaze pressing against him.

'I came in. I walked in. I'm sorry to disturb you. I didn't realise it was still early.'

'You should walk out the same way you came in then turn right on the road and keep going for a day or so.'

Luisa said something to the old man in Italian, under her breath. The old man sighed and said, 'The first town you go through, the town not the few separate houses, there are people there who can help you.'

'Thank you, sir. Thank you, sir. Thank you.' Ray

looked at Luisa who looked down at her plate. She seemed angry. There was nothing he could say.

As he walked out of the room, Luisa looked up again to see his back retreating. He had tried to make his uniform as neat as possible. The beard on his face had looked so thick in the light, black as beetles. She was stuck to her chair, losing him. Nothing she could do, no power. And even if she could run after him, what would she be able to say? If she moved to Paris she might have a life, or Rome. Here in this life there was nothing. She had on her plate two peaches from the garden. She picked up her knife, trembling.

51

The world blazed into Ray's eyes full of a million things. Light poured down. The sound of insects pulsed out of trees and bushes. He tried to whistle with his dry mouth, tried to remember how soldiers walked. His legs were shaking. After the gloom of the attic, the light was blinding. It hurt like diamonds crushed into his eyes. He hung his head and walked, the road around him leaping up in explosions that didn't happen. If you're not dead you carry on. He said, *George, I'm coming.* Wind raced against his skin. He kept walking.

A noise getting louder behind him: the crunch of footsteps. Ray assumed the final end. He closed his eyes. His shoulders stiffened. His hands closed. He heard his name. 'Ray. Ray.' It was her voice.

It was strange to see the Princess outside, in the real light of day. She stood in front of him, small and blinking. Her hair moved in the wind. She seemed very clear and separate. Her skin was paler than indoors. She raised a hand of delicate fingers to her forehead to make a visor against the sun.

'Where are you going? You should say goodbye. You shouldn't just go like that.'

'I'm sorry. I did. I wanted to.'

'It's not nice just to go like this.'

Her voice sounded different. She stood there detached from the long dream of his days in hiding.

'I wanted to say thank you to you.'

'Where are you going?'

'I said. I have to go to Palermo. I have to go back. I'm sorry.'

The Princess was looking down, her eyes in her hand's shadow. The soft flesh of her lower lip was caught between her teeth.

'But . . .'

'I'm sorry,' he said. 'You've been so kind to me.'

'It doesn't matter. You have to go. I don't know what I'm doing following you. I don't know what I'm doing.'

'I'm really grateful.'

'Are you? Wait. Will you wait? I've had an idea. I can drive you to Palermo. I can get the car and a driver. I can take you all the way.'

'You don't have to . . .'

'I know I don't but I want to. Will you wait? Will you stay here?'

'Sure.'

'Stay here.'

The Princess turned and hurried away. Ray watched her go. She went with rapid steps that lifted and broke into a run that was awkward to maintain against her long skirt. In that effort and urgency, Ray saw something. Maybe he was wrong, but it looked like love. For him. For another person. For no reason, just given, just happening. It was love that made her hurry. He couldn't keep it; it wouldn't last. He had to get back to Palermo and do whatever came next but there it was. It would keep him safe a little while longer, for this journey in her car.

52

Everything was very clear.

Angilù sat opposite the church and waited. A lizard flickered onto the wall beside him, quick on its tiny fingers, its small tail lashing. It froze, picked up its head, the flat mouth fixed in a smile. Angilù saw its throat pulse. It darted away. Making the decision had been difficult, like stepping through a flaming doorway and out through an avenue of burning trees. But now he was beyond, he was calm. He could see everything.

Blind Tinu was folded in the shadows of the church doorway. Always there, empty as a clock, feeling the passing of the hours, hearing the clatter of the bell. Tinu was never a witness. He never said anything, never made sense. You gave him a coin or a piece of bread and it was like tossing it into a well, his reaction just splash and echoes and silence again.

Angilù had to be careful about other people seeing him. He was not one of them. He would not be treated as invisible. The others did not fear him enough to erase him from their sight. Nevertheless, he felt peaceful and secure in his purpose. The decision was like a final acquiescence. Angilù had given in and become part of the place. Resisting it with other methods had been exhausting and useless. Now he had recognised his fate, embraced it, married it. He was pleased and placid as a bridegroom.

The gun was wedged in his waistband and he sat so that no one could see. The church had sucked in its widows for Mass and exhaled them out again and still no sign. Angilù couldn't wait for ever. He'd left his wife and children alone. He might be in the wrong place. He might be too late.

He gave it one more hour.

Angilù got up and walked across the square and up the steep road, past the church and mindless Tinu to the house where Silvio had lived until he'd been killed. He cleared his throat at the door and knocked then put his hand to the handle of the pistol.

The door was opened by a child. Albanese sat smoking in the middle of the whitewashed space. His eyes focused sharply when he saw Angilù. Albanese knew immediately. But he exhaled smoke slowly before he said, 'What do you want?'

Angilù wanted to say something frightening like 'Those are beautiful children' but he couldn't think of a whole sentence and his throat was too dry. Instead, he stared, his hand on the gun.

Albanese ordered the children out of the room. To Angilù, this preparation made it seem as though Albanese wanted it to happen too, as though there was an agreement between the two men. The children were hurried out by the oldest boy. He pushed them out with his feet but he didn't leave. Angilù turned to look at him. Albanese said, 'You're doing this all wrong. You don't know what you're doing.' Then Albanese started to move in his seat so Angilù pulled out the gun and shot him. A red circle smacked over one eye and the top of his nose. His mouth fell open as his head lolled back. Angilù shot him twice more in the chest, the shots making a huge din in the closed room. He'd done this before. This had happened before. Firing into the dark up in the mountains. Albanese went over backwards on the wooden chair. His feet bounced as he landed. Angilù moved the gun across to point at the boy, not to kill him but to keep him still. The boy was panting. After the pistol smoke had cleared there was still smoke coming from Albanese. Angilù thought his shirt might have caught fire and glanced across and saw a cigarette still alight between his fingers. A spreading puddle was reaching his wrist. Angilù nodded at the cigarette and said to the boy, 'It will burn him.' The boy, holding the door frame, looked confused. Angilù turned and walked out.

He walked down the little street. He turned left at the bottom and headed out of Sant'Attilio, back to his house and family. He realised that he was lost but he wasn't worried for his family yet. He was full of his accomplishment, very calm and fulfilled, relieved, although it occurred to him that he hadn't got round to telling his wife where he'd buried some money, wrapped up in a bag with the gold ring the Prince had given him years and years ago. They could make use of that. Angilù walked the familiar road. He was unsurprised to hear footsteps running up behind him and to feel the boy on his back. He got his hand up quickly enough that the knife sliced his fingers instead of his throat.

Swerving around, bucking like a goat trying to leap

out of a pen, Angilù got free of the boy's grasp. He went for the gun in his pocket but had to use the wrong hand. The boy rushed at him and stabbed him a few times. Angilù didn't feel the blade going in, just thumps to his body like punches. He threw his arms around the boy's neck to slow him and felt stripes of narrow itchiness appear across his back. The boy shook Angilù off and he fell to the ground. The boy thumped him a few more times. Angilù felt tired and irritable. The boy didn't need to keep going on like that. It was unnecessary. He stopped. Angilù was wet and cold. There were stones under his face. He was where he'd always been, lying on the ground. He couldn't move at all.

Mattia stood over the body, swearing. He was stained with Cassini's blood and angered by the humiliation of discovering that some of the wetness on his trousers was his own urine. He bent down and took the man's gun out of his pocket. There'd still be three bullets in that. He prodded the body with his foot. Nothing. Mattia didn't know what to do now except go home and wash. After he could go to the police and show them Albanese's body like he'd just run from the house. Later, he would seek out Alvaro Zuffo. Zuffo would look after him. He would know what to do.

53

The razor tugged at the long hairs of his beard, cutting squares and rectangles into the foam. His full face inched back into view in the spotted mirror above the sink.

The new uniform was loose on him but still Ray felt decent, fresh and ordinary. He was one of the men. He walked the corridors, perfectly upright, trying not to think or remember.

But before he could do anything else, he needed to explain the course of events, to excuse himself. Opposite him, a man sat at a typewriter. The man hunched forwards and produced a burst of preliminary typing. He said, 'If you want to smoke, go right ahead.'

'That's okay.' Ray wondered what sort of person this man was, where he came from. There wasn't anything that gave him away.

'So, start at the beginning. You were with Anthony Geminiano.'

'That's right.'

'And then what?'

'Well, ah. Ah. It was . . . Jesus, what happened?'

'Look, don't worry.' The man sat back from the typewriter, his hands in his lap. 'I don't think there'll be trouble. You were gone awhile but you're back.

Happened to a lot of guys. Coming back is not deser-
tion, is it?'

'No, it isn't. I didn't.'

'Like I said. Now, you said there was a blast?'

'That's right.'

'So. Amnesia. And now you're back.'

'I'm back. I see. That is what happened. It is. That's
what happened.'

'Fine. Tell me from the beginning.'

'We came through the fighting. We got lost. We
were really lost.'

'Okay. Go on.'

ACKNOWLEDGEMENTS

I'd like to express my gratitude to Gea Schirò, Beatrice Monti della Corte von Rezzori, the Planeta family, Prof. Salvatore Lupo, Robin Robertson, Mitzi Angel, Anna Webber and Sarah Chalfant. These generous people tried to educate me and to improve this book, the failings of which are all mine.